Prais

'The novels of Andrea Camilleri breathe out
the sense of place, the sense of humour, and the sense
of despair that fill the air of Sicily. To read him is
to be taken to that glorious, tortured island'
Donna Leon

'Both farcical and endearing, Montalbano is a cross between
Columbo and Chandler's Philip Marlowe, with the added
culinary idiosyncrasies of an Italian Maigret . . . The smells,
colours and landscapes of Sicily come to life'
Guardian

'Sly and witty . . . Montalbano must pick his way through a
labyrinth of corruption, false clues, vendettas – and delicious
meals. The result is funny and intriguing with a fluent
translation by New York poet Stephen Sartarelli'
Observer

'Delightful . . . funny and ebulliently atmospheric'
The Times

'This savagely funny police procedural proves that
sardonic laughter is a sound that translates ever so smoothly
into English'
New York Times Book Review

'Camilleri is as crafty and charming a writer as
his protagonist is an investigator'
Washington Post

EXCURSION TO TINDARI

Andrea Camilleri is one of Italy's most famous contemporary writers. His Montalbano series has been adapted for Italian television and translated into several languages. He lives in Rome.

Stephen Sartarelli is an award-winning translator. He is also the author of three books of poetry, most recently *The Open Vault*. He lives in France.

Also by Andrea Camilleri

ANDREA CAMILLERI

EXCURSION TO TINDARI

Translated by Stephen Sartarelli

PICADOR

First published 2005 by Viking Penguin,
a member of Penguin Putnam Inc., New York

First published in Great Britain 2006 by Picador

First published in paperback 2006 by Picador
an imprint of Pan Macmillan
The Smithson, 6 Briset Street, London ECIM 5NR
Associated companies throughout the world
www.panmacmillan.com

ISBN 978-0-330-49303-1

Originally published in Italian as *La gita a Tindari* by Sellerio Editore, Palermo.

28

A CIP catalogue record for this book is available from
the British Library.

Typeset by SetSystems Ltd, Saffron Walden, Essex
Printed and bound by
CPI Group (UK) Ltd, Croydon, CR0 4YY

EXCURSION TO TINDARI

ONE

He realized he was awake, as his mind was functioning logically and not following the absurd labyrinths of dream. He could hear the rhythmic swashing of the sea; a pre-dawn breeze was blowing through the open window. Yet he stubbornly kept his eyes closed, knowing that the ill humour boiling inside him would come spewing out the moment he opened his eyes, leading him to say or do something stupid he would later regret.

The sound of whistling on the beach reached his ears. At that hour, surely someone walking to work in Vigàta. The tune was familiar, but he couldn't recall the title or lyrics. What did it matter? He never had been able to whistle himself. Not even by sticking a finger up his arse.

He stuck a finger in his arsehole
and gave a shrill whistle,
the prearranged signal
of the cops on patrol.

Some dumbshit ditty a Milanese friend at the police academy used to sing to him sometimes, which had stuck in his memory ever since. His inability to whistle had made him the favourite victim of his childhood schoolmates, all masters of the art of whistling like shepherds, sailors, mountaineers, even adding fanciful variations. School-mates! That's what had ruined his night's sleep! He'd been remembering them after reading in the newspaper, shortly before going to bed, that Carlo Militello, not yet fifty years old, had been named president of the second most important bank in Sicily. The paper had expressed its heartfelt best wishes to the new president and had printed a photograph of him: spectacles, almost certainly gold-rimmed, designer suit, impeccable shirt, exquisite tie. A successful man, a man of order, defender of Values (that is, stock-market values as well as Family, Country and Freedom). Montalbano remembered him well. Not as a classmate in primary school, but as a comrade in 1968!

'We'll hang the enemies of the people with their ties!'

'Banks are only good for being robbed!'

Carlo Militello, nicknamed Carlo Martello – Italian for Charles Martel – because of his supreme-commander attitudes and his penchant for confronting adversaries with words like hammer blows and punches worse than hammer blows, was the most intransigent, most inflexible of anyone. Compared to him, the Ho Chi Minh so often invoked by demonstrators seemed like a social-democratic reformist. Martello forced everyone to stop smoking cigarettes so as not to enrich the state monopoly. Joints, yes, to their heart's content. Only once in his life, he claimed, had Comrade Stalin done the right thing, and that was when he'd set about bleeding the banks to finance the Party. 'State' was a word that gave them all nightmares, throwing them into a rage like bulls before a red cape. What Montalbano remembered most from those days was a poem by Pasolini, defending the police against the students at Valle Giulia, in Rome. All his friends had spat on those verses, whereas he, Montalbano, had tried to defend them. 'But it's a beautiful poem.' If they hadn't restrained him, Carlo Martello would've broken his nose with one of his deadly punches. But why hadn't that poem bothered him? Had he read his future as a cop in it? At any rate, over the years he'd seen his friends, the legendary comrades from 68, all turn 'reasonable'. And by dint of reason, their abstract fury had softened and finally settled into concrete acquiescence. And now, with the exception of one who, with extraordinary dignity, had been putting up with trials and incarceration for over a decade for a crime he'd neither committed nor ordered, and another who'd died in obscure circumstances, the rest had all made out rather well, hopping from left to right and back again, ending up as chief editors of newspapers, television producers, high government functionaries, senators and chamber deputies. Unable to change society, they'd changed themselves. Or perhaps they hadn't even needed to change, since in 68 they had only been play-acting, donning the costumes and masks of revolutionaries.

That appointment of Carlo Martello-Militello had really not gone down well. Especially because it had triggered another thought in his mind, by far the most troubling of all.

But aren't you cut from the same cloth as these people you're criticizing? Don't you serve the same state you fought so ferociously at age eighteen? Or are you just griping out of envy, since you're paid a pittance while they're earning billions?

A gust of wind rattled the shutter. No, he wouldn't close it, not even at the command of the Almighty. Fazio was always hassling him about it.

'Chief, excuse me for saying so, but you're really asking for trouble! You not only live in an isolated house, you also leave your window open at night! So if anyone wants to do you harm — and there are people out there who do — they can come right in, whenever and however they please!'

Then there was that other hassle named Livia.

'No, Salvo, not at night, no!'

'But don't you, in Boccadasse, sleep with the window open?'

'What's that got to do with anything? First of all, I live on the third floor, and, secondly, in Boccadasse we don't have all the burglars you have here.'

And so, when Livia phoned him one night, all upset, to tell him that the burglars of Boccadasse had cleaned out her apartment when she was out, he gave silent thanks to Genoa's thieves, then managed to express his dismay, though not as much as he should have.

The telephone started ringing.

His first reaction was to shut his eyes even more tightly, but it didn't work. It's a well-known fact that sight and hearing are not the same thing. He should have plugged his ears, but he preferred to bury his head under the pillow. Nothing doing. The ringing, faint and distant, continued. He got up, cursing the saints, went into the other room and picked up the receiver.

'Montalbano here. I should say hello, but I won't. I'm not ready to.'

There was a long silence at the other end. Then the sound of the phone hanging up. What now, after that brilliant move? Go back to bed and continue to stew over the new President of Interbanco, who, when he was still Comrade Martello, once publicly shat on a tray full of ten-thousand-lire notes? Or put on his bathing suit and have a nice swim in the freezing water? He opted for the second course. It might help him simmer down. He jumped in the water and immediately became half-paralysed. Would he ever get it through his head that, at age fifty, this was no longer a good idea? That the time for such bravado was over? He headed gloomily back to the house and could already hear the phone ringing from thirty feet away. His only choice was to accept things as they were. And, for starters, to answer the phone.

It was Fazio.

'Tell me something. Was it you who called fifteen minutes ago?'

'No, Chief, it was Catarella. He said you said you weren't ready to say hello. So I let a little time pass and then rang back myself. Feel ready now, Chief?'

'How can you be so funny first thing in the morning, Fazio? Are you at the office?'

'No, Chief. Somebody got killed. Zap!'

'What's that supposed to mean, "zap"?'

'He got shot.'

'No. A pistol shot goes "bang", a *lupara* goes "boom", a machine gun goes "ratatatatat", and a knife goes "swiss".'

'Then it was a bang, Chief. Just one shot. To the face.'

'Where are you?'

'At the scene of the crime. Isn't that what they call it? Via Cavour 44. You know where it is?'

'Yeah, I know. Was he shot at home?'

'He was just coming home, sticking his key in the front door. They left him sprawling on the pavement.'

*

Can a murder ever be said to happen at the right moment? No, never. A death is always a death. Nevertheless, it was a concrete, incontrovertible fact that Montalbano, while driving to Via Cavour 44, felt his bad mood passing. Jumping right into an investigation would help to chase away the dark thoughts that had cluttered his mind upon awakening.

*

When he got there he had to fight his way through the crowd. Like flies drawn to shit, even though it was barely dawn, an excited throng of men and women blocked the street. There was even a girl with a baby in her arms. The little thing gaped wide-eyed at the scene, and the mother's teaching methods made his balls spin.

'Everybody out of here!'

A few people started to move away at once, while others had to be shoved by Galluzzo. But one could still hear moaning, a kind of sustained whimper. It was a woman of about fifty, dressed all in black; she was being restrained by two men to prevent her from throwing herself on the corpse, which lay belly-up on the pavement, face rendered unrecognizable by a gunshot wound between the eyes.

'Get that woman out of here.'

'But she's his mother, Chief.'

'She can go and cry at home. She's only in the way. Who informed her? Did she hear the shot and come running?'

'No, sir. She couldn't have heard the shot, since she lives in Via Autonomia Siciliana 12. Apparently somebody informed her.'

'And was she just sitting there, all ready with her black dress on?'

'She's a widow, Chief.'

'All right, be nice, but get her out of here.'

Whenever Montalbano talked this way, it was hopeless. Fazio approached the two men, muttered something to them, and they dragged the woman away.

The inspector walked up beside Dr Pasquano, who was crouching over the victim's head.

'Well?' he asked.

'Not well at all,' the doctor replied. And he went on, even more rudely than Montalbano, 'Do I really need to explain what happened? They shot him once. Bull's eye, in the middle of the forehead. The exit wound took out half his cranium in the back. See those little clots? They're bits of his brain. Satisfied?'

'When did it happen, in your opinion?'

'A few hours ago. Around four or five in the morning.'

A short distance away, Vanni Arquà, the new chief of forensics, was examining the most ordinary of stones with the eye of an archaeologist who's just discovered a Palaeolithic artefact. Montalbano wasn't fond of Arquà, and his antipathy was openly returned.

'Did they kill him with that?' asked the inspector, indicating the stone, a look of seraphic innocence on his face.

Vanni Arquà looked at him with undisguised disdain.

'Don't be ridiculous! It was a firearm.'

'Have you recovered the bullet?'

'Yes. It ended up embedded in the wood of the front door, which was still closed.'

'And the cartridge?'

'Look, Inspector, I'm not required to answer your questions. The case is going to be handled by the captain of the Flying Squad. Commissioner's orders. You're to play only a supporting role.'

'What do you think I'm doing? You don't call this support?'

Judge Tommaseo, the assistant prosecutor, was nowhere to be seen. They would have to wait before they could move the victim's body.

'Fazio, why isn't Inspector Augello here?'

'He's on his way. He spent the night with friends in Fela. We called him on his mobile phone.'

Fela? It would take him another hour to get to Vigàta. And in what condition! Dead tired and sleepless! Friends, right! He'd likely spent the night with some woman whose husband was out getting his fun somewhere else.

Galluzzo came up.

'Tommaseo just phoned. Asked if we could go and pick him up in one of our cars. He crashed into a pole about two miles outside Montelusa. What should we do?'

'Go and get him.'

Nicolò Tommaseo rarely got where he wanted to go in his car. He drove like a dog on drugs. The inspector didn't feel like waiting for him. Before leaving, he had a look at the corpse.

11

A kid barely twenty years old, in jeans and sports jacket, with a ponytail and earring. The shoes must have cost him his inheritance.

'Fazio, I'm going to the office. You wait for the judge and the Flying Squad captain. See you later.'

*

He decided to go to the port instead. Leaving the car on the wharf, he began walking slowly, one step at a time, along the eastern jetty, towards the lighthouse. The sun had risen bright red, apparently happy to have managed it one more time. On the horizon were three black dots, motor trawlers returning late to shore. He opened his mouth wide and took a deep breath. He liked the smell of Vigàta's port.

'What are you talking about? All ports have the same stink,' Livia once said to him.

It wasn't true. Every harbour had a different smell. Vigàta's combined, in perfect doses, wet cordage, fishing nets drying in the sun, iodine, rotten fish, dead and living algae and tar with, deep in the background, a hint of petrol. Incomparable. Before reaching the flat rock under the lighthouse, he bent down and picked up a handful of pebbles.

At the rock, he sat down. Gazing at the water, he thought he saw the face of Carlo Martello appear indistinctly before him. He angrily threw the handful of pebbles at it. The image broke apart, flickered and vanished. Montalbano lit a cigarette.

*

'Oh, Chief, Chief, Chief!' Catarella assailed him as soon as he came through the front door of headquarters. 'Doctor Latte, the one with an *s* at the end, called three times! He wants to talk to you poissonally in poisson! Says it's rilly rilly urgint!'

He could guess what Lattes, the chief of the commissioner's cabinet, nicknamed 'Caffè-Lattes' for his nervous, unctuous manner, had to say.

Commissioner Luca Bonetti-Alderighi, Marquis of Villabella, had been explicit and severe. Montalbano never looked his superior in the eye, but always slightly higher; he was fascinated by the man's hair, which was very thick, with a great big shock on top that curled back like certain human shit piles deposited in the open countryside. Noticing that the inspector was averting his gaze, the commissioner had made the mistake of believing he'd finally intimidated his subordinate.

'Montalbano, now that the new captain of the Flying Squad, Ernesto Gribaudo, has arrived, I'm going to tell you once and for all: you're going to play a supporting role from here on in. Your department will only handle little things; the big stuff will be handled by the Flying Squad in the person of Captain Gribaudo or his second-in-command.'

Ernesto Gribaudo, a living legend. Once, when glancing at the chest of a man who'd been killed by a burst of Kalashnikov fire, he'd declared the victim dead from a dozen stab wounds inflicted in rapid succession.

'Excuse me, Mr Commissioner, could you give me a few practical examples?'

Luca Bonetti-Alderighi had beamed with pride and satisfaction as Montalbano stood before him on the other side of his desk, leaning slightly forward, a humble smile playing on his lips. Indeed, the inspector's tone had been almost beseeching. The commissioner had him in the palm of his hand!

'Please be more explicit, Montalbano. What sort of examples do you mean?'

'I'd like to know what things I should consider little and what things I should consider big.'

Montalbano, too, was congratulating himself. His imitation of Paolo Villaggio's immortal Fantozzi was succeeding marvellously.

'What a question, Montalbano! Petty theft, domestic quarrels, small-time drug-dealing, brawls, ID checks on immigrants, that's the small stuff. Murders, that's big.'

'Mind if I take notes?' Montalbano had asked, pulling a piece of paper and a pen out of his pocket.

The commissioner had looked at him in bewilderment. And the inspector, for a moment, had felt frightened, thinking he'd pulled the other's leg a little too hard and the commissioner had caught on.

But no. The commissioner had actually been scowling in disdain.

'Go right ahead.'

And now Lattes was about to reiterate the commissioner's explicit orders. A murder did not fall within his province. It was a matter for the Flying Squad. Montalbano dialled the cabinet chief's number.

'Montalbano, old boy! How are you? Eh? And how's the family?'

Family? He was an orphan and not even married.

'They're all fine, thanks. And yours?'

'All well, by the Virgin's good graces. Listen, Montalbano, on the matter of that murder committed last night in Vigàta, the commissioner—'

'I already know, Dr Lattes. It's not my concern.'

'That's not true! Who ever said that? I called you, in fact, because the commissioner actually *wants* you to take the case.'

Montalbano felt a mild shock. What could this mean? He didn't even know the victim's vital statistics. Want to bet it will turn out the boy was the son of some bigwig? Were they trying to get him to take on some tremendous headache? Not a hot potato, but a glowing firebrand?

'I'm sorry, Dr Lattes. I was at the crime scene, but I didn't start any investigation. You can understand. I didn't want to tread on anyone's turf.'

'Of course I understand, Montalbano! We have some extremely sensitive people in this police department, thanks be to God!'

'Why isn't Captain Gribaudo on the case?'

'You don't know?'

'I know nothing.'

'Well, last week Captain Gribaudo had to go to Beirut for an important conference on—'

'I know. Was he held up in Beirut?'

'No, no, he's back, but, upon his return, he immediately came down with a violent case of dysentery. We were worried it might be some sort of cholera – it's not so unusual in those places, you know – but then, by the Virgin's good graces, it turned out not to be.'

Montalbano himself thanked the Virgin for having forced Gribaudo not to stray more than a foot and a half from the nearest toilet.

'What about his second-in-command, Lieutenant Foti?'

'He was in New York for a conference organized by Rudolph Giuliani, you know, the "zero tolerance" mayor. The conference dealt with the best ways to maintain order in a large metropolis—'

'Didn't that end two days ago?'

'Yes, of course, but, you see, afterwards, Lieutenant Foti decided to explore Manhattan a little and got shot in the leg by some muggers who stole his wallet. He's in hospital at the moment. Nothing serious, thank God.'

＊

Fazio didn't turn up until after ten.

'Why so late, Fazio?'

'Please, Chief, I don't want to hear about it. First we had to wait for the assistant prosecutor's assistant. Then—'

'Wait. Explain.'

Fazio looked up to the heavens. Having to rehash the whole affair brought back all the nervous agitation he'd suffered that morning.

'OK. When Galluzzo went to pick up Assistant Tommaseo, who'd wrapped his car around a tree—'

'Wasn't it a pole?'

'No, Chief. He thought it was a pole, but it was a tree. To cut a long story short, Tommaseo hurt his forehead and was bleeding. Galluzzo took him to the emergency department at Montelusa Hospital. From there, Tommaseo, who by then also had a headache, called to ask for a replacement. But it was early and there was nobody in the office. So Tommaseo called a colleague of his at home, Judge Nicotra. So then we had to wait for Judge Nicotra to get dressed, have breakfast, get in his car and drive to the crime scene. Meanwhile, Captain Gribaudo was nowhere to be seen. Ditto his lieutenant. After the ambulance finally arrived and the body was taken away, I waited another ten minutes for the Flying Squad. Seeing that nobody was coming, I left. If Captain Gribaudo wants me, he can come and look for me here.'

'What did you find out about the murder?'

'What the fuck do you care, Chief, with all due respect? It's the Flying Squad's case!'

'Gribaudo's not coming, Fazio. He's holed up in a toilet somewhere, shitting his soul out. Foti got shot in New York. Lattes called and told me. The case is ours.'

Fazio sat down, eyes gleaming with contentment. He immediately pulled from his pocket a piece of paper covered with minuscule writing. He began reading.

'Emanuele Sanfilippo, known as Nenè, son of Gerlando Sanfilippo and Natalina Patò—'

'That's enough,' said Montalbano.

He was irritated by what he called Fazio's 'records-office complex', but what irked him most was the tone of voice his sergeant used when citing birth dates, relatives, marriages, etc. Fazio understood at once.

'Sorry, Chief.' But he didn't put the piece of paper back in his pocket. 'I'll keep it as a reminder,' he said by way of justification.

'How old was this Sanfilippo?'

'Twenty-one years and three months.'

'Was he a drug user? Dealer?'

'Apparently not.'

'Have a job?'

'No.'

'Did he live in Via Cavour?'

'Yes, sir. Third-floor flat, with living room, two bed-rooms, bathroom and kitchen. He lived alone.'

'Did he rent it or own it?'

'Rented. Eight hundred thousand lire a month.'

'Did his mother pay for it?'

'His mother? She's penniless, Chief. Lives on a pension of five hundred thousand a month. If you ask me, things went as follows: around four o'clock in the morning, Nenè Sanfilippo parks his car right in front of the main entrance, he crosses the street, and—'

'What kind of car?'

'A Fiat Punto. But he's got another one in the garage. A Duetto. Get the picture?'

'Ill-gotten gains?'

'I'd say so. You should see what he had in his flat. All the latest stuff, TV, satellite dish on the roof, computer, VCR, video camera, fax, refrigerator ... And I didn't even get a good look. There are video cassettes, diskettes and CD-ROMs for the computer.... We'll have to check it all out.'

'Any news of Mimì?'

Fazio, who had got all worked up, seemed disoriented.

'Who? Oh, right. Inspector Augello? He showed up shortly after the assistant's assistant showed up. Had a look around and left.'

'Any idea where?'

'Dunno. Anyway, as I was saying, Nenè Sanfilippo inserts the key in the lock and, at that exact moment, somebody calls his name.'

'How do you know this?'

'Because he was shot in the face, Chief. Hearing his

name called, Sanfilippo turns around and takes a few steps towards the person who called him. It must have happened very fast, mind you, because he left the key in the lock.'

'Was there a struggle?'

'Apparently not.'

'Did you look at the keys?'

'There were five keys. Two for Via Cavour: main door and flat door. Two for his mother's place, main door and flat door. And the fifth is one of those ultra-modern keys that locksmiths say can't be duplicated. We don't know what door that one was for.'

'Interesting kid, this Sanfilippo. Were there any witnesses?'

Fazio started laughing.

'Are you kidding, Chief?'

TWO

They were interrupted by some heated shouting in the lobby. There was decidedly a row in the making.

'Go and have a look.'

Fazio went out, the voices calmed down, and a few minutes later he returned.

'There's a man who got upset with Catarella because he wouldn't let him in. He insists on speaking to you.'

'He can wait.'

'He seems pretty worked up, Chief.'

'Let's hear him, then.'

In came a bespectacled man of about forty, neatly dressed, with hair parted on the side and the look of a respectable clerk.

'Thank you for agreeing to see me. You're Inspector Montalbano, aren't you? My name is Davide Griffo and I feel mortified for having raised my voice, but I couldn't understand what that policeman was saying to me. Is he a foreigner?'

Montalbano preferred not to answer.

'I'm listening.'

'Well, I live in Messina and work at city hall. And I'm married. My parents live here, in Vigàta, and I'm an only child. I'm very worried about them.'

'Why?'

'I phone them twice a week from Messina, every Thursday and Sunday. Two nights ago, last Sunday, they didn't answer, and I haven't heard from them since. Every hour's been hell, so finally my wife suggested I get in the car and drive to Vigàta. Yesterday I phoned the concierge to find out if she had the key to my parents' flat. She said no. So my wife said I should turn to you. She's seen you a couple of times on TV.'

'Do you want to file a report?'

'First I'd like to get authorization to break down the door...' His voice began to crack. 'Something serious may have happened to them, Inspector.'

'All right. Fazio, get Gallo for me.'

Fazio went out and returned with his colleague.

'Gallo, please accompany this gentleman. He needs to have the door to his parents' flat broken down. He has had no word of them since last week. Where did you say they live?'

'I hadn't told you yet. In Via Cavour, number 44.'

Montalbano's jaw dropped.

'*Madunnuzza santa!*' said Fazio.

Gallo started coughing violently and left the room in search of a glass of water.

Davide Griffo, now pale and spooked by the effect of his words, looked around.

'What did I say?' he asked in a faint voice.

*

As Fazio pulled up in front of Via Cavour 44, Davide Griffo stepped out of the car and rushed inside the main door.

'Where do we start?' Fazio asked the inspector as he was locking the car.

'We start with the missing old people. The dead man's already dead and can wait.'

In the main doorway they ran into Griffo, who was racing back like a bat out of hell.

'The concierge said somebody was murdered last night! Somebody who lived in this building!'

Only then did he notice Nenè Sanfilippo's silhouette, outlined in white on the pavement. He began to tremble violently.

'Calm down,' the inspector said to him, putting a hand on his shoulder.

'No . . . it's just that I'm afraid that—'

'Mr Griffo, are you thinking that your parents might be somehow involved in this murder?'

'Are you joking? My parents are—'

'Well, then, forget the fact that someone was killed in front of the building this morning. Let's go and have a look.'

Signora Ciccina Recupero, the concierge, was pacing about her six-by-six-foot porter's lodge like one of those bears that go insane in their cages and start rocking first on one leg, then another. She could allow herself this luxury because she was all bones, and the little bit of space she had available was more than enough for her to shuffle about in.

'Oh God oh God oh God! *Madunnuzza santa!* What is happening in this building? What on earth is happening? Has somebody cast a spell on it? We must call a priest at once for some holy water!'

Montalbano grabbed her by the arm — or, rather, by the bone of her arm — and forced her to sit down.

'Cut out the theatrics. Stop crossing yourself and answer my questions. When did you last see the Griffos?'

'Last Saturday morning, when Mrs Griffo came back from shopping.'

'Today is Tuesday. Weren't you worried?'

The concierge bristled.

'Why should I be? Those two never said a word to anyone! Stuck up, they were! And I don't give a damn if their son hears me say it! They'd go out, come back with their groceries, lock themselves up in their flat, and three days'd go by before anyone saw them again! They had my phone number. They could phone if they needed anything!'

'And did that ever happen?'

'Did what ever happen?'

'Did they ever phone you?'

'Yeah, it happened a few times. When Signor Fofò, the husband, was sick, he phoned me for help when his wife was out at the chemist's. Another time when a hose on the washing machine broke and their flat got flooded. Another time—'

'That's enough, thanks. You said you haven't got the key?'

'I didn't just say it, I don't have it! Mrs Griffo left me the key last summer when they went to see their son in Messina. She wanted me to water the plants she keeps on the balcony. But then they asked for it back without a word of thanks – nothing – like I was their servant or something! And I'm supposed to be worried about them? Hell, if I went up to the fourth floor to ask them if they needed anything, they'd probably tell me to fuck off!'

'Shall we go up?' the inspector asked Davide Griffo, who was leaning against the wall. He looked a little weak in the knees.

They took the lift to the fourth floor. Davide shot out at once. Fazio brought his mouth to the inspector's ear.

'There are four flats on each floor. Nenè Sanfilippo lived in the one directly under the Griffos,' he said, gesturing with his chin toward Davide, who was pressing all his weight against the door of number 17 and wildly ringing the doorbell.

'Stand aside, please.'

Davide, seeming not to hear him, kept pushing the doorbell. They could hear it ringing inside, remote and useless. Fazio stepped forward, grabbed the man by the shoulders and moved him aside. The inspector extracted a large key ring from his pocket. From it hung a dozen or so variously shaped picklocks, a gift from a burglar with whom he'd become friends. He fiddled with the lock for a good five minutes.

The door finally opened. Montalbano and Fazio opened their nostrils wide to smell the odour inside. Fazio was holding back Davide, who wanted to rush in, by the arm. Death, after a few days, begins to stink. But there was nothing. The apartment merely smelled stuffy. Fazio let go and Davide sprang forward, immediately crying out, 'Papa! Mama!'

Everything was in perfect order. The windows shut, the bed made, the kitchen tidy, the sink empty of dirty dishes. Inside the fridge, a packet of prosciutto, some olives, a bottle of white wine, half empty. In the freezer, four slices of meat and two mullets. If they'd indeed gone away, they certainly left with the intention of returning soon.

'Do your parents have any relatives?'

Davide was sitting on a chair in the kitchen, head in his hands.

'Papa, no. Mama, yes. A brother in Comiso, and a sister in Trapani who died.'

'Do you think they could have gone to——'

'No, Inspector, it's not possible. They haven't heard from my parents for a month. They're not very close.'

'So you have absolutely no idea where they might have gone?'

'No. If I did, I'd have tried to find them.'

'The last time you spoke to them was last Thursday evening, correct?'

'Yes.'

'They didn't say anything that might have—'

'Nothing whatsoever.'

'What did you talk about?'

'The usual things, health, the grandchildren ... I have two boys, Alfonso, named after my father, and Giovanni. Six and four years old. My parents are very fond of them. Whenever we came to Vigàta they would shower them with presents.'

He made no effort to hold back his tears.

Fazio, who'd had a look around the flat, returned with a shrug.

'Mr Griffo, there's no point in us remaining here. I hope to have some news for you very soon.'

'Inspector, I took a few days off from my job. I can stay in Vigàta at least until tomorrow evening.'

'As far as I'm concerned, you can stay as long as you like.'

'Actually, what I meant was: could I sleep here tonight?'

Montalbano thought it over a moment. In the dining

room, which also doubled as a living room, there was a small desk with papers on it. He wanted to go over these at his convenience.

'No, you can't sleep here, I'm sorry.'

'But what if somebody rings . . . ?'

'Who, your parents? Why would they ring, knowing there's nobody at home?'

'No, I meant if somebody rings with news . . .'

'You're right. I'll have somebody tap the phone right away. Fazio, you take care of it. Mr Griffo, I need a photo of your parents.'

'I've got one right here, Inspector, in my pocket. I took it myself when they came to Messina. Their names are Alfonso and Margherita.'

He started sobbing as he handed the photo to Montalbano.

*

'Five times four is twenty, twenty minus two is eighteen,' said Montalbano on the landing, after Griffo had left more bewildered than convinced.

'Trying to pick the winning numbers?' asked Fazio.

'As sure as one and one makes two, there should be twenty flats in this building, since it has five floors. But in fact there are only eighteen, if we exclude the Griffo and Sanfilippo flats. Which means we've got no less than eighteen families to interrogate, and two questions to ask each family. What do you know about the Griffos? And what do you know about Nenè Sanfilippo? If that little son of a bitch Mimì were here to give us a hand—'

Speak of the devil. At that moment, Fazio's mobile phone rang.

'It's Inspector Augello. Wants to know if we need his help.'

Montalbano's face turned red with rage.

'Tell him to get here immediately, and if he's not here in five minutes, I'll break his legs.'

Fazio gave him the message.

'While we're waiting,' the inspector suggested, 'let's go and get ourselves a cup of coffee.'

*

When they returned to Via Cavour, Mimì was already there waiting for them. Fazio walked discreetly away.

'Mimì,' the inspector began, 'I'm really at my wits' end with you. I'm speechless. What on earth is going through your head? Do you or don't you know that—'.

'I know,' Augello interrupted him.

'What the hell do you know?'

'What I'm supposed to know. That I fucked up. The fact is, I feel weird, confused.'

The inspector's rage subsided. Mimì was standing before him with a look he'd never had before. Not the usual devil-may-care attitude. On the contrary, there was something resigned about him, something humble.

'Mimì, would you tell me what's up with you?'

'I'll tell you later, Salvo.'

Montalbano was about to place a consoling hand on his subordinate's shoulder when a sudden suspicion stopped him. What if this son of a bitch Mimì was play-acting the same way he himself had done with Bonetti-Alderighi, pretending to be servile when in fact he was taking him for a ride? Augello, who had a poker face worthy of a tragedian, was capable of this and more. In doubt, the inspector refrained from the affectionate gesture. Instead, he filled him in on the disappearance of the Griffos.

'You'll handle the tenants on the first and second floors, Fazio will take the fifth and ground floors, and I'll do the third and fourth floors.'

＊

Third floor, flat 12. The widow Concetta Lo Mascolo, née Burgio, in her late fifties launched into the most impassioned of monologues.

'Don't talk to me about this Nenè Sanfilippo, Inspector! Don't mention that name! The poor boy was murdered, may he rest in peace! But he damned my soul, he did! During the day he was never at home, but at night, oh yes, he certainly was. And that, for me, was when the hell began! Every other night! Hell! You see, Mr Inspector, my bedroom shares a wall with Sanfilippo's bedroom. And the walls in this building are paper-thin! You can hear everything, every last little thing! And after they'd been playing music loud enough to break my eardrums, they would start in with another kind of music! A symphony! Clunkety clunkety clunkety clunk! And the bed would knock against the wall and play percussion! And the slut of the hour would go ah ah ah ah! And then clunkety clunkety clunkety clunk all over again, from the top! And I would start to think wicked thoughts. So I would say ten Hail Marys. Twenty Hail Marys. Thirty Hail Marys. But it was hopeless! I couldn't get the thoughts out of my head. I'm still a young woman, Inspector! He was damning my soul! Anyway, no, sir, I know nothing about the Griffos. They never said a word to anyone. If nobody tells me anything, why should I tell you anything? Am I right?'

*

Third floor, flat 14. The Crucillà family. Husband: Stefano Crucillà, retired, former accountant at the fish market. Wife: Antonietta, née De Carlo. Elder son: Calogero, mining engineer, working in Bolivia. Younger daughter: Samanta with no *h* between the *t* and the *a*, maths teacher, unmarried, living at home with her parents. Samanta spoke for them all.

'You see, Inspector, just to give you an idea of how unsociable the Griffos were, one day I ran into Mrs Griffo as she was coming through the front door of the building with her shopping trolley filled to bursting and two plastic shopping bags in each hand. Since you have to climb three steps to get to the lift, I asked if I could help her. She rudely said no. And the husband was no better.

'As for Nenè Sanfilippo, good-looking guy, full of life, very nice. What did he do? What young people always do at his age, when they're free.'

With this, she shot a glance at her parents, sighing. She, alas, was not free. Otherwise she could have shown a thing or two to Nenè Sanfilippo, rest his soul.

*

Third floor, flat 15. Dr Ernesto Assunto, dentist.

'This is only my office, Inspector. I live in Montelusa and only come here during the day. All I can tell you is that I ran into Mr Griffo once when his left cheek was swollen with an abscess. When I asked him if he had a dentist, he said no. So I suggested he drop in at the office. For my trouble I was given only a firm no. As for Sanfilippo, you know what, Inspector? I never met him and don't even know what he looked like.'

*

Montalbano began climbing the flight of stairs that led to the floor above when he happened to look at his watch. It was one thirty and, seeing what time it was, he felt, by conditioned reflex, a tremendous hunger pang. The lift passed him on its way up. He heroically decided to suffer the hunger and continue his questioning, since at that hour he was more likely to find people at home. In front of flat 16 stood a fat, bald man holding a black, misshapen tote bag in one hand and trying with the other to insert his key in the door. He saw the inspector stop behind him.

'You looking for me?'

'Yes, Mr....'

'Mistretta. Who are you?'

'I'm Inspector Montalbano.'

'What do you want?'

'I want to ask you a few questions about the young man who was murdered last night—'

'Yeah, I heard. The concierge told me everything when I was leaving for the office this morning. I work at the cement plant.'

'And about the Griffos.'

'Why, what did the Griffos do?'

'They're missing.'

Mr Mistretta opened the door and stood aside.

'Please come in.'

Montalbano took one step inside and found himself in a flat in utter disorder. Two mismatched, threadbare socks adorned a shelf near the entrance. He was shown into a room that must have once been a living room. Newspapers, dirty plates, grimy glasses, clean and unwashed laundry, ashtrays overflowing with butts and ash.

'It's a little messy,' Mr Mistretta admitted, 'but my wife's been away for two months in Caltanissetta, with her ailing mother.'

From the black tote bag he extracted a tin of tuna, a

lemon and a loaf of bread. He opened the tin and emptied its contents onto the first plate within reach. Pushing aside a pair of pants, he grabbed a fork and a knife. He cut the lemon and squeezed it onto the tuna.

'Care to join me? Look, Inspector, I don't want to waste your time. I was thinking of filling your ear with bullshit just to keep you here awhile and have a little company. But then I realized it wouldn't be right. I probably saw the Griffos a couple of times. But we didn't even say hello. And I never even saw the young man who was killed.'

'Thanks. Good day,' said the inspector, standing up.

Even among all the filth, seeing somebody eat had redoubled his appetite.

*

Fourth floor. Beside the door to flat 18, under the doorbell, was a plaque that said: Guido and Gina De Dominicis. He rang the bell.

'Who is it?' asked a little kid's voice.

What to say to a child?

'A friend of your papa's.'

The door opened and a boy of about eight, a mischievous glint in his eye, appeared before the inspector.

'Is your papa there? Or your mama?'

'No, but they'll be back soon.'

'What's your name?'

'Pasqualino. What's yours?'

'Salvo.'

At that moment Montalbano became convinced he smelled something burning inside the flat.

'What's that smell?'

'Nothing. I set the bed on fire.'

The inspector sprang forward, pushing Pasqualino aside. Black smoke was pouring out of a doorway. It was the bedroom. A quarter of the double bed had caught fire. He took off his jacket, saw a wool blanket folded up on a chair, grabbed this, opened it and threw it onto the flames, patting it hard with his hands. A malicious little tongue of fire consumed half of one of his shirt cuffs.

'If you put out my fire I'll just start another one somewhere else,' said Pasqualino, brandishing a box of kitchen matches menacingly.

The little demon! What to do? Disarm him or continue to extinguish the blaze? The inspector opted for the fireman's role, repeatedly getting singed and seared. Then a woman's shrill cry paralysed him.

'Guiiiiidoooo!'

A young blonde, boggle-eyed, was clearly about to faint. Montalbano hadn't had time to open his mouth when a bespectacled, broad-shouldered young man, a kind of Clark Kent, materialized beside the young woman. Without saying a word, Superman, with a single, extremely elegant gesture, pushed his jacket aside, and at once a pistol the size of a cannon was pointing at the inspector.

'Hands up.'

Montalbano obeyed.

'He's a pyromaniac! A pyromaniac!' the young woman babbled, weeping and embracing her precious little angel.

'Mama! Mama! He said he wanted to burn the whole house down!'

It took a good half-hour to clear matters up. Montalbano learned that the husband worked as a cashier in a bank, which explained why he went around with a gun, and that Signora Gina had come home late because she'd been to see the doctor.

'Pasqualino's going to have a brother,' the woman confessed, lowering her eyes modestly.

*

Against a background of screams and cries from the child, who'd been spanked and locked in a small dark room, Montalbano learned that even when the Griffos were at home, it was as if they weren't there.

'Never a cough, or even, say, the sound of something dropped on the floor, or a word spoken a little louder than the rest. Nothing!'

As for Nenè Sanfilippo, Mr and Mrs De Dominicis didn't even know the murder victim had lived in their building.

THREE

The last station on the Via Crucis was flat 19, fourth floor. Leone Guarnotta, lawyer.

Filtering out from under the door was a fragrance of ragù sauce that made Montalbano feel faint.

'Ah, you're Inspector Montaperto,' said the big, mannish woman who answered the door.

'Montalbano.'

'I never get names right, but it's enough for me to see a face just once on TV and I never forget it!'

'Who is it?' asked a male voice from inside the flat.

'It's the inspector, Leo. Come in, come in.'

As Montalbano entered, a skinny man of about sixty appeared, a napkin stuck into his shirt collar.

'Guarnotta's the name, pleased to meet you. Make yourself comfortable. We were about to eat. Come into the living room.'

'The living room!' the mannish woman intervened. 'If

you waste time talking, the pasta's going to turn to glue. Have you eaten, Inspector?'

'Actually, no, not yet,' said Montalbano, feeling his heart flutter with hope.

'Well, then, there's no problem,' Mrs Guarnotta concluded. 'You can sit down with us for a dish of pasta, and that way it'll be easier for all of us to talk.'

The pasta had been drained at the right moment ('Knowin' when it's time to drain the pasta is an art,' his housekeeper Adelina had once proclaimed). And the meat in the sauce was savoury and tender.

But, except for filling his belly, the inspector had come up empty again, as far as the investigation was concerned. He had made, as the Sicilians say, another hole in the water.

*

Around four o'clock that afternoon, finding himself in his office with Mimì Augello and Fazio, Montalbano couldn't help but notice that he'd in fact made three holes in the water.

'Not to mention that with you, one plus one does not make two,' said Fazio, 'since there are actually twenty-three apartments in that building.'

'Twenty-three?' said Montalbano, flummoxed because he was truly hopeless with numbers.

'There are three on the ground floor, Chief, all offices. And they don't know the Griffos, much less Sanfilippo.'

In conclusion, the Griffos had lived in the building for years, but it was as if they were made of air. As for Sanfilippo, forget about it. There were tenants who hadn't even heard of him.

'You two,' said Montalbano, 'before the news of the disappearance becomes official, I want you to go around town and try to find out more. Rumours, gossip, hearsay, backbiting, that sort of thing.'

'Why? Do you think people's answers will change after they hear of the disappearance?' asked Augello.

'Oh, they'll change all right. Something that at first seems normal is seen in a different light after something abnormal happens. And while you're at it, ask them about Sanfilippo, too.'

Fazio and Augello left the office less than convinced.

Montalbano picked up the keys to Sanfilippo's place, which Fazio had left on the table, put them in his pocket, went out and called Catarella, who for the last week had been busy trying to solve a crossword puzzle for beginners.

'Cat, I want you to come with me. I'm entrusting you with an important mission.'

Overcome with emotion, Catarella couldn't open his mouth, not even after they'd entered the murdered young man's flat.

'See that computer, Cat?'

'Yessir. It's rilly nice.'

'Well, get to work on it. I want to know everything

that's inside it. Then put in all the diskettes and ... what are they called?'

'Ziti roms, Chief.'

'Have a look at all of them, too. And report to me when you're done.'

'There's also some video cassettes.'

'Leave the cassettes alone.'

✻

He got in his car and headed towards Montelusa. His friend Nicolò Zito, newsman for the Free Channel television station, was about to go on the air. Montalbano handed him the photograph.

'These are the Griffos, Alfonso and Margherita. You're to say only that their son Davide is worried because he has no news of them. Please mention it on tonight's news.'

Zito, who was an intelligent person and a good journalist, looked at the photo and asked a question the inspector had been expecting.

'Why are you concerned about the disappearance of these two?'

'I feel sorry for them.'

'I'm sure you do. But I'm also sure that's not the only reason. Is there some connection, by any chance?'

'With what?'

'With that kid, Sanfilippo, who was murdered in Vigàta.'

'They lived in the same building.'

Nicolò literally leapt out of his chair.

'But that's big news—'

'Which you're not going to mention. There may be a connection, but then again there may not. Do as I say, and the first major developments will be all yours.'

*

He sat on the veranda, having savoured the *pappanozza* he'd been wanting for a while. A humble dish: potatoes and onions boiled a long time, mashed into a porridge with the back of a fork, then dressed with an abundance of olive oil, strong vinegar, freshly ground black pepper and salt. To be eaten preferably with a tin fork (he had two which he jealously guarded), scorching the tongue and palate and cursing the saints with each bite.

On the nine p.m. news programme, Nicolò Zito did his job, showing the photo of the Griffos and saying their son was worried.

The inspector turned off the television and decided to start reading the latest novel by Vázquez Montalbán, which featured Pepe Carvalho as the protagonist and took place in Buenos Aires. He read the first three lines and then the phone rang. It was Mimì.

'Am I disturbing you, Salvo?'

'Not in the least.'

'Are you busy?'

'No. Why do you ask?'

'I'd like to talk to you. I'll come over to your place.'

So Mimì's attitude when he'd reproached him that morning had been sincere, not just an act. What could have happened to the poor guy? In matters of women, Mimì was easy to please and belonged to that line of male thinking according to which every neglected woman is lost to her mate. Maybe there'd been a scene with a jealous husband. Like the time he was caught by Perez, the accountant, while kissing the naked breasts of his lawfully wedded spouse. Things turned nasty, and an official grievance was filed with the Office of the Commissioner. But Mimì had wiggled out of it, because the commissioner – the old one, that is – had managed to settle the matter. If it had been the new commissioner, Bonetti-Alderighi, that would have been it for the career of Deputy Inspector Mimì Augello.

Somebody rang the doorbell. It couldn't possibly be Mimì, since he'd called not a moment before. But it was.

'Did you fly to Marinella from Vigàta?'

'I wasn't in Vigàta.'

'Where were you, then?'

'Here, nearby. I called you from my mobile phone. I've been circling the area for an hour.'

Uh-oh. Mimì'd been wandering around the neighbourhood before deciding to call. A sign that the matter was more serious than he had imagined.

Suddenly, a terrible thought occurred to him: what if Mimì had caught a disease from all his whoring?

'How's your health, Mimì?'

Mimì gave him a confused look.

'My health? Fine.'

Oh, God. If the burden he was bearing didn't involve the body, then it must concern the opposite realm. The soul? The mind? Who are we kidding? What did Mimì know about any of that?

As they were heading toward the veranda, Mimì said, 'Would you do me a favour, Salvo? Could you pour me a couple of shots of whisky, neat?'

He was trying to get up nerve, clearly. Montalbano started to feel extremely agitated. He set the bottle and glass down in front of Mimì, waited for him to pour out a substantial serving and then spoke.

'Mimì, I'm getting sick of this charade. Tell me what the hell is happening to you.'

Augello downed the drink in a single gulp and, looking out at the sea, said in a very low voice, 'I've decided to take a wife.'

Montalbano reacted on impulse, prey to an uncontrollable rage. With his left hand he swept the glass and bottle off the table, while with his right he dealt Mimì, who'd turned towards him, a ringing slap on the cheek.

'You stupid shit! What the fuck are you saying? As long as I'm alive, I'll never let you do a thing like that! I won't allow it! How could you ever think of such a thing? For what reason?'

Augello, meanwhile, had stood up, back against the wall, a hand on his reddened cheek, wide-eyed and terrified.

The inspector managed to get hold of himself, realizing he'd overreacted. He came towards Augello with his arms extended. Mimì managed to flatten himself even closer to the wall.

'For your own good, Salvo, don't touch me.'

So it was definitely contagious, Mimì's disease.

'Whatever it is you have, Mimì, it's still better than death.'

Mimì's jaw literally dropped.

'Death? Who ever said anything about death?'

'You did. Just now, you said: "I've decided to take my life." Do you deny it?'

Mimì didn't answer, but began to slide down the wall. He had his hands on his belly as if in unbearable pain. Tears came from his eyes and began to roll down beside his nose. The inspector felt a sense of panic come over him. What to do? Call a doctor? Who could he wake up at that hour? Mimì, meanwhile, had jumped to his feet, cleared the balustrade in a single bound, recovered the whisky bottle, unbroken, from the sand, and was now guzzling its contents. Montalbano froze. Then he gave a start, as Augello began to howl. But, no, he wasn't howling. He was laughing. What the hell was so funny? At last Mimì managed to speak.

'I said "wife", Salvo, not "life"!'

The inspector felt simultaneously relieved and pissed off. He went into the house, into the bathroom, put his head in the sink, turned on the cold water and stayed there for a bit. When he returned to the veranda, Augello was sitting down again. Montalbano took the bottle from his hands, brought it to his lips and polished it off.

'I'll go and get another.'

He returned with a brand-new bottle.

'You know, Salvo, when you reacted like that, you scared the shit out of me. I thought you'd become a fag and were in love with me!'

'Tell me about the girl,' Montalbano cut in.

Her name was Rachele Zummo. Mimì had met her in Fela, at the house of some friends. She worked in Pavia, in the north, but was visiting her parents.

'What's she do in Pavia?'

'Want to hear something funny? She's a policewoman!'

They laughed. And they kept laughing for another two hours, finishing the bottle.

*

'Hello, Livia? It's me, Salvo. Were you asleep?'

'Of course I was asleep. What's happening?'

'Nothing. I wanted to—'

'What do you mean, nothing? Do you know what time it is? It's two o'clock in the morning!'

'Oh, really? I'm sorry. I didn't realize it was so late ... or so early. No, really, it's nothing, just some silly matter, believe me.'

'Well, even if it's some silly matter, you're going to tell me anyway.'

'Mimì Augello said he's going to get married.'

'Well, isn't that the latest news! He already told me, three months ago, and begged me not to tell you.'

An extremely long pause.

'Are you still there, Salvo?'

'Yeah, I'm here. So you and Mr Augello have your little secrets and keep me in the dark, is that how it is?'

'Oh, come on, Salvo!'

'No, Livia, allow me for once to be pissed off!'

'And you allow me the same!'

'Why?'

'Because you called marriage a silly matter, arsehole! When in fact you should follow Mimì's example! Good night!'

*

He woke up around six o'clock in the morning, his mouth gluey, his head throbbing slightly. He drank half a bottle of cold water and tried to go back to sleep. No dice.

What to do? The question was answered by the ringing telephone.

At that hour? It was probably that idiot Mimì calling to tell him he'd changed his mind about getting married. He slapped his forehead. So that's what created the misunderstanding last night! Since when does a Sicilian 'take a wife'? In Sicily, one simply gets married! He picked up the receiver.

'Have you changed your mind?'

'No, Chief, I haven't. That'd be rather difficult, since I don't know what I would've changed my mind about. Care to tell me?'

'Sorry, Fazio, I thought you were someone else. What's up?'

'Sorry to wake you at this hour, but . . .'

'But?'

'We can't find Catarella. He disappeared yesterday afternoon, leaving the office without saying where he was going. And nobody's seen him since. We even asked at Montelusa Hospital . . .'

Fazio kept on talking, but the inspector was no longer listening. Catarella! He'd completely forgotten about him!

'I'm sorry, Fazio, I apologize to all of you. He went to do something for me and I forgot to tell you. There's nothing to be worried about.'

He distinctly heard Fazio sigh with relief.

*

It took him about twenty minutes to shower, shave and get dressed. He felt battered. When he arrived at Via Cavour 44, the concierge was sweeping the street in front of the door. She was so skinny that there was practically no difference between her and the broomstick. She looked remarkably like Olive Oyl, Popeye's girlfriend. He took the lift, got off on the third floor and opened the door to Nenè Sanfilippo's flat with a picklock. The lights were on inside. Catarella was sitting in front of the computer in his shirtsleeves. Upon seeing his superior, he immediately shot to his feet, put on his jacket and adjusted the knot of his tie. He was unshaven, his eyes red.

'Awaiting your orders, Chief!'

'You still here?'

'Just finishing up, Chief. Another coupla hours oughta do it.'

'Find anything?'

'Beggin' pardon, Chief, but d'you wan' me to talk technical or simple?'

'As simple as possible, Cat.'

'All right. I din't find a goddamn thing in this computer.'

'What do you mean?'

'I mean what I said, Chief. It's got no interneck connection. Inside it's only got sumpin he's writing...'

'And what's that?'

'Looks to me like a novel book, Chief.'

'And what else?'

'Then there's copies of all the litters 'e wrote and alla those writ to him. There's a lot of 'em.'

'Business?'

'No bizniss, Chief. They're skin litters.'

'I don't understand.'

Catarella blushed.

'It's like love litters, but—'

'I get the picture. And what's on those diskettes?'

'A lotta filth, Chief. Guys wit' girls, guys wit' guys, girls wit' girls, girls wit' animals...'

Catarella's face looked like it was about to catch fire at any moment.

'OK, OK, Cat. Print 'em up for me.'

'All of 'em? The guys wit' girls, guys wit' guys, girls—'

Montalbano halted the litany.

'I meant the novel book and the litters. But right now we're going to do something else. You're coming with me to a cafe, you're going to have a *caffellatte* and a couple of croissants and then I'll bring you back here.'

*

The moment he returned to his office, Imbrò, who'd been assigned to the switchboard, came in.

'Chief, the Free Channel called with a list of the names and phone numbers of all the people who contacted them after seeing the Griffos' photo on TV. I wrote 'em all down here.'

Fifteen or so names. At a glance, the phone numbers all looked to be from Vigàta. So the Griffos were not as evanescent as they had first seemed. Fazio came in.

'Jesus, what a scare we got when we couldn't find Catarella! We didn't know he'd been sent on a secret mission. You know what that wicked Galluzzo called him? Agent Double-oh-oh.'

'Spare me the comedy. Got any news?'

'I went to see Sanfilippo's mother. The poor lady has no idea what her son did for a living. She told me that at age eighteen, with his passion for computers, he got a good job in Montelusa. Pretty well paid, and with his mother's pension they got on OK. Then all of a sudden Nenè quit his job, had a personality change and went off to live by himself. He had a lot of money, but he let his mother go around with holes in her shoes.'

'Tell me something, Fazio. Did they find any money on his person?'

'Are you kidding? Three million lire in cash and a cheque for two million.'

'Good, so at least Mrs Sanfilippo won't have to go into debt to pay for the funeral. Who was the cheque from?'

'From Manzo and Company of Montelusa.'

'Try to find out what it was for.'

'All right. As for the Griffos—'

'Have a look at this,' Montalbano interrupted him. 'It's a list of people with information on the Griffos.'

✢

The first name on the list was Saverio Cusumano.

'Hello, Mr Cusumano. This is Inspector Montalbano.'

'What do you want from me?'

'Wasn't it you who called the television station when you saw the photo of Mr and Mrs Griffo?'

'Yes, sir, that was me. But what's that got to do with you?'

'We're handling the case.'

'Nobody ever told me that! I'm only talking to their son Davide. Goodbye.'

A joyous start is the best of guides, as Matteo Maria Boiardo once said.

The second name on the list was Gaspare Belluzzo.

'Hello, Mr Belluzzo? This is Inspector Montalbano, Vigàta Police. You called the Free Channel about Mr and Mrs Griffo.'

'Right. Last Sunday, the wife and I saw them, they were on the bus with us.'

'Where were you going?'

'To the Sanctuary of the Madonna of Tindari.'

Tindari, gentle as I know you – the line by Quasimodo echoed in his head.

'And what were you going there for?'

'It was an excursion organized by Malaspina Tours in Vigàta. The wife and I went on one last year, too, to San Calogero di Fiacca.'

'Tell me something. Do you remember the names of the other passengers?'

'Sure, there was Mr and Mrs Bufalotta, the Continos, the Domenidòs, the Raccuglias … There were about forty of us in all.'

Messrs Bufalotta and Contino were on the list of those who'd phoned.

'A final question, Mr Belluzzo. When you got back to Vigàta, did you see the Griffos with everyone else?'

'To be honest, I can't really say. You know, Inspector, it was late, eleven o'clock at night, it was dark, we were all tired...'

*

There was no point wasting more time with other phone calls. He summoned Fazio.

'Listen, all these people went on an excursion to Tindari last Sunday. The Griffos were there too. The trip was organized by Malaspina Tours.'

'I know them.'

'Good. Go there and get the whole list. Then call everyone who went on the tour. I want them all at the station at nine o'clock tomorrow morning.'

'And where are we going to put them?'

'I don't give a damn where we put them. Set up a field hospital or something, because the youngest of the lot's probably sixty-five. Another thing: find out from Malaspina who was driving the bus that Sunday. If he's in Vigàta and he's not working, I want him here within the hour.'

*

Catarella — eyes even redder than before, hair standing on end, making him look like a textbook maniac — came in with a fat stack of pages under his arm.

'Here's all of it, Chief, all printed up and all.'

'Good. Leave it here and go and get some sleep. I'll see you late this afternoon.'

'Whatever you say, Chief.'

Jesus! Now he had a ream of at least six hundred pages on his desk!

Mimì came in looking splendid, and a twinge of envy came over Montalbano, who immediately remembered the spat he'd had over the phone with Livia. His mood darkened.

'Listen, Mimì, about that Rebecca...'

'What Rebecca?'

'Your fiancée, no? The girl you want to *marry*, not *take as wife*, as you said...'

'It means the same thing.'

'No, it doesn't, believe me. Anyway, about this Rebecca—'

'Her name is Rachele.'

'Fine, whatever. I think I remember you saying she's a policewoman in Pavia, right?'

'Right.'

'Has she requested a transfer?'

'Why would she do that?'

'Mimì, try to think for a minute. What are you going to do after you're married? Stay in Vigàta while Rebecca stays in Pavia?'

'C'mon, get it straight! Her name is Rachele. No, she hasn't requested a transfer. That would be premature.'

'But, sooner or later, she'll have to, won't she?'

Mimì took a deep breath, as if preparing to dive underwater.

'I don't think she will.'

'And why not?'

'Because we've decided that I should be the one to ask for a transfer.'

Montalbano's eyes turned into a serpent's: motionless, gelid.

Now a forked tongue's going to dart out of his mouth, thought Augello, feeling himself bathed in sweat.

'Mimì, you're a motherfucking son of a bitch. Last night, when you came to my house, you sang only half the Mass. You talked to me about marriage, not about reassignment, which for me is the more important of the two, and which you know perfectly well.'

'I was going to tell you, Salvo, I swear it! If not for your crazy reaction, which threw me for a loop...'

'Mimì, look me in the eye and tell me the whole truth: have you already put in your request?'

'I have, but—'

'And what did Bonetti-Alderighi say?'

'He said it would take a little time. And also that ... never mind.'

'Speak.'

'He said he was pleased, and that it was high time that band of mafiosi at Vigàta Police – his exact words – started to break up.'

'And what'd you do?'

'Well...'

'Come on, out with it.'

'I took back the request that was on his desk. I told him I needed to think it over.'

Montalbano sat there in silence for a while. Mimì looked like he'd just walked out of a shower. The inspector then gestured towards the stack of pages Catarella had brought him.

'This is everything that was in Nenè Sanfilippo's computer. There's a novel and a lot of letters — let's call them love letters. Who better than you to read this stuff?'

FOUR

Fazio rang to give him the name of the man who'd driven the bus from Vigàta to Tindari and back: one Filippo Tortorici, son of Gioacchino and ... He stopped himself in time. Even over the telephone, he could sense the inspector's growing exasperation. He added that the driver was out on a job, but Mr Malaspina, with whom he was compiling a list of the people who'd gone on the excursion, had assured him he would send Tortorici on to police headquarters as soon as he got back, which would be around three in the afternoon. Montalbano looked at his watch: he had two free hours.

He automatically headed towards the Trattoria San Calogero. The owner put a seafood appetizer in front of him, and, without warning, the inspector felt a kind of pincer close the opening to his stomach. It was impossible to eat. In fact, the sight of the squid, baby octopus and clams nauseated him. He sprang to his feet.

Calogero, the waiter-owner, came running up, worried.

'Inspector, what's wrong?'

'Nothing, Calò, I just don't feel like eating any more.'

'Don't turn your nose up at that appetizer, Inspector. It doesn't come any fresher!'

'I know. Please give it my apologies.'

'You don't feel so good?'

An excuse came to mind.

'Ah, I don't know. I feel a little chill, maybe I'm coming down with the flu.'

He left, knowing this time where he was headed. To the lighthouse, to sit down on the flat rock beneath it, which had become a kind of rock of tears. He had sat there the day before as well, when he couldn't get that friend from 68 out of his head, what was his name? He couldn't remember. The rock of tears. And he had once shed tears in earnest there, liberating tears, when he first learned that his father was dying. Now he was back there again, because of another end foretold, over which he would shed no tears, but which deeply saddened him. An end, yes, that was not an exaggeration. It didn't matter that Mimì had withdrawn his request for a transfer. The fact remained that he had submitted it at all.

Bonetti-Alderighi was a notorious imbecile, and he brilliantly confirmed this when he called the inspector's police department a 'band of mafiosi'. In reality it was a team, tightly knit and compact, a well-oiled machine, where every little cog had a function and – why not? – a personality of its own. And the belt that made the whole mechanism run was none other than Mimì Augello. One had to recognize the problem for what it was: a crack, the beginning of a break. The beginning of an end. How long would Mimì be able to hold out? Another two months? Three? Eventually he would give in to Rebecca's tears and pressure – that is, Rachele's tears and pressure – and then, goodbye, it was nice knowing you.

'And what about me?' he asked. 'What the hell am I doing?'

One of the reasons he so feared promotion and the inevitable transfer was the certainty that he would never again be able, anywhere else, to put together a team like the one he'd managed, miraculously, to assemble in Vigàta. But even as he was thinking this, he knew that it wasn't the real reason for what he felt at that moment, the truth behind his suffering – *There, goddamn it, you've finally managed to say the word! What, were you ashamed? Go on, repeat it: suffering.* He was very fond of Mimì. He considered him more than a friend, rather like a kid brother, and this was why his pre-announced abandonment had hit him right in the chest with the force of a gunshot. The word 'betrayal' had flitted through his brain for a moment. And Mimì'd had the gall to confide in Livia, utterly certain that she would never – Christ! – say a word to him, her man. And he'd even mentioned his possible transfer to her, and even this she had withheld from him, complicitous in every respect with her friend Mimì! What a pair!

He realized that his suffering was turning into senseless,

stupid rage. He felt ashamed. What he was thinking at that moment wasn't really him.

✻

Filippo Tortorici showed up at three forty-five, a bit out of breath. He was a scrawny little man somewhere in his fifties, with a little crest of hair in the middle of his head and bald everywhere else. He looked exactly like a bird Montalbano had once seen in a documentary on the Amazon rainforest.

'What did you want to talk to me about? My boss, Mr Malaspina, ordered me to come here right away but didn't give me no explanation.'

'Were you the driver for the Vigàta to Tindari excursion last Sunday?'

'Yes, sir, I was. When the company organizes these tours, they always turn to me. The customers ask for me personally. They want me for their driver. They trust me. I'm calm and patient. You have to understand them; they're all old and have a lot of needs.'

'Do you do these tours often?'

'In the warm season, at least once every couple of weeks. Sometimes we go to Tindari, sometimes to Erice, sometimes to Siracusa, sometimes—'

'Is it always the same passengers?'

'There's about ten who're always there. The rest are different.'

'As far as you know, were Alfonso and Margherita Griffo on Sunday's excursion?'

'Sure they were! I've got a good memory! Why do you ask?'

'Don't you know? They've disappeared.'

'*O Madunnuzza santa!* What you mean, disappeared?'

'They haven't been seen since they went on the tour. It was even mentioned on television. They said the son was desperate.'

'I didn't know, I really didn't.'

'Listen, did you know the Griffos before the excursion?'

'No, never seen 'em before.'

'So how do you know the Griffos were on the bus?'

'Because before we leave, the boss always gives me the list of passengers. And before we leave, I tick their names off on my list.'

'And do you do it again for the return trip?'

'Of course! And the Griffos were there.'

'Tell me what happens on these excursions.'

'Normally we set out at seven in the morning. It depends on how long it will take to get to where we're going. The passengers are all getting on in years, retired, that kind of people. They go on the tour not so they can see, say, the Black Madonna of Tindari, but so they can spend a day in the company of other people. You know what I mean? Their kids are grown up and far away, they don't have any friends ... During the drive, there's always somebody in the coach to entertain them, selling things, like, I dunno, household goods, blankets, that sort of thing. And we always arrive in time for the midday Mass. For lunch they go to a restaurant the boss has an arrangement with. The cost of the meal is included in the ticket. And you know what happens after they eat?'

'No, I don't. Tell me.'

'They go back to the bus for a little nap. After they wake up, they take a stroll around town, buy little gifts and souvenirs. At six – in the evening, that is – I make sure they're all there and we leave. At eight, by prior arrangement, we stop at a cafe at the halfway point, and they have coffee and biscuits. That's also included in the price of the ticket. Then we're supposed to be back in Vigàta around ten o'clock.'

'Why did you say "supposed to be"?'

''Cause it always ends up being later.'

'Why's that?'

'As I said, Inspector, the passengers are all old folks.'

'So?'

'If one of 'em asks me to stop at the first cafe or service station because they need a lavatory, what'm I gonna say – no? So I stop.'

'I see. And do you remember if anyone on last Sunday's return trip asked you to stop?'

'Inspector, they made it so we didn't get back until almost eleven! Three times we stopped! And the last time we weren't but half an hour from Vigàta! I even asked if they could wait, we were so close. Nothing doing. And you know what happens then? One of 'em gets out, they all get out. They all need a lavatory, and we end up losing a lot of time.'

'Do you remember who it was that asked you to make the last stop?'

'No, sir, I honestly don't remember.'

'Did anything strange or unusual happen, anything out of the ordinary?'

'What could possibly happen? If anything did, I didn't notice.'

'Are you sure the Griffos made it back to Vigàta?'

'Inspector, once we're back, I don't have to check the names again. If any of these people didn't get back on the bus after one of the stops, the others would have noticed. Anyway, before leaving, I always toot the horn three times and wait for at least three minutes.'

'Do you remember where you made the extra stops on the way back?'

'Yes, sir. The first was on the Enna highway, at the Cascino service station. The second was on the Palermo–Montelusa expressway, at the Trattoria San Gerlando; and the last was at the bar-trattoria Paradiso, a half-hour drive from here.'

✻

Fazio straggled back at about seven o'clock.

'You took your time.'

Fazio didn't reply. Whenever the inspector chided him for no reason, it merely meant he needed to let off steam. Answering would have made things worse.

'Anyway, Chief. There were forty people who went on that excursion. Eighteen married couples, which makes thirty-six, two old ladies, which makes thirty-eight, and the Laganà brothers, twins, who never miss a single one of these tours, who aren't married, and who live together in the same house. The Laganà brothers were the youngest of the bunch, fifty-eight years old. And the passengers also included the Griffos, Alfonso and Margherita.'

'Did you tell them all to be here tomorrow morning at nine?'

'I did. And I didn't do it by phone, but by going door-to-door. You should also know that two of them can't come tomorrow. We'll have to go to their place if we want to question them. The name's Scimè: the wife is sick with the flu, and the husband has to stay by her side and can't go anywhere. I took one liberty, Inspector.'

'What was that?'

'I divided them up into groups. They'll come in ten at a time, one hour apart. There'll be less confusion that way.'

'Good idea, Fazio. Thanks. You can go now.'

Fazio didn't move. The moment had come for avenging the unjustified reproach of a few minutes before.

'As for taking my time, I wanted to mention that I also went to Montelusa.'

'What for?'

What was happening to the inspector? Was he forgetting things?

'You don't remember? I went to do what you told me to do. To talk to the people at Manzo and Company, the ones who wrote the cheque for the two million we found in Nenè Sanfilippo's pocket. All above board. Mr Manzo paid the kid a million lire a month to keep an eye on his computer and fix anything that needed fixing ... Last month there was a snag and he didn't get paid, and that's why the cheque was for double the amount.'

'So Nenè worked.'

'Worked? With the money Manzo paid him he could barely pay the rent! Where'd he get the rest?'

*

When Mimì Augello stuck his head inside the door it was already dark outside. His eyes were red. For a moment Montalbano thought Mimì had been crying, having suddenly repented. Which was the fashion, in any case: everyone, from the Pope to the latest mafioso, was repenting about something. But, no, nothing of the sort! In fact, the first thing Augello said was, 'This is wrecking my eyes, going through Nenè Sanfilippo's papers! I'm only halfway through the letters.'

'Are there only letters from him?'

'Are you kidding! It's a regular correspondence. Letters from him and letters from a woman, but hers aren't signed.'

'How many are there?'

'About fifty from each. For a while they exchanged letters every other day ... They'd do it and then comment on it.'

'I don't understand.'

'I'll explain. Let's say they slept together on a Monday. On Tuesday, they would write to each other, commenting, in detail, on everything they'd done the day before. From her perspective and from his. On Wednesday, they'd get together again and the next day they'd write to each other. The letters are pure filth. They had me blushing at moments.'

'Are the letters dated?'

'All of them.'

'Seems fishy to me. With our postal system, how could the letters always arrive punctually the next day?'

Mimì shook his head no.

'I don't think they were posted.'

'So how did they send them?'

'They didn't. They handed them to each other next time they met. They probably read them in bed, and then started fucking. Sounds like an excellent stimulant.'

'I can see you're an expert in these things. Aside from the date, do the letters mention the place of origin?'

'Nenè's always come from Vigàta. Hers are from Montelusa or, on rarer occasions, from Vigàta. Which bolsters my hypothesis, which is that they would get together sometimes here, sometimes in Montelusa. She's married. Both he and she often mention the husband, but they never say his name. The period they saw each other most often coincided with a trip abroad by the husband. Who, as I said, is never mentioned by name.'

'That gives me an idea, Mimì. Isn't it possible the whole thing is a pile of bullshit dreamed up by the boy? Isn't it possible this woman doesn't exist, that she's a product of his erotic fantasies?'

'I think the letters are authentic. He typed them into the computer and then destroyed the originals.'

'What makes you so sure the letters are authentic?'

'What she writes. They minutely describe what a woman feels when she's making love. They give details that would never remotely occur to us men. They do it in every way possible: normal, oral, anal, in all the positions, on different occasions, and every time, she says something new, intimately new. If it was all made up by the boy, he would surely have turned out to be a great writer.'

'How far did you get?'

'I've got about twenty left. Then I'll get started on the novel. You know, Salvo, I have a feeling I might know who the woman is.'

'Tell me.'

'Not yet. I have to think it over.'

'I have a vague idea about it too.'

'What's that?'

'I think we're dealing with a woman who's not so young

any more, and who took on a twenty-year-old lover. Whom she paid handsomely.'

'I agree. Except that if it's the woman I think it is, she's not middle-aged. She's rather young. And there's no money involved.'

'So you think it's a question of infidelity?'

'Why not?'

'Maybe you're right.'

No, Mimì wasn't right. Montalbano sensed instinctively, in his gut, that behind the killing of Nenè Sanfilippo there must be something big. So why was he agreeing with Mimì's hypothesis? To keep him happy? What was the proper verb? Ah, yes: to cajole him. He was pandering to him shamelessly. Perhaps he was behaving like that newspaper editor in the movie *The Front Page*, who resorts to every expedient on earth and in heaven to keep his ace reporter from moving, for love, to another city. It was a comedy with Matthau and Lemmon, and he remembered that he died laughing. Why was it that thinking back on it now, he didn't even crack a smile?

*

'Livia? Hi, how are you? I want to ask you two questions, and then tell you something.'

'What are their numbers?'

'What are what's numbers?'

'The questions. What are their reference numbers?'

'Come on . . .'

'Don't you realize you're talking to me as if I was some kind of office?'

'I'm sorry. I really didn't mean—'

'Go ahead, ask me the first one.'

'Livia, imagine we've made love—'

'I can't. The prospect is too remote.'

'Please, I'm being serious.'

'All right, but give me a minute while I collect my memories. OK. Go on.'

'Would you ever think, the day after, to write me a letter describing everything you'd felt?'

There was a pause, and it lasted so long that Montalbano thought Livia had hung up on him.

'Livia? You there?'

'I was trying to think. No, I, personally, wouldn't do that. But another woman, in the throes of a violent passion, might.'

'The second question is this: when Mimì Augello confided in you that he planned to get married—'

'Oh, God, Salvo, you're such a bore when you put your mind to it!'

'Let me finish. Did he also say he was going to ask to be transferred? Did he?'

This time the pause was even longer than before. But Montalbano knew she was still at the other end, because her breathing had grown heavy. Then, in a faint voice, she asked, 'Did he do that?'

'Yes, Livia, he did. Then, because the commissioner made an asinine comment, he withdrew his request. But only temporarily, I think.'

'Salvo, believe me, he never said anything to me about leaving Vigàta. And I don't think he had that in mind when he talked about his marriage plans. I'm sorry. Very sorry. And I realize how sorry you must be. What was it you wanted to tell me?'

'That I miss you.'

'Really?'

'Yes, a lot.'

'How much is a lot?'

'A lot a lot.'

There, that's how you do it. Trust in the most utterly obvious thing. And surely the truest.

*

He went to bed with the book by Vázquez Montalbán and began rereading it from the beginning. At the end of the third page, the telephone rang. He thought about it a moment; the desire not to answer was strong, but the caller was liable to persist until his nerves were frayed.

'Hello? Am I speaking to Inspector Montalbano?'

He didn't recognize the voice.

'Yes.'

'Inspector, I beg your pardon for disturbing you at this hour, when you're finally enjoying some much-desired rest with your family . . .'

What family? Had everyone gone batty, from Dr Lattes to this stranger, with this idea of his nonexistent family?

'Who is this?'

'... but I was certain to find you at home. I am Orazio Guttadauro, the lawyer. I don't know if you remember me...'

How could he not remember Guttadauro, the Mafia's favourite lawyer, who during the investigation into the murder of the beautiful Michela Licalzi had tried to entrap the then captain of the Montelusa Flying Squad? A worm had a deeper sense of honour than Orazio Guttadauro.

'Would you excuse me a moment?'

'By all means! I should be the one asking you...'

He let him go on talking, went into the bathroom, emptied his bladder and gave his face a good washing. When talking to Guttadauro one had to be alert and vigilant, to catch even the most fleeting nuances in the words he used.

'Here I am, Counsel.'

'This morning, my dear Inspector, I went to see my old friend and client Don Balduccio Sinagra, whom you certainly must know, at least by name, if not personally.'

Not only by name, but also by reputation. Sinagra was head of one of the two Mafia families — the other being the Cuffaro family — that were vying for territorial control over the Montelusa province and this led to at least one death per month, on each side of the fence.

'Yeah, I know the name.'

'Good. Don Balduccio is very advanced in years, and celebrated his ninetieth birthday the day before yesterday. He's got a few aches and pains, as is normal for his age, but his mind is still extremely lucid. He remembers everything and everyone, and keeps up with the newspapers and television. I go to see him often because the man simply charms me with his memories and, I humbly confess, with his enlightened wisdom. Just think . . .'

Was this lawyer joking? Had he phoned him at home at one o'clock in the morning just to give him details on the mental and physical health of a hood like Balduccio Sinagra, who would make the world a better place if he were to die tomorrow?

'Mr Guttadauro, don't you think—'

'Forgive me the long digression, Inspector, but when I start talking about Don Balduccio, for whom I harbour feelings of deep veneration—'

'Look, Mr Guttadauro—'

'Please please please excuse me. Forgiven? Forgiven. I'll get to the point. This morning, when talking of this and that, Don Balduccio mentioned your name.'

'Was it during the this or the that?'

The remark came out before Montalbano could stop it.

'I don't understand,' said the lawyer.

'Never mind.'

And he said no more. He wanted Guttadauro the lawyer to do the talking, and so he pricked up his ears all the more.

'He asked about you. If you were in good health.'

A chill ran down the inspector's spine. If Don Balduccio asked after somebody's health, in ninety per cent of the cases that person, a few days later, would be climbing the hill to Vigàta Cemetery in a hearse. But again he didn't open his mouth, to encourage Guttadauro to keep talking. Stew in your juices, arsehole.

'The fact is, he would really like to see you,' the lawyer shot out, finally coming to the point.

'That's not a problem,' said Montalbano with the aplomb of an Englishman.

'Thank you, Inspector, thank you! You cannot imagine how happy I am with your answer! I was sure you would satisfy the wishes of an elderly man who, despite everything people say about him—'

'Will he be coming to the police station?'

'Who?'

'What do you mean, who? Mr Sinagra. Didn't you just say he wanted to see me?'

Guttadauro cleared his throat twice in embarrassment.

'Inspector, the fact is that Don Balduccio has a great deal of difficulty moving about. He can't stand on his feet. It would be very painful for him to come in to the police station. Surely you understand...'

'I certainly do understand how painful it would be for him to come to the police station.'

The lawyer preferred not to notice the irony. He remained silent.

'So where can we meet?' the inspector asked.

'Er, Don Balduccio suggested that . . . well, if you would be so kind as to come to his place . . .'

'I've no objection. Naturally, I'll have to inform my superiors first.'

Naturally, he had no intention whatsoever of mentioning it to that imbecile Bonetti-Alderighi. But he wanted to have a little fun with Guttadauro.

'Is that really necessary?' the lawyer asked in a whiny voice.

'Yes, I'd say so.'

'Because, you see, Inspector, what Don Balduccio had in mind was a more private conversation, a very private conversation, possibly a preamble to some important developments . . .'

'A preamble, you say?'

'Yes, indeed.'

Montalbano sighed noisily, in resignation, like a pedlar forced to sell cheap.

'In that case . . .'

'How about tomorrow evening around six thirty?' the lawyer promptly replied, as if fearing the inspector might reconsider.

'All right.'

'Thank you again, Inspector, thank you. Neither Don Balduccio nor I had any doubts as to your gentlemanly grace, your ...'

FIVE

The moment he stepped out of his car at eight thirty the next morning, he could hear, from the street, a tremendous uproar inside the police station. He went in. The first ten people summoned – five husbands and their respective wives – had shown up extremely early and were behaving exactly like children in a nursery school. They were laughing, joking, pushing one another, embracing. It immediately occurred to him that someone should perhaps consider creating community nursery schools for the aged.

Catarella, assigned by Fazio to maintain public order, had the unfortunate idea to shout out, 'The inspector himself in person has arrived!'

In the twinkling of an eye, that kindergarten playground turned inexplicably into a battlefield. Barrelling into one another, tripping each other up or holding one another back by an arm or by the coat-tails, all present assailed the inspector, trying to get to him first. And during the struggle, they spoke and shouted so loudly that a deafened Montalbano understood not a word amidst the clamour.

'What is going on here?' he asked in a military voice.

Relative calm ensued.

'No favourites, now!' shouted one, barely taller than a midget, nestling up under the inspector's nose. 'We must proceed in strick flabettical order!'

'No, sir, no, sir! We'll proceed in order of age!' another proclaimed angrily.

'What's your name?' the inspector asked the quasi-midget, who'd managed to speak first.

'Abate's the name, first name Luigi,' he said, looking around, as if to rebut any differences of opinion.

Montalbano congratulated himself for guessing right. He'd made a bet with himself that the pipsqueak who was advocating that they proceed in alphabetical order was named either Abate or Abete, since there were no names like Alvar Aalto in Sicily.

'And yours?'

'Arturo Zotta. And I'm the oldest person here!'

The inspector was right about the second one, too.

Having wended his adventure-filled way through those ten people, who seemed more like a hundred, the inspector barricaded himself in his office with Fazio and Galluzzo, leaving Catarella on guard to contain any further geriatric riots.

'But why are they all here already?'

'If you really want to know the full story, Inspector,

four of the people you summoned, two husbands with their wives, showed up at eight o'clock this morning,' Fazio explained. 'What do you expect? They're old, they don't get enough sleep, the curiosity was eating them alive. Just think, there's a couple out there that wasn't supposed to be here till ten.'

'Listen, let's agree on a plan. You're free to ask whatever questions you think most appropriate. But there are a few that are indispensable. Write this down. First question: did you know the Griffos before the excursion? If so, where, how and when? If anyone says they knew the Griffos beforehand, don't let them leave, because I want to talk to them. Second question: where were the Griffos sitting on the bus, both on the way there and on the way back? Third question: during the excursion, did the Griffos talk to anyone? And if so, what about? Fourth question: do you know what the Griffos did during the time they spent at Tindari? Did they meet anyone there? Did they go into anyone's house? Any information they may have is essential. Fifth question: did the Griffos get off the bus at any of the three extra stops made on the way back at the request of the passengers? If so, at which of the three? Did they see them get back on the bus? Sixth and final question: do they remember seeing the Griffos after the bus returned to Vigàta?'

Fazio and Galluzzo looked at each other.

'Sounds like you think something happened to the Griffos on the way back,' said Fazio.

'It's just a conjecture. But it's what we're going to work with. If someone then comes out and says he saw them get off in Vigàta and go quietly home, we'll take our conjecture and stick it where the sun doesn't shine, and we'll start all over again. One important thing, however. Try not to get sidetracked; if we give these people too much rope, they're likely to tell us their life stories. And another thing: when questioning couples, arrange it so that one of you gets the wife and the other the husband.'

'Why?'

'Because otherwise the one will affect what the other says, in all good faith. You two will take three apiece, I'll take the rest. If you do as I say, with the Virgin's blessing we'll be done in no time.'

*

From the first interrogation, the inspector realized that he'd almost certainly been wrong in his prediction, and that every dialogue could easily stray into absurdity.

'We met a few minutes ago. I believe your name is Arturo Zotta, is that right?'

'Of course it's right. Arturo Zotta, son of Giovanni Zotta. My father had a cousin who was a tinsmith, an' people often mistook him for my father. But my father—'

'Mr Zotta, I—'

'I also wanted to say that I'm very pleased.'

'About what?'

''Cause you did as I said you should do.'

'And what's that?'

'Go by age. 'Cause I'm the oldest of the lot, I am. I'll be seventy-seven in three months and five days. You gotta respect the elderly. That's what I keep tellin' my grandchildren, who're a nasty bunch. It's lack of respect that's screwin' up the whole stinking world! You weren't even born in Mussolini's day. With Mussolini around, there was respect and plenty of it. And if you didn't have no respect, wham! He'd cut your head right off. I remember—'

'Mr Zotta, to be honest, we decided not to follow any order at all, alphabetical or—'

The old man giggled to himself, all in *ee* sounds.

'Was I right, eh? Was I? I'da bet my life on it! In this place, which should be a temple of order – no sir! They don't give a good damn about order! Arse-backwards, that's how they do things here! Anything goes! Pell-mell, harum-scarum, topsy-turvy! You like walking on your hands? That's what I say. And then we complain when our kids take drugs and steal and kill . . .'

Montalbano cursed himself. How did ever let himself get trapped by this ancient blabbermouth? He had to stop the avalanche. Immediately, or he would be inexorably swept away by it.

'Mr Zotta, please, let's not digress.'

'Wha'?'

'Let's not get off the subject!'

'Who's gettin' off the subject? You think I got up at six in the morning just to come here and talk about the first thing that comes into my head? You think I don't got better things to do? I know I'm retired and all, but—'

'Did you know the Griffos?'

'The Griffos? Never seen 'em before the tour. And after the tour, neither, can't say as I met 'em even then. The name, yes. I heard 'em call it out when the driver was ticking the names off his list before leaving, and they said, "Present." We didn't even say hello or talk. Not a peep. They were very quiet and all by themselves, mindin' their own business. Now I say, Mr Inspector, these excursions are nice when everybody stays together. You joke, you laugh, you sing songs. But if—'

'Are you sure you never met the Griffos?'

'Where would I a met 'em?'

'I don't know, at the market, the tobacco shop...'

'My wife does the shopping an' I don't smoke. On the other hand...'

'On the other hand?'

'I used to know a guy named Pietro Giffo. Mighta been a relative, only the r was missing. This Giffo was a travelling salesman, the kind of guy who liked a good joke. One time—'

'Did you by any chance run into the Griffos at any time during the day you spent in Tindari?'

'Me and the wife, we never see anyone from the group when we get to where we're going. We go to Palermo? I got a brother-in-law there. We go down to Erice? I got a cousin lives there. They roll out the red carpet, invite us to lunch. And Tindari, forget about it! I got a nephew there, Filippo, he come to pick us up at the bus stop, took us to his house, and his wife served us a *sfincione* for the first course, and for the second—'

'When the driver called out the names for the return home, were the Griffos present?'

'Yes, sir, I heard 'em answer.'

'Did you notice if they got off the bus at any of the three extra stops the bus made on the way back?'

'I was just telling you, Inspector, what my nephew Filippo gave us to eat. Well, we couldn't even get up out of our seats, that's how stuffed we were! On the way back, when we stopped for *caffellatte* like we planned, I didn't even want to get off the bus. But then the wife reminded me it was all paid for anyway. What we gonna do? Waste our money? So I just had a little spot of milk with two biscuits. And immediately I started to feel sleepy. Always happens to me after I eat. Anyway, I nodded off. And it's a good thing I didn't have any coffee! 'Cause, lemme tell you, when I drink coffee—'

'You can never get to sleep. Once you got back to Vigàta, did you see the Griffos get off the bus?'

'Dear Inspector, at that hour, dark as it was, with me practically not knowing if my own wife was gettin' off the bus!'

'Do you remember where you sat?'

'That I do. I remember where we was sittin', the wife and me. Right in the middle of the bus. In front of us was the Bufalottas, behind us was the Raccuglias and beside us the Persicos. We already knew all of them, it was our fifth tour together. The Bufalottas, poor things, they need to take their mind off their troubles. Their oldest boy, Pippino, died when—'

'Do you remember where the Griffos were seated?'

'In the last row, I think.'

'The one with five seats in a row, without armrests?'

'I think so.'

'Good. That's all, Mr Zotta, you can go now.'

'What do you mean?'

'I mean we're finished. You can go home.'

'What? What the hell is this anyway? You trouble a seventy-seven-year-old man and a seventy-five-year-old woman for this kind of bullshit? We got up at six in the morning for this! You think that's right?'

*

When the last of the old people had left it was nearly one o'clock, and the police station looked as if it had been the site of a very crowded picnic. Granted, there was no grass in the office, but where are you going to find grass nowadays? That stuff that still manages to grow on the outskirts of town — you call that grass? Four stunted, half-yellowed blades where, if you stick your hand, chances are ninety-nine out of a hundred you'll get pricked by a hidden syringe?

With these fine thoughts, a bad mood was descending again on the inspector when he realized that Catarella, assigned clean-up duty, had come to a sudden halt, broom in one hand and something not clearly identifiable in the other.

'My, my, my! Wouldja look at that!' Catarella muttered, flabbergasted as he eyed what he'd picked up off the floor.

'What is it?'

All at once Catarella's face turned a flaming red.

'A profellattict, Chief!'

'Used?!' the inspector asked, astonished.

'No, Chief, still in its wrapper.'

There: that was the only difference from the rubbish left behind at a real picnic. As for everything else, the same depressing filth, tissue paper, cigarette butts, cans of Coca-Cola and orangeade, bottles of mineral water, pieces of bread and biscuits, even an ice-cream cone slowly melting in a corner.

*

As Montalbano had already tabulated from an initial comparison of the answers given to him, Fazio and Galluzzo – and this, no doubt, was another, if not the main reason for his foul mood – it turned out that they knew not a whit more about the Griffos than they had before.

The bus had exactly fifty-three seats, not counting the driver's. The forty passengers had all gathered in the front part of the coach, twenty on one side of the aisle, twenty on the other. The Griffos, on the other hand, had sat in two of the five seats in the final row, on both the outward and return journeys, with the big rear window behind them. They had spoken to no one and no one had spoken to them. Fazio reported that one of the passengers had said to him, 'You know what? After a while we forgot all about them. It was as if they weren't travelling in the same coach as us.'

'But,' the inspector cut in, 'we still don't have the deposition of that couple whose wife is sick. Scimè, I think they're called.'

Fazio gave a little smile.

'Did you really think Mrs Scimè was going to miss the party? With all her girlfriends there? No, she came, together with her husband, though she could barely stand up. She had a fever of a hundred and two. I talked to her, Galluzzo talked to the husband. No dice. The lady could have spared herself the strain.'

They looked at each other in dejection.

'A night wasted, and it's a girl,' commented Galluzzo, quoting the proverbial saying — *Nottata persa e figlia fimmina* — of the husband who has spent a whole night beside his wife in labour, only to see her give birth to a baby girl instead of that much-desired son.

'Shall we go and eat?' asked Fazio, getting up.

'You two go ahead. I'm going to stay a little while yet. Who's on duty?'

'Gallo.'

*

Left to himself, he started studying the sketch Fazio had made of the bus's layout. There was a small isolated rectangle at the top with the word 'driver' written inside, followed by twelve rows of four little rectangles, each bearing the name of its occupant, or left empty when vacant.

Eyeing it, the inspector became aware that Fazio must have resisted the temptation to draw much larger rectangles with the vital statistics of each occupant inside: first and last name, father's name, mother's maiden name, etc. In the last row of five seats, Fazio had written 'Griffo' in such a way that each of the letters occupied one of the five little rectangles, except for the double *f*. Apparently he hadn't managed to find out which of the five places the vanished couple had sat in.

Montalbano started to imagine the journey to himself. After the initial greetings, a few minutes of inevitable silence as people got comfortable, unburdening themselves of scarves, caps and hats, checking bags or pockets for reading glasses, house keys, etc. Then the first signs of cheer, the first audible conversations, the overlapping phrases . . . And the driver asking: 'Want me to turn on the radio?' A chorus of 'no' . . . And maybe, from time to time, somebody turning around towards the back, towards the last row where the Griffos sat next to each other, immobile and as though deaf, since the eight vacant seats between them and the other passengers formed a kind of barrier against the sounds, the words, the noise, the laughter.

At this point Montalbano slapped himself on the

forehead. He'd forgotten! The driver had told him something very specific, and he'd let it completely slip his mind.

'Gallo!'

What came out of his mouth was less the name than a strangled cry. The door flew open, a frightened Gallo appeared.

'What's wrong, Inspector?'

'Get me the bus company on the double, I forget the name. If there's anyone there, let me talk to them.'

He was in luck. The accountant answered.

'I need some information. On the excursion to Tindari last Sunday, was there anyone else in the coach besides the driver and passengers?'

'Of course. You see, Inspector, our company allows sales representatives for certain businesses to present their products. Kitchenware, detergents, knickknacks, that sort of thing...'

This was said in the tone of a king granting a favour.

'How much do you get paid for this?' asked Montalbano, the disrespectful subject.

The accountant's regal tone turned into a kind of painful stammering.

'Well ... you h-have to c-consider ... that the percentage—'

'I'm not interested. I want the name and telephone number of the salesperson who went on that excursion.'

'Hello? Is this the Dileo household? Inspector Montalbano here. I'd like to speak to Mrs or Miss Beatrice Dileo.'

'This is Beatrice Dileo, Inspector. And it's "miss". I was wondering when you would get around to questioning me. If you hadn't called by the end of the day, I was going to come to the station tomorrow.'

'Have you finished your lunch?'

'I haven't started yet. I just got back from Palermo. I had an exam at the university. Since I live alone, I ought to be preparing something to eat, but I don't really feel like it.'

'Would you like to meet me for lunch?'

'Sure, why not?'

'Meet me in half an hour at the Trattoria San Calogero.'

*

The eight men and four women eating in the trattoria at that moment all stopped, one after another, forks in mid-air, to stare at the girl who'd just walked in. A real beauty, tall, slender, long blonde hair, blue eyes. The kind one sees on the covers of magazines, except that this one had the look of a nice family girl. What was she doing in the Trattoria San Calogero? The inspector had barely the time to ask himself this question when the creature headed straight for his table.

'You're Inspector Montalbano, aren't you? I'm Beatrice Dileo.'

She sat down. Montalbano remained standing for a moment, at a loss. Beatrice Dileo hadn't a trace of make-up on her face; she looked that way naturally. Perhaps that was why the women present continued to eye her without envy. How can one envy a jasmine flower?

'What'll it be?' asked Calogero, approaching their table. 'Today I've got a risotto in squid ink that's really special.'

'Sounds good to me. And what'll you have, Beatrice?'

'I'll have the same, thanks.'

Montalbano was pleased to note that she didn't add the typically female admonition: not too much, mind you. Just two spoonfuls. One spoonful. Three grains of rice, no more. Unbearable.

'For the second course, there's last night's catch of sea bass, or else—'

'Forget the "or else". I'll have the bass. How about you, Beatrice?'

'The bass.'

'For you, Inspector, the usual mineral water and Corvo white. For you, signorina?'

'The same.'

What were they – married?

'By the way, Inspector,' Beatrice said with a smile, 'I have a confession to make. When I'm eating, I'm unable to speak. So you should interrogate me now, before the risotto comes, or between courses.'

Jesus! So it was true: the miracle of meeting one's spiritual twin did sometimes happen. Too bad that, at a glance, she looked to be twenty-five or so years younger than him.

'Never mind the interrogation. Tell me about yourself instead.'

And so before Calogero arrived with the special risotto, which was more than simply special, Montalbano learned that Beatrice was indeed twenty-five years old, had finished her coursework in literature at the University of Palermo, and served as a representative of Sirio Kitchenware to support herself while continuing her studies. Sicilian despite appearances, surely of Norman extraction, she was born at Aidone, where her parents still lived. Why did she herself live and work in Vigàta? Simple: two years earlier in Aidone, she'd met a boy from Vigàta, also a student at Palermo, but in law. They fell in love, she had a terrible quarrel with her parents, and she followed the boy to Vigàta. They took a flat on the sixth floor of an ugly tenement in Piano Lanterna, but at least from the bedroom balcony you could see the sea. After four months of bliss, Roberto — that was her boyfriend's name — left her a polite little note telling her he was moving to Rome, where his fiancée, a distant cousin, was waiting for him. She hadn't had the nerve to go back to Aidone. End of story.

Then, with their noses, palates and throats invaded by the heavenly scent of the risotto, they fell silent, as agreed.

They resumed speaking while waiting for the bass. The subject of the Griffos was broached by Beatrice herself.

'That couple who disappeared—'

'Excuse me, but if you were in Palermo, how did you know—'

'The manager of Sirio phoned me yesterday and said you'd summoned all the passengers for questioning.'

'OK, go on.'

'I naturally have to bring a collection of samples with me. If the coach is full, the samples – which are cumbersome and fill two big boxes – are put in the luggage compartment. But if the coach isn't full, I usually put them in the last row, the one with five seats. I fit the two boxes into the two seats furthest from the exit, so as not to get in the way of people getting on or off the bus. Well, the Griffos went straight to the last row and sat down there.'

'Which of the three remaining places did they take?'

'Well, he sat in the centre seat, the one with the aisle in front of it. His wife sat beside him. The seat left unoccupied was the one closest to the exit. When I arrived at seven thirty that morning—'

'With the samples?'

'No. The boxes had already been put on the bus the evening before, by an employee of Sirio. The same employee also comes and takes them away when we return to Vigàta.'

'Go on.'

'When I saw them sitting right next to the boxes, I suggested they might want to find better seats, since the coach was still almost entirely empty and no places were reserved. I pointed out that since I had to display the merchandise, I might be a nuisance to them, always going back and forth. The woman didn't even look at me. She only stared straight ahead; I thought she was deaf. The husband, on the other hand, looked worried – no, not worried, but tense. He replied that I could do whatever I needed to do, but they preferred to stay where they were. Halfway through the journey, when I had to get down to work, I asked him to move. You know what he did? He bumped his hip against his wife's, forcing her to move into the free seat beside the exit, and slid into her seat, so I could get my frying pan. But when I turned around, with my back to the driver, microphone in one hand and frying pan in the other, the Griffos were already back in their old places.'

She smiled.

'I feel pretty ridiculous when I do that routine. But then ... There's one passenger who's almost always there, Cavaliere Mistretta, who's forced his wife to buy three full sets. Get it? He's in love with me! You can't imagine the looks his wife gives me. Anyway, to each buyer we give a complimentary talking watch, the kind the *vù cumprà* sell for ten thousand lire apiece. But all passengers get a free ballpoint pen with the company name, Sirio, written on it. Well, the Griffos didn't even want the pen.'

The fish arrived and, once again, silence reigned.

'Would you like some fruit? Coffee?' Montalbano asked when, sadly, all that was left of the bass were the bones and the heads.

'No,' said Beatrice, 'I like to keep that aftertaste of the sea.'

Not just a twin, but a Siamese twin.

'Anyway, Inspector, the whole time I was giving my sales talk, I kept looking over at the Griffos. They just sat there, stock-still, only he turned around a few times to look back through the rear window. As if he was afraid some car might be following the bus.'

'Or the opposite,' said the inspector. 'To make sure that some car *was* still following the bus.'

'Maybe. They didn't eat with us in Tindari. When we all got off the bus, they remained seated. When we got back on, they were still there. On the drive back they didn't once get out, not even when we stopped for *caffellatte*. Of one thing I'm certain, however: it was Mr Griffo who asked that we stop at the cafe-trattoria Paradiso. We were almost home, and the driver wanted to keep going. But he protested. And in the end almost everybody got out. I stayed inside. Then the driver honked the horn, the passengers reboarded and the bus left.'

'Are you sure the Griffos also got back on?'

'I can't say for certain. During the stop, I started listening to music on my Walkman, so I was wearing headphones, and my eyes were closed. In the end, I dozed off. I didn't reopen my eyes till we were back in Vigàta and most of the passengers had already got off the bus.'

'So it's possible the Griffos were already walking back home.'

Beatrice opened her mouth as if to say something, then closed it again.

'Go on,' the inspector said. 'Whatever it is, even if it seems silly to you, might be of use to me.'

'OK. When the company employee went into the bus to take away the samples, I gave him a hand. As I was pulling the first of the big boxes toward me, I leaned one hand on the seat where Mr Griffo should have been sitting just a few minutes before. Well, it was cold. If you ask me, those two did not get back on the bus after the stop at the cafe-trattoria Paradiso.'

SIX

Calogero brought the bill, Montalbano paid, Beatrice stood up, and the inspector did likewise, though with a twinge of regret. The girl was a veritable wonder of nature, but there was nothing to be done. It ended there.

'Let me give you a lift,' said Montalbano.

'I've got my own car,' replied Beatrice.

At that very moment, Mimì Augello walked in. Seeing Montalbano, he headed straight for him, then all at once stopped dead in his tracks, eyes agape. It was as though the angel of popular legend had passed, the one that says, 'Amen,' and everyone remains exactly as they were, frozen. Apparently he had brought Beatrice into focus. He suddenly turned around and made as if to leave.

'Were you looking for me?' the inspector asked, stopping him.

'Yes.'

'So why were you leaving?'

'I didn't want to disturb you.'

'What do you mean, disturb me! Come, Mimì. Miss Dileo, this is my right-hand man, Deputy Inspector Augello. This young woman travelled with the Griffos last Sunday and has told me some interesting things.'

Mimì knew only that the Griffos had disappeared, but was entirely ignorant of the investigation. In any case he was unable to open his mouth, his eyes still fixed on the girl.

It was at that moment that the Devil, the one with a capital *D*, materialized beside Montalbano. Invisible to all present except the inspector, he was wearing his traditional costume: hairy skin, cloven feet, pointed tail, short horns. The inspector felt his fiery, sulphurous breath burn his left ear.

'Let them get to know each other better,' the Devil ordered him.

Montalbano bowed to His Will.

'Have you got another five minutes?' he asked Beatrice with a smile.

'Sure. I'm free all afternoon.'

'And you, Mimì, have you eaten?'

'Uh ... n-no, not yet.'

'Then sit down in my place and order something while the young lady tells you what she told me about the Griffos. I, unfortunately, have an urgent matter to attend to. See you later at the office, Mimì. And thank you again, Miss Dileo.'

Beatrice sat back down. Mimì lowered himself into his

chair, as stiff as if he was wearing a suit of armour. He still couldn't grasp how this gift of God had fallen to him, but the topper was the fact that Montalbano had been so unusually nice to him.

The inspector, meanwhile, left the trattoria humming to himself. He had planted a seed. If the ground was fertile (and he had no doubt as to the fertility of Mimi's ground), that seed would grow. Which meant goodbye Rebecca, or whatever the hell her name was, goodbye transfer request.

'Excuse me, Inspector, but don't you think you're being a bit of a stinker?' asked the indignant voice of Montalbano's conscience.

'Jesus, what a pain in the arse!' was his reply.

*

In front of the Caffè Caviglione stood its owner, Arturo, leaning against the doorframe and basking in the sun. He was dressed like a beggar, in stained, threadbare jacket and trousers, despite the four to five billion lire he'd made loan-sharking. A skinflint from a legendary family of skinflints. He had once shown the inspector an old sign, yellowed and covered with fly shit, that his grandfather used to display in the cafe at the start of the century: 'Anyone sitting at a table must also drink a glass of water. And a glass of water costs two cents.'

'Have a coffee, Inspector?'

They went inside.

'A coffee for the inspector!' Arturo ordered the barman as he dropped into the till the coins Montalbano had extracted from his pocket. The day Arturo decided to offer a few scraps of brioche free of charge would be the day the world witnessed a cataclysm to delight Nostradamus.

'What is it, Artù?'

'I wanted to talk to you about this Griffo business. I know them. In the summer, every Sunday evening, they sit down at a table, always by themselves, and order two pieces of ice-cream cake: cassata for him and hazelnut with cream for her. I saw them that morning.'

'What morning?'

'The morning they left for Tindari. The bus stop is just down the street, in the piazza. I open at six, give or take a few minutes. Well, the Griffos were already here that morning, standing in front of the closed shutters. And the bus wasn't supposed to leave until seven! Work that one out!'

'Did they have anything to eat or drink?'

'They each had a hot brioche the baker brought to me about ten minutes later. The bus pulled in at six thirty. The driver, whose name is Filippo, came in and ordered a coffee. Mr Griffo went up to him and asked if they could board the bus. Filippo said yes, and they left without even saying goodbye. What were they afraid of, missing the bus?'

'Is that everything?'

'Well, yes.'

'Listen, Artù. That boy that was killed, did you know him?'

'Nenè Sanfilippo? Until a couple of years ago he used to come in regularly to play pool. Then he started showing up a lot less. Only at night.'

'What do you mean, at night?'

'I close at one a.m., Inspector. He'd come in sometimes and buy a few bottles of whisky, gin, that kind of thing. He'd pull up in his car, and there'd almost always be a girl inside.'

'Did you ever recognize anybody?'

'Nah. He probably brought 'em here from Palermo, or Montelusa, or wherever the hell he found them.'

*

Pulling up outside the entrance to headquarters, Montalbano didn't feel like going in. A teetering pile of papers to be signed awaited him on his desk; the mere thought of it made his right arm ache. Checking his pocket to make sure he had enough cigarettes, he got back in his car and headed in the direction of Montelusa. Exactly halfway between the two towns was a little country road, hidden behind an advertising hoarding which led to a ramshackle rustic cottage, behind which stood an enormous Saracen olive tree that was easily two hundred years old. It looked like a fake tree, a stage prop, something out of the imagination of Gustave Doré, perhaps an illustration for Dante's *Inferno*.

The lowest branches dragged and twisted along the ground, unable, try as they might, to hoist themselves skyward, and thus at a certain point in their progress they reconsidered their effort and decided to turn back towards the trunk, creating a kind of elbow-like bend or, in some cases, an out-and-out knot. Shortly thereafter, however, they changed their minds and turned around again, as if frightened at the sight of the powerful though pocked, burnt, time-wrinkled trunk. And in turning around, the branches took a different direction from the one before. They looked just like vipers, pythons, boas and anacondas that had suddenly metamorphosed into olive branches. And they seemed to despair, forever damned by the sorcery that had frozen them – 'crystallized' them, the poet Montale might have said – in an eternity of tragic, impossible flight. The middle branches, having reached more or less a yard in length, were immediately beset by doubt as to whether they should head skyward or turn earthward to rejoin the roots.

When it wasn't sea air he was after, Montalbano, instead of his customary walk along the eastern jetty, would pay a visit to the olive tree. Straddling one of the lower branches, he would light a cigarette and begin to reflect on problems in need of resolution.

He had discovered that, in some mysterious way, the entanglement, contortion, overlapping, in short, the labyrinth of branches, almost mimetically mirrored what was happening inside his head, the intertwining hypotheses and accumulating arguments. And if some conjecture happened to seem at first too reckless or rash, the sight of a branch tracing an even more far-fetched path than his thought would reassure him and allow him to proceed.

Ensconced amidst the silvery-green leaves, he could stay there for hours without moving. His immobility was only interrupted from time to time to make the movements needed to light a cigarette, which he would smoke without ever removing it from his mouth, or to carefully extinguish the butt, which he would rub against the heel of his shoe. He would keep so still that ants, undisturbed, would climb all over his body, creep into his hair, walk across his hands and his forehead. Once he got down from the branch, he would have to shake out his clothes very carefully, and at that moment, along with the ants, a little spider or two, or a few lucky ladybirds, would also come tumbling out.

*

Having settled onto his branch, he asked himself a question fundamental to what direction the investigation would take: was there any connection between the disappearance of the old couple and the murder of the boy?

Raising his head to let the first drag of smoke go down better, the inspector noticed a branch of the olive tree tracing an impossible path of sharp corners, tight curves, bounds forward and back. At one point it actually looked like an old-fashioned three-lobed radiator.

'No, I won't fall for it,' Montalbano muttered, rejecting

the invitation. There was no need for acrobatics, not yet. For the moment the facts, and only the facts, were enough.

All the residents of Via Cavour 44, including the concierge, unanimously maintained they had never seen the old couple and the boy together. Not even in some chance encounter, as might happen when waiting for the lift. They kept different hours, led entirely different lives. Come to think of it, how the hell could two unsociable, bad-tempered old bears, who never spoke to a living soul, have any kind of relationship at all with a twenty-year-old with too much money in his pockets who brought a different woman home every other night?

It seemed best, at least for now, to keep the two things separate. And to consider the fact that the two missing persons and the murder victim lived in the same building a pure and simple coincidence. For the moment. Besides, hadn't he already decided this, without openly saying so? He'd given Mimì Augello Nenè Sanfilippo's papers to study, and thus had implicitly assigned him the murder investigation. It was up to him, the inspector, to look into the Griffos.

Alfonso and Margherita Griffo, who would hole up in their flat for up to three or four days in a row, as if besieged by solitude, giving not the slightest sign of being physically at home, not even a sneeze or a cough, nothing, as though rehearsing their eventual disappearance ... Alfonso and Margherita Griffo, who, as far as their son could remember, had been outside of Vigàta only once in their lives, to go to Messina. Then one fine day, Alfonso and Margherita suddenly decide to make an excursion to Tindari. Were they devotees of the Madonna? But they never even went to church!

And they were so keen on that excursion!

According to what Arturo Caviglione told him, they arrived an hour before departure time and were the first to get on the still-empty bus. And though they were the sole passengers at that point, with fifty seats at their disposal, they went and chose the decidedly most uncomfortable ones, which were already encumbered by two giant boxes containing Beatrice Dileo's collection of samples. Did they make that choice out of inexperience, unaware that one feels the sharp turns most keenly in the last row and ends up with a queasy stomach? At any rate, the hypothesis that they chose those seats so they would be more isolated and not have to talk to their fellow passengers didn't hold water. If one wants to remain silent, one can, even if there are hundreds of people around. So why the last row?

The answer might lie in what Beatrice had told him. The girl had noticed that from time to time, Alfonso Griffo would turn around and look back through the big rear window. From that position, he could watch the cars that were behind them. But he could also, in turn, be seen, say, by a car that was following the bus. To see and be seen: this would not have been possible had he been seated anywhere else in the coach.

After arriving in Tindari, the Griffos didn't budge. In Beatrice's opinion, they never got off the bus. They hadn't joined the others and weren't seen about town. What, then, was the reason for that excursion? Why was it so important to them?

Again it was Beatrice who had revealed something important. Namely, that it was Alfonso Griffo who had the driver make the final extra stop, barely half an hour from Vigàta.

Maybe, until the day before departure, it had never even occurred to the Griffos to go on that excursion. Maybe their intention had been to spend that Sunday the way they had spent hundreds of others. Except that something had happened which forced them, against their will, to make that journey. Not just any journey, but that one. They'd been given some kind of explicit order. But who could have given that order, and what sort of power did he have over the old couple?

'Just to give this some coherence,' Montalbano said to himself, 'let's say it was a doctor that ordered them.'

But he was in no mood for joking.

And we are talking about a doctor so conscientious that he decided to follow the bus with his car, both on the way out and the way back, to make sure that his patients were in their seats the whole time. After it gets dark, and they're not far outside of Vigàta, the doctor flashes his headlights in some special way. It's a prearranged signal. Alfonso Griffo asks the driver to stop. And at the cafe-trattoria Paradiso, the couple disappear without a trace. Maybe the conscientious doctor asked the elderly pair to get in his car; maybe he urgently needed to check their blood pressure.

*

At this point Montalbano decided it was time to stop playing Me Tarzan, You Jane and return, as it were, to civilization. As he was shaking the ants out of his clothes, he asked himself one last question: what mysterious illness did the Griffos suffer from, making it necessary for their ever-so-conscientious family doctor to intervene?

*

Shortly before the descent that led into Vigàta, there was a public telephone. Miraculously, it worked. Mr Malaspina, owner of the tour-bus company, took barely five minutes to answer the inspector's questions.

No, Mr and Mrs Griffo had never gone on any of these tours before.

Yes, they had booked their seats at the last minute, at exactly one p.m. on Saturday afternoon, the deadline for signing up.

Yes, they had paid in cash.

No, the person who made the booking was neither Mr nor Mrs Griffo. Totò Bellavia, the employee at the counter, was ready to swear on a stack of Bibles that it was a distinguished-looking man of about forty, calling himself the Griffos' nephew, who signed them up and paid.

How did Mr Malaspina happen to be so well informed on the subject? Simple, the whole town was doing nothing but talking about the disappearance of the Griffos, and he'd become curious and decided to inform himself.

✶

'Chief, that would be the old people's son waiting for you in Fazio's office.'

'Would be or is?'

Catarella didn't miss a beat.

'Both, Chief.'

'Let him in.'

Davide Griffo came in looking frazzled: unshaven, red-eyed, suit rumpled.

'I'm going back to Messina, Inspector. What's the use in staying around here? I can't fall asleep at night, with the same thought in my head all the time ... Mr Fazio said you still haven't managed to find anything out.'

'Unfortunately, that's right. But rest assured that as soon as there's any news, we'll let you know immediately. Do we have your address?'

'Yes, I left it for you.'

'One question, before you leave. Do you have any cousins?'

'Yes, one.'

'How old is he?'

'About forty.'

The inspector pricked up his ears.

'Where does he live?'

'In Sydney. He works there. He hasn't been to see his father in three years.'

'How do you know?'

'Because every time he comes, we arrange to see each other.'

'Could you leave this cousin's address and telephone number with Fazio?'

'Certainly. But why do you want it? Do you think . . . ?'

'I don't want to leave any stone unturned.'

'Look, Inspector, the mere idea that my cousin could have anything to do with this disappearance is utterly insane . . . if you'll excuse my saying so.'

Montalbano stopped him with a gesture.

'Another thing. You must know that, in these parts, we give names like cousin, uncle, nephew to people with whom we have no blood relation. We do it out of affection, because we like them . . . Think hard. Do you know of anyone your parents might refer to as nephew?'

'Inspector, you obviously don't know my father and mother! God forbid any of us should have such a disposition! No, sir, I do not think it possible that they would ever call anyone a nephew who wasn't their nephew.'

'Mr Griffo, you'll forgive me if I make you repeat

something you've already said to me, but, you must understand, it's as much in your interest as mine. Are you
absolutely certain your parents mentioned nothing to
you about the excursion they were planning to go on?'

'They said nothing, Inspector, absolutely nothing. We
weren't in the habit of writing to each other; we only talked
over the phone. I was always the one who rang, every
Thursday and Sunday, always between nine and ten p.m.
On Thursday, the last time I spoke to them, they made no
mention of going to Tindari. Actually, Mama, before
hanging up, said, "We'll talk again on Sunday, as usual." If
they were already planning on going on that tour, they
would have told me not to worry if they weren't at home,
and to call back a little later, in case the bus was late.
Doesn't that seem logical to you?'

'Yes, of course.'

'But since they didn't say anything, I phoned them on
Sunday at nine fifteen, and nobody answered. And that's
when my torments began.'

'The bus returned to Vigàta around eleven o'clock that
evening.'

'And I called and called until six the next morning.'

'Mr Griffo, we must, unfortunately, consider every
possibility. Even those that we find repugnant. Did your
father have any enemies?'

'Inspector, if I didn't have this lump in my throat I
would laugh out loud. My father is a good man, even if he

has an unpleasant personality. Like my mother. Papa's been retired ten years. Never has he spoken of anyone wanting to do him harm.'

'Is he rich?'

'Who, my father? He gets by on his pension. He was able to buy the flat they're living in by liquidating their savings.'

Griffo lowered his eyes, disheartened.

'I can't think of any reason why my parents would have wanted to disappear, or anything that would have forced them to disappear. I even went and spoke to their doctor. He said they were doing well, given their age. And they had no signs of arteriosclerosis.'

'Sometimes, after a certain age,' said Montalbano, 'people become more susceptible to certain influences, more easily persuaded . . .'

'I don't understand.'

'Well, I don't know, some acquaintance may have spoken to them about the miracles of the Black Madonna of Tindari . . .'

'What would they have needed miracles for? Anyway, they were pretty lukewarm about anything to do with God.'

*

He was getting up to go to his rendezvous with Balduccio Sinagra when Fazio walked into his office.

'Sorry, Chief, you got any news of Inspector Augello?'

'I saw him at lunchtime. He said he'd be by later. Why?'

'Central Police of Pavia are looking for him.'

At first Montalbano didn't make the connection.

'Pavia? Who was it?'

'It was a woman, but she didn't tell me her name.'

Rebecca! Surely worried about her beloved Mimì.

'This woman from Pavia didn't have his mobile-phone number?'

'Yeah, she's got it, but she said it's not connected. Turned off. She said she's been trying to reach him for hours, since just after lunch. What should I tell her if she rings back?'

'You're asking me?'

Deep down, even as he was answering Fazio with feigned irritation, he felt quite pleased. Want to bet the seed was beginning to grow?

'Listen, Fazio, don't worry about Inspector Augello. He'll turn up sooner or later. I was about to tell you I'm leaving.'

'Going home to Marinella?'

'Fazio, I don't have to tell you where I'm going or not going.'

'Jesus, what did I ask! And what's got your goat, anyway? I asked you a simple, innocent question. Sorry I was so bold.'

'Listen, I'm the one who should apologize. I'm a little on edge.'

'I can see.'

'Don't tell anyone what I'm about to tell you. I'm on my way to an appointment with Balduccio Sinagra.'

Fazio turned pale and looked at him boggle-eyed.

'Are you kidding me?'

'No.'

'The guy's a wild animal, Chief!'

'I know.'

'Chief, get as angry as you like, but I'll say it anyway: in my opinion, you shouldn't go to this appointment.'

'I've got news for you. Mr Balduccio Sinagra, at this point in time, is a free man.'

'Well, hurray for freedom! The guy spent twenty years in the slammer and has at least twenty murders on his conscience! At least!'

'Which we haven't been able to prove yet.'

'Proof or no proof, he's still a piece of shit.'

'I agree. But have you forgotten that it's our job to deal with shit?'

'Well, if you really want to go, Chief, I'm coming with you.'

'You're not moving from this office. And don't make me tell you that's an order, 'cause it pisses me off no end when you guys make me say things like that.'

SEVEN

Don Balduccio Sinagra lived with his entire populous
family in a gigantic country house at the very top of a hill
known since time immemorial as Ciuccàfa, halfway between
Vigàta and Montereale.

Ciuccàfa Hill had two peculiarities that distinguished
it. The first was that it was entirely bald, lacking even the
tiniest blade of green grass. Never had a tree managed to
grow on that land, or even so much as a stalk of sorghum,
a caper bush or a clump of milk vetch. There was, true
enough, a cluster of trees surrounding the house, but these
had been transplanted, fully grown, by Don Balduccio, to
create a little shade. And to prevent them from drying up
and dying, he'd had truckloads of special soil brought in.
The second peculiarity was that, except for the Sinagra
house, no other dwelling, be it cottage or villa, was
anywhere to be seen on the hill, no matter what side one
was looking at. One saw only the snaking ascent of the
broad, paved road, two miles long, that Don Balduccio had

built for himself at his own expense, as he liked to say. There were no other houses not because the Sinagras had bought up the entire hill, but for another, subtler reason.

Despite the fact that the land on Ciuccàfa had been declared suitable for building by the new development plan some time ago, the landowners, a lawyer named Sidoti and the Marchese Lauricella, did not dare, though both short of cash, to divide up and sell the land, for fear of gravely offending Don Balduccio, who had indeed summoned them and, through metaphors, proverbs and anecdotes, had given them to understand that the presence of outsiders would be an unbearable nuisance to him. As a precaution against any dangerous misunderstandings, the lawyer Sidoti, who owned the land on which the road had been built, had also staunchly refused to be compensated for the unwanted expropriation. Indeed, in town there were malicious whispers that the two landowners had agreed to share the damages fifty-fifty. The lawyer gave up the land, while the marchese graciously made a gift of the road to Don Balduccio, shouldering the costs of the labour. The gossips also said that whenever, due to bad weather, any potholes or bumps appeared in the road surface, Don Balduccio would complain to the marchese, and, in the twinkling of an eye, pockets ever at the ready, the latter would see to it that the road was again smooth as a billiard table.

*

For some three years now, things hadn't been going so well for either the Sinagras or the Cuffaros, the two families fighting for control of the province.

Masino Sinagra, Don Balduccio's sixty-year-old first-born, had finally been arrested and sent to jail under a pile of indictments so vast that even if, during trial preparations, it had been decided in Rome to abolish life sentences, the legislature would have had to make an exception for him, reinstating it for this one case. Japichinu, son of Masino and beloved grandson of Don Balduccio, a boyish thirty-year-old endowed by nature with a face so sweet and honest that retirees would have trusted him with their life savings, was forced to go into hiding, pursued by a slew of arrest warrants. Bewildered and disturbed by this utterly unprecedented offensive on the part of justice after decades of somnolent languor, Don Balduccio, who'd felt rejuvenated by a good thirty years upon hearing of the murder of two of the island's most valiant magistrates, had plummeted back into the throes of old age when he learned that the new chief prosecutor was the worst thing possible: Piedmontese, and with a whiff of communism about him. One day, when watching the evening news, he'd seen the new magistrate kneeling in church.

'What's he doing, going to Mass?' he had asked in dismay.

'Yes, sir, the man's religious,' someone had explained.

'Wha'? Didn't the priests teach him nuthin'?'

Don Balduccio's younger son, 'Ngilino, had gone

completely mad, and began speaking an incomprehensible tongue he claimed was Arabic. And from that moment on, he'd begun dressing like an Arab as well, so that in town he became known as 'the sheikh'. The sheikh's two sons spent more time abroad than in Vigàta. Pino, known as the 'reconciler' for the diplomatic skill he was able to summon up at difficult moments, was constantly travelling back and forth between Canada and the United States. Caluzzo, on the other hand, spent eight months of the year in Bogotá. The burden of conducting the family's business had therefore fallen back onto the shoulders of the patriarch, who was now being lent a hand by a cousin, Saro Magistro. It was rumoured that this Magistro, after killing one of the Cuffaros, had eaten the man's liver, roasted on a spit.

As for the Cuffaros, it could not be said things were going any better for them. One Sunday morning two years ago, the ultra-octogenarian head of the family, Don Sisìno Cuffaro, got in his car to attend Holy Mass, as he was devoutly and unfailingly in the habit of doing. At the wheel was his youngest son, Birtino. When the latter turned on the ignition, there was a terrible blast that shattered windows up to three miles away. One Arturo Spampinato, accountant, who had nothing whatsoever to do with any of this, thinking a frightful earthquake was taking place, threw himself out of a sixth-floor window, smashing himself to bits. All that was found of Don Sisìno were his left arm and right foot; of Birtino, only four charred bones.

The Cuffaros did not hold this against the Sinagras, as everyone in town had expected. The Cuffaros as well as the Sinagras knew that the deadly bomb had been put in the car by some third party, elements of an emergent new Mafia, ambitious young thugs with no respect and ready to do anything, who'd got it in their heads to fuck over the two historic families and take their place. And there was an explanation for this. If the narcotics road had always been rather wide, it had now become a six-lane superhighway. One therefore needed young, determined manpower with good hands and the ability to use Kalashnikovs and computers with equal skill.

*

All these things were going through the inspector's head as he drove to Ciuccàfa. A tragicomic scene he'd witnessed on television also came back to him. In it, some bloke from the Anti-Mafia Commission who'd arrived in Fela after the tenth murder in a single week had been dramatically ripping up his own clothes while asking in a strangled voice, 'Where is the state?'

Meanwhile, the handful of carabinieri, four policemen, two coast guard agents and three assistant prosecutors who represented the state in Fela, risking their own skin each day, looked at him in amazement. The distinguished anti-Mafia commissioner was apparently suffering a memory lapse. He had forgotten that he, at least in part, *was* the state. And if things were what they were, it was he, along with others, who had made them what they were.

*

At the very bottom of the hill, where the solitary paved road leading to Don Balduccio's house began, stood a one-storey cottage. As Montalbano's car drew near, a man appeared at one of the two windows. He eyed the car and brought a mobile phone to his ear. Those in charge had been alerted.

On either side of the road were electrical and telephone poles, and every hundred and fifty yards or so there was an open space, a kind of rest area. Without fail, in each rest area, there was a person, now inside a car, plumbing the depths of his nose with his finger, now standing and counting the crows overhead, now pretending to fix a motor scooter. Sentinels. There were no weapons anywhere to be seen, but the inspector knew full well that should the need arise, they would promptly appear from behind a pile of rocks or a telephone pole.

The great cast-iron gate, sole opening in the high defensive wall surrounding the house, was wide open. In front of it stood Guttadauro the lawyer, a bright smile slicing across his face, bowing frantically.

'Go straight, then immediately turn right. There you'll find somewhere to park.'

In the parking area were some ten cars, from luxury to

economy models. Montalbano stopped and got out, as Guttadauro came running up, breathless.

'I never once doubted your sensibility, understanding and intelligence! Don Balduccio will be most pleased! Come, Inspector, I'll show you in.'

The start of the entrance lane was marked by two giant monkey-puzzle trees. Under each tree, on either side, was an odd sort of sentry box, odd because they looked like playhouses for children. And, in fact, one could see transfers of Superman, Batman and Hercules on their walls. But the sentry boxes also each had a little door and a window. The lawyer intercepted the inspector's gaze.

'Those are playhouses Don Balduccio had built for his grandchildren, I mean, his great-grandchildren. One of them's called Balduccio, like him, and the other is Tanino. They're ten and eight years old. Don Balduccio's just crazy about those kids.'

'Excuse me, Counsel,' Montalbano asked with an angelic expression on his face, 'but that man with the beard who came to the window in the playhouse on the left, was that Balduccio or Tanino?'

Guttadauro gracefully ignored the question.

They were now in front of the main door, a monumental affair of copper-studded black walnut, vaguely reminiscent of an American-style coffin.

In one corner of the garden — all prissy beds of roses, vines and flowers, and graced by a pool of goldfish (where the hell did the bastard get the water?) – was a big, powerful cage with four Dobermanns inside. In utter silence, they were sizing up the weight and texture of the guest, with a manifest desire to eat him alive with all his clothes on. Apparently the cage was opened at night.

'No, Inspector,' said Guttadauro when he saw Montalbano heading towards the coffin serving as the front door. 'Don Balduccio is waiting for you in the parterre.'

They went towards the left-hand side of the villa. The 'parterre' was a vast space, open on three sides, with the terrace of the floor above serving as the ceiling. Through the six slender arches that marked its boundary on the right, one enjoyed a splendid view of the landscape. Miles of beach and sea, interrupted on the horizon by the jagged profile of Capo Rossello. On the opposite side, the panorama left much to be desired: a prairie of cement without the slightest breath of green, and Vigàta, distant, drowning in it.

In the parterre were a sofa, four comfortable armchairs and a low, broad coffee table. Ten or so chairs were lined up against the only wall, for use, no doubt, in plenary meetings.

Don Balduccio, little more than a skeleton in clothes, was sitting on the two-seater sofa with a plaid blanket over his knees, even though it wasn't cold and no wind was blowing. Sitting beside him in an armchair was a ruddy-faced priest of about fifty in collar and gown, who rose when the inspector came in.

'And here's our dear Inspector Montalbano!' Gutta-dauro joyously announced in a shrill voice.

'Excuse me for not getting up,' said Don Balduccio in a faint voice, 'but I can't stand on my own two legs anymore.'

He made no sign of wanting to shake the inspector's hand.

'This is Don Saverio, Saverio Crucillà, who was and still is the spiritual father of Japichinu, my blessèd young grandson, slandered and hounded by evil men. It's a good thing he's a boy of deep faith; he suffers his persecution by offering it up to God.'

'Having faith is always best!' sighed Father Crucillà.

'If you don't sleep, you still can rest,' Montalbano chimed in.

Don Balduccio, Guttadauro and the priest all looked at him in shock.

'I beg your pardon,' said Don Crucillà, 'but I think you're mistaken. The proverb is about the bed, and it goes like this: "Of all things the bed is best / If you can't sleep you still can rest." No?'

'You're right, I was mistaken,' the inspector admitted.

He really was mistaken. What the fuck did he think he was doing, cracking a joke by mangling a proverb and paraphrasing the hackneyed line about religion being the opium of the people? If only religion actually was an opium for a murderous thug like Balduccio Sinagra's precious grandson!

'I think I'll be going,' said the priest.

He bowed to Don Balduccio, who gestured with both hands in reply, then he bowed to the inspector, who replied with a slight nod of the head, then he took Guttadauro by the arm.

'You're coming with me, aren't you, Counsel?'

They had clearly planned in advance to leave him alone with Don Balduccio. The lawyer would reappear later, after allowing enough time for his client – as he liked to call the man who in reality was his boss – to say what he had to say to Montalbano, without witnesses.

'Make yourself comfortable,' the old man said to the inspector, gesturing towards the armchair in which Father Crucillà had been sitting.

Montalbano sat down.

'Have anything to drink?' asked Don Balduccio, extending his hand towards a three-button control panel on the arm of the sofa.

'No, thank you.'

Montalbano couldn't help but wonder what those other two buttons were for. If the first one rang for the maid, the second probably summoned the in-house killer. And the third? Maybe that one set off a general alarm capable of unleashing something along the lines of World War Three.

'Tell me something – I'm curious,' said the old man, readjusting the blanket over his legs. 'A moment ago, when you came in, if I'da held out my hand to you, would you have shaken it?'

Good question, you son of a bitch! thought Montalbano.

He decided at once to answer sincerely.

'No.'

'Can you tell me why?'

'Because you and I stand on opposite sides of the barricade, Mr Sinagra. And for now, at least – though perhaps not for long – no armistice has been declared.'

The old man cleared his throat. Then he cleared it again, and only then did the inspector realize that Don Balduccio was laughing.

'Not for long?'

'There are already signs.'

'Let's hope so. But let's get down to serious matters. You, Inspector, must be curious to know why I wanted to see you.'

'No.'

'Is that all you know how to say: no?'

'To be honest, Mr Sinagra, I already know everything about you that might interest me as a cop. I've read all the dossiers on your case, even the ones that go back to before I was born. As a man, you don't interest me at all.'

'So then why did you come?'

'Because I don't rate myself so highly that I can say no to someone who asks to speak to me.'

'Right answer,' said the old man.

'Mr Sinagra, if you have something to say to me, fine. Otherwise . . .'

Don Balduccio seemed to hesitate. He bent his turtle-like neck even further towards Montalbano and stared at him fixedly, straining his glaucoma-glazed eyes.

'When I was a boy, my vision was so good it was scary. Now I see more and more fog, Inspector. Fog that's getting thicker and thicker. And I'm not just talking about the disease in my eyes.'

He sighed and leaned against the back of the sofa as if to sink down into it.

'A man should live only as long as is right. Ninety years, that's a lot. Too long. And it gets even harder if you're forced to pick things back up that you thought you were rid of. And this business with Japichinu's worn me out, Inspector. I'm so worried I can't sleep. He's even got TB. So I said to him: give yourself up to the carabinieri, at least they'll cure you. But Japichinu's a boy, stubborn like all boys. Anyway, I had to think about taking control of the family again. And it's hard, really hard. 'Cause in the meanwhile, time's gone by and people have changed. You don't understand how they think any more, you don't understand what's going through their heads. Used to be — just to give you an example — used to be, you had a problem, you could reason about it. Even for a long time, maybe days and days, maybe even till things got hot and tempers flared, but you could still reason. Nowadays people don't wanna reason any more, they don't wanna waste time.'

'So what do they do?'

'They shoot, Inspector, they shoot. And we're all really good at shooting, even the dumbest of the bunch. Right now, for instance, if you pull your gun out of your pocket—'

'I haven't got one, I don't carry a gun.'

'Really?' Don Balduccio's astonishment was sincere. 'But that's very careless, Inspector! With all the criminals running around these days—'

'I know. But I don't like weapons.'

'I didn't like 'em either. But as I was saying, if you point a gun at me and say, "Balduccio, get down on your knees," I've got no choice. Since I'm unarmed, I've got to get down on my knees. That's logical, no? But it doesn't mean you're a man of honour, it only means – pardon my language – that you're a piece of shit with a gun in your hand.'

'And how does a man of honour act?'

'Not how does he act, Inspector, but how *did* he *used to* act. You come to my place unarmed and you talk to me, you explain the problem to me, you give me the pros and cons, and if at first I don't agree with you, next day you come back and we reason, we talk it out until I'm convinced that the only solution is for me to get down on my knees like you asked, for my own good and everyone else's.'

Suddenly, a passage from Manzoni's *Colonna Infame* flashed through the inspector's brain, the one where some poor wretch is driven to the point where he can only utter,

'Tell me what you want me to say,' or something along those lines. But Montalbano didn't feel like getting into a discussion about Manzoni with Don Balduccio.

'But I'm under the impression that even in the happy times you mention, the custom was to kill people who wouldn't get down on their knees.'

'Of course!' the old man said with gusto. 'Of course! But killing a man for refusing to obey, you know what that used to mean?'

'No.'

'It meant you lost the battle, because that man's courage left you no other choice. You get my point?'

'Yeah, I get it. But, you see, Mr Sinagra, I didn't come here to listen to you tell me the history of the Mafia from your point of view.'

'But you already know the history from the point of view of the law!'

'Of course. But you're a loser, Mr Sinagra, or almost. And history is never written by the losers. For the moment, it's the people who won't reason and just shoot who're more likely to write it. The winners of the moment. And now, if you don't mind...'

He made as if to rise, but the old man stopped him with a gesture.

'Excuse me. Us old folks, along with all our other ailments, we've got big mouths. In two words, Inspector: it's possible we made some big mistakes. Really big mistakes. And I say "we" because I'm also talking on behalf of the late Sisìno Cuffaro and his people. He was my enemy for as long as he was alive.'

'What, are you starting to repent?'

'No sir, Inspector, I'll never repent before the law. Before the Good Lord in heaven, yes, when the moment comes. What I wanted to say is this: we made some really big mistakes, but we always knew there was a line that should never be crossed. Never. Because, you cross that line, and there ain't no difference between a man and a beast.'

He closed his eyes, exhausted.

'I understand,' said Montalbano.

'But do you really understand?'

'Really.'

'Both things?'

'Yes.'

'Then I've said what I wanted to say to you,' the old man continued, opening his eyes. 'If you wanna go, you're free to go. Goodbye.'

'Goodbye,' the inspector replied, getting up. He retraced his steps through the courtyard and down the lane and didn't encounter anybody. When passing the two playhouses under the monkey puzzles, he heard children's voices. In one of the houses was a little boy with a water pistol in hand, in the opposite playhouse another little boy was holding an intergalactic machine gun. Apparently Guttadauro had turned out the bearded watchman and promptly replaced him with Don Balduccio's great-grandsons so the inspector wouldn't get the wrong idea.

'Bang! Bang!' said the boy with the pistol.

'Ratatatatatat!' answered the boy with the machine gun.

They were training for when they became adults. But maybe they didn't even need to grow up. The previous day, in fact, at Fela, the police had arrested someone the papers called the 'killer baby', a boy barely eleven years old. One of those people who'd decided to squeal (Montalbano couldn't bring himself to call them 'repenters', much less state's witnesses) had revealed that a kind of public school existed where children were taught how to shoot and kill. Of course, Don Balduccio's great-grandsons had no need to attend such a school. They could get all the education they wanted at home.

No sign of Guttadauro anywhere. At the gate was a man with a beret, who tipped his cap as the inspector drove past, then immediately closed the gate behind him. Descending the hill, Montalbano couldn't help but notice how perfect the road surface was. Not a single pebble, not the tiniest crack in the asphalt. The maintenance must have cost the Marchese Lauricella his estate. In the rest areas, the situation hadn't changed, even though more than an hour had passed. One man watched crows in the sky, a second was smoking inside his car, the third was still trying to fix his motorbike. Seeing the latter, Montalbano felt tempted to fuck with the man's head. When he was in front of him, he stopped.

'Won't start?' he asked.

'No,' replied the man, dumbfounded.

'Want me to have a look at it?'

'No thanks.'

'I could give you a lift.'

'No!' the man yelled, exasperated.

The inspector continued on his way. In the cottage at the end of the road, the man with the mobile phone was back at the window, obviously relaying the message that Montalbano was about to leave the confines of the kingdom of Don Balduccio.

*

It was getting dark. Back in town, the inspector headed to Via Cavour. He pulled up in front of number 44, opened the glove compartment, grabbed the keys and got out. The concierge wasn't in, and he didn't see anybody on his way to the lift. He opened the door to the Griffos' flat and, once inside, closed it. The place smelled stuffy. He turned on the light and got down to work. It took him an hour to gather all the papers he could find, which he then put in a rubbish bag he took from the kitchen. He also found a tin box of Lazzaroni biscotti, stuffed full of cashier's receipts. Looking at the Griffos' papers was something he should have done at the very start of the investigation, but he'd neglected to do so. Too distracted by other concerns. Those papers might just contain the secret of the Griffos' illness, the one that had made their conscientious doctor follow them in his car.

He was turning off the light in the hall when he

remembered Fazio's concern about his meeting with Don Balduccio. The telephone was in the dining room.

'Hallo! Hallo! Whoozzat onna line? Dis is Vigàta police!'

'Cat, it's Montalbano. Is Fazio there?'

'I'll put 'im right true immediatelike.'

'Fazio? I just wanted to let you know I'm back safe and sound.'

'I know, Chief.'

'Who told you?'

'Nobody, Chief. Right after you left, I followed behind. I waited for you near the cottage where the guards stay. When I saw you coming out, I went back to headquarters.'

'Any news?'

'No, Chief, except for that lady that keeps calling from Pavia looking for Inspector Augello.'

'She'll find him sooner or later. Listen, you want to know what was said at the meeting with that person?'

'Of course, Chief. I'm dying of curiosity.'

'Well, I'm not going to tell you. You can die for all I care. And you know why I won't tell you? Because you disobeyed my orders. I told you not to move from headquarters, and you came and followed me anyway. Satisfied?'

He turned off the light and left the Griffos' home with the rubbish bag slung over his shoulder.

EIGHT

He opened the fridge and let out a whinny of sheer delight. His housekeeper, Adelina, had made him two imperial mackerels in onion sauce, a dinner he would obviously spend the whole night wrestling with, but it was worth the trouble. To cover his rear, before starting to eat he made sure there was a packet of bicarbonate of soda in the kitchen, bless its little heart. Sitting on the veranda, he scrupulously scarfed down the whole dish. All that remained on his plate were the fishes' skeletons and heads, picked so clean they could have been fossils.

Then, having cleared the table, he emptied out the rubbish bag stuffed with the papers he'd taken from the Griffos' home. Maybe a phrase, a line, a hint somewhere would reveal a reason, any reason, for the elderly couple's disappearance. They'd saved everything – letters, greeting cards, photographs, telegrams, electrical and phone bills, income statements, invoices and receipts, advertising brochures, bus tickets, birth certificates, marriage certificates, retirement booklets, medical-service cards, expired cards. There was even a copy of the 'certificate of living existence', that nadir of bureaucratic imbecility. What might Gogol, with his dead souls, have concocted from such a document? Had a copy fallen into his hands, Franz Kafka would surely have come up with another of his anguishing short stories. And now that we had 'self-certification', how was one supposed to proceed? What was the protocol, to use a word dear to government offices? Did one simply write on a sheet of paper something like: 'I, the undersigned, Salvo Montalbano, hereby declare myself to be in existence', sign it and turn it in to the appointed clerk?

At any rate, the papers telling the story of the Griffos' living existence didn't amount to much, barely a kilo of sheets and scraps. It took Montalbano till three in the morning to examine them all.

Nottata persa e figlia fimmina, as they say. He put the papers back in the bag and went to bed.

*

Contrary to his fears, the imperial mackerels placidly let themselves be digested without any flicks of the tail. Thus he was able to wake at seven, after four hours of restful, sufficient sleep. He stayed in the shower longer than usual, even if it meant wasting all the water he had left in the reserve tank. There he reviewed his entire dialogue, word by word, silence by silence, with Don Balduccio. He wanted to be sure he understood the two messages the old man had given him before taking any action. In the end he was convinced he'd interpreted them correctly.

*

'Inspector, I wanted to tell you Augello called half an hour ago,' said Fazio. 'Says he'll be in around ten.'

The sergeant braced himself — as was only natural, since it had happened many times before — for an angry outburst from Montalbano at the news that his second-in-command was once again taking things easy. But this time the inspector remained calm and even smiled.

'Yesterday evening, after you got back here, did the woman from Pavia call?'

'I'll say she did! Three more times before giving up hope.'

As he was talking, Fazio was shifting his weight from one foot to the other, the way somebody does when he is about to dash off but is held back by something. But Fazio was not about to dash off anywhere; he was being eaten alive by curiosity, but didn't dare open his mouth to ask what Sinagra had said to his boss.

'Close the door.'

Fazio sprang up, locked the door, came back and sat down on the edge of a chair. Upper body leaning forward and eyes aglitter, he looked like a famished dog waiting for its master to throw it a bone. He was therefore a little disappointed by Montalbano's first question.

'Do you know a priest named Saverio Crucillà?'

'I've heard him mentioned, but I don't know him personally. I know he's not from around here. If I'm not mistaken, he's from Montereale.'

'Try to find out everything you can about him. Where he lives, what his habits are, what his church hours are, who he associates with, what people say about him. Get the whole lowdown. And after you've done this – which I want you to do before the day is out—'

'I come and report back to you.'

'Wrong. You don't report anything to me. You start to follow him, discreetly.'

'Leave it to me, Chief. He won't see me, even if he's got eyes in the back of his head.'

'Wrong again.'

Fazio looked stunned. 'Chief, when you're tailing someone, the rule is that the person isn't supposed to know. Otherwise, what's the point?'

'Things are different in this case. I want the priest to know you're following him. In fact, I want you to make it clear to him that you're one of my men. It's very important, see, that he realizes you're a cop.'

'I've never done anything like that before.'

'Nobody else, however, under any circumstances, must know that you're following him.'

'Can I be honest with you, Chief? I haven't understood a word you said.'

'No problem. You don't have to understand. Just do as I say.'

Fazio looked offended.

'Inspector, when I do things without understanding them, they come out bad. So you're going to have to deal with that.'

'Fazio, Father Crucillà is expecting to be followed.'

'But why, for the love of God?'

'Because he's supposed to lead us somewhere. But he's supposed to pretend he doesn't know he's doing it. It's an act, get it?'

'I'm beginning to understand. And who's gonna be waiting for us in this place the priest is gonna take us to?'

'Japichinu Sinagra.'

'Holy shit!'

'Your polite euphemism leads me to think that you finally realize what an important matter this is,' said the inspector, talking the way they do in books. Fazio, meanwhile, had started eyeing him suspiciously.

'How did you ever discover that this Father Crucillà knows where Japichinu Sinagra is hiding? The whole world is looking for Japichinu — the Anti-Mafia Commission, the Flying Squad, the ROS, the Secret Service — and nobody's been able to find him.'

'I didn't discover anything. He told me. Actually, no, he didn't tell me, he insinuated it.'

'Who, Father Crucillà?'

'No. Balduccio Sinagra.'

Something like a mild earthquake seemed to pass

through the room. Fazio, his face fire-red, staggered, taking one step forward, two steps back.

'His grandfather?!' he asked, breathless.

'Calm down, you look like a character in the puppet theatre. Yes indeed, his grandfather. Wants the boy to go to jail. Japichinu, however, is probably not entirely convinced. Messages between grandfather and grandson are conveyed by the priest, who Balduccio wanted to introduce me to at his house. If he had no interest in my meeting him, he would have sent him away before I arrived.'

'I just don't get it, Chief. What's he thinking? Japichinu's going to get life, not even God can save him from that!'

'Maybe God can't, but someone else might.'

'How?'

'By killing him, Fazio. In prison he's got a good chance to save his skin. The punks in the new Mafia are really sticking it to all these guys, the Sinagras as well as the Cuffaros. So, maximum-security prison means security not just for people on the outside, but for those on the inside, too.'

Fazio thought it over a little, and finally seemed convinced.

'Do I have to sleep in Montereale, too?'

'I don't think so. I don't think the priest goes out at night.'

'How's Father Crucillà going to let me know when he's leading me to Japichinu's hideout?'

'Don't worry, he'll find a way. But when he shows you the place, I'm warning you, don't get any bright ideas, don't make any move at all. You're to contact me immediately.'

'OK.'

Fazio stood up and headed slowly towards the door. Halfway there, he stopped and turned around to look at Montalbano.

'What is it?'

'Chief, I've known you too long not to see that you're not telling me the whole story.'

'For instance?'

'Don Balduccio must've told you something else.'

'You're right.'

'Can I know what it is?'

'Certainly. He said it wasn't them. And he assured me that it wasn't the Cuffaros, either. So the culprits must be the new guys.'

'The culprits for what crime?'

'I don't know. At the moment, I don't know what the hell he was referring to. But I'm beginning to get an idea.'

'Can you tell me what that is?'

'It's too early.'

Fazio barely had time to turn the key in the lock when he was pushed violently against the wall by the door, which Catarella had thrown open.

'You almost broke my nose!' said Fazio, holding his hand over his face.

'Chief, Chief!' gasped Catarella. 'Sorry to bust in here like dis, but it's hizzoner the commissioner in poisson!'

'Where is he?'

'Onna phone, Chief.'

'Put him through.'

Catarella dashed out like a hare, and Fazio waited for him to pass before going out himself.

Commissioner Bonetti-Alderighi sounded like he was talking inside a freezer, so cold was his voice.

'Montalbano? A preliminary question, if you don't mind. Do you drive a Fiat Tipo with licence plate AG 334 JB?'

'Yes.'

Now Bonetti-Alderighi's voice was coming directly from a polar ice floe. In the background one could hear bears howling (but do bears howl?).

'Come to my office immediately.'

'I'll be there in about an hour, so I can—'

'Don't you understand Italian? I said immediately.'

*

'Come in and leave the door open,' the commissioner ordered, as soon as he saw Montalbano in the doorway. It must have been a very serious matter, since a minute earlier, in the hallway, Lattes had pretended not to see him. As Montalbano approached the desk, Bonetti-Alderighi stood up and went to open the window.

I must have turned into a virus, thought Montalbano. *The man's afraid I'll infect the air.*

The commissioner sat back down without signalling to Montalbano to do the same. It was like when he was in school, when the headmaster would call him into his office for a solemn tongue-lashing.

'Great,' said Bonetti-Alderighi, looking him up and down. 'Just great. Fantastic.'

Montalbano didn't breathe. Before deciding how to act, he needed to learn the reason behind his superior's anger.

'This morning,' the commissioner continued, 'I had barely set foot in this office when I discovered a bit of news I won't hesitate to call unpleasant. Extremely unpleasant, in fact. It was a report that threw me into a rage. And this report was about you.'

Mouth shut! the inspector commanded himself severely.

'This report says that a Fiat Tipo, licence number . . .' He paused, leaning forward to read the sheet of paper on his desk.

'AG 334 JB?' Montalbano timidly suggested.

'Be quiet. I'll do the talking. A Fiat Tipo, licence number AG 334 JB, drove past our checkpoint yesterday evening, on its way to the home of notorious Mafia boss Balduccio Sinagra. After the required search was done, they ascertained that the car belongs to you, and felt duty-bound to inform me. Now, tell me: are you stupid enough to imagine that that villa would not be under constant surveillance?'

'No! Of course not! How can you say that?' said

Montalbano, play-acting at great astonishment. And over his head, no doubt, appeared one of those bright rings that saints customarily wear. He let his face assume a worried expression and muttered through clenched teeth, 'Damn! Bad move!'

'You have every reason to be worried, Montalbano! I demand an explanation. And a satisfactory one. Otherwise your controversial career ends right here. Your methods border on illegality all too often, and I've been tolerating them far too long!'

The inspector hung his head, letting it fall into a pose of contrition. Seeing him this way, the commissioner grew bolder and let fly.

'You see, Montalbano, with someone like you, it's not that far-fetched to imagine some kind of collusion! Unfortunately there are plenty of notorious precedents, which I won't cite for you, since you're already well aware of them! And anyway, I'm sick and tired of you and the whole Vigàta police force! It's not clear whether you're policemen or mafiosi!'

Apparently he liked the line of argument he'd used with Mimì Augello.

'I'm going to clean the place out!'

As if following a script, Montalbano first wrung his hands, then took a handkerchief out of his pocket and wiped his face. He spoke haltingly.

'I've got a heart like a lion and another like a donkey, Mr Commissioner.'

'I don't understand.'

'I'm in an awkward position. Because, the fact is that, after talking to me, Balduccio Sinagra had me give my word that . . .'

'That?'

'That I wouldn't mention a word of our meeting to anyone.'

The commissioner slammed his hand down on the desk with such force that he surely must have broken some bones.

'But do you realize what you're saying to me? Nobody was supposed to know! And in your opinion, am I, the commissioner, nobody? It is your duty, I repeat, your duty—'

Montalbano raised his hands in a gesture of surrender. Then he ran his handkerchief rapidly over his eyes.

'I know, I know, Mr Commissioner,' he said, 'but if you only knew how torn I feel between my duty on the one hand and my word of honour on the other . . .'

He secretly congratulated himself. What a fine language Italian was! 'Torn' was exactly the word required in this case.

'You're raving, Montalbano! You don't realize what you're saying! You're putting your duty on the same level as a promise made to a criminal!'

The inspector repeatedly nodded his head.

'You're right! You're right! Your words are the gospel truth!'

'So now, without beating about the bush, tell me why you met Sinagra! I demand a full explanation!'

Now came the climax of the whole performance he'd been improvising. If the commissioner swallowed the bait, the whole business would end right then and there.

'I think he might want to turn himself in,' he murmured, in a low voice.

'What's that?' said the commissioner, who'd understood not a word.

'I think Balduccio Sinagra has half a mind to turn himself in.'

As if propelled in the air by an explosion in the very spot in which he was seated, Bonetti-Alderighi shot out of his chair, ran anxiously over to the window and door and shut them both, giving the latter a turn of the key for good measure.

'Let's sit over here,' he said, pushing the inspector towards a small sofa. 'So we won't have to raise our voices.'

Montalbano sat down and lit up a cigarette, knowing full well that the commissioner went ape-shit, had out-and-out attacks of hysteria, whenever he saw the slightest shred of tobacco. But this time Bonetti-Alderighi didn't even notice. With a faraway smile and dreamy eyes, he was imagining himself surrounded by squabbling, impatient journalists, in the glare of the floodlights, a cluster of microphones extended towards his mouth, while he explained in brilliant turns of phrase how he'd managed to persuade one of the most bloodthirsty bosses in the Mafia to cooperate with justice.

'Tell me everything, Montalbano,' he entreated, his tone conspiratorial.

'What can I say, Mr Commissioner? Yesterday Sinagra rang me up personally to tell me he wanted to see me at once.'

'You could at least have let me know!' the commissioner reproached him, wagging his index finger in the air as if to say, 'Naughty, naughty.'

'I didn't have the time, believe me. Actually, no, wait . . .'

'Yes?'

'Now I remember: I did call you, but was told you were busy, I don't know, in a meeting or something . . .'

'That's possible, very possible,' the other admitted. 'But let's come to the point: what did Sinagra tell you?'

'Surely, Mr Commissioner, you must know from the report that it was a very brief conversation.'

Bonetti-Alderighi got up, glanced at the sheet of paper on his desk, then came and sat back down.

'Forty-five minutes is not brief.'

'Granted, but in those forty-five minutes you've got to include the drive up there and back.'

'You're right.'

'Anyway, Sinagra didn't really tell me anything outright. Rather, he gave me to understand his intentions. Better yet, he left it all up to my intuition.'

'Sicilian-style, eh?'

'Yeah.'

'Could you try to be a little more specific?'

'He said he was beginning to feel tired.'

'I can imagine. He's ninety years old!'

'Exactly. He said his son's arrest and his grandson's life on the run were hard blows to take.'

It sounded like a line from a B-movie, and it had come out well. The commissioner, however, looked a tad disappointed.

'Is that all?'

'It's already a lot, Mr Commissioner! Think about it. Why did he want to tell *me* about his situation? You know these guys: they usually take things really slow. We need to remain calm, patient and tenacious.'

'Of course, of course.'

'He said he'd call me back soon.'

Bonetti-Alderighi's momentary discouragement turned into enthusiasm again.

'He said that?'

'Yes he did, sir. But we need to be very cautious; one false step could send it all up in smoke. The stakes are extremely high.'

He felt disgusted by the words coming out of his mouth. A clutch of clichés. But that was just the sort of language that worked at that moment. He wondered how much longer he could keep up the charade.

'Yes, of course, I understand.'

'Just think, Mr Commissioner, I didn't tell any of my men about this. You never know where there might be a mole.'

'I promise to do the same!' the commissioner vowed, holding up his hand.

It was as if they were at Pontida. The inspector stood up.

'If you have no further orders . . .'

'Fine, fine, Montalbano, you can go. And thanks.'

They shook hands energetically, looking one another in the eye.

'However . . .' said the commissioner, drooping.

'What is it?'

'There's still that damned report. I can't ignore it, you realize. I have to respond in one way or another.'

'Mr Commissioner, if somebody begins to suspect that there's any contact, however minimal, between us and Sinagra, the rumour will spread and the whole deal will fall through. I'm sure of it.'

'Right, right.'

'And that's why, a few minutes ago, when you told me my car had been spotted, I felt a twinge of disappointment.'

How good he was at talking this way! Had he perhaps found his true mode of expression?

'Did they photograph the car?' he asked after an appropriately long pause.

'No. They just took down the licence-plate number.'

'Then there might be a solution. But I don't dare tell you what it is, since it would offend your unshakeable honesty as a man and civil servant.'

Bonetti-Alderighi heaved a long sigh, as if on death's doorstep.

'Tell me anyway.'

'Just tell them they copied the number wrong.'

'But how would I know they got it wrong?'

'Because during that very same half hour they claim I was at Sinagra's place, you were having a long conversation with me on the phone. No one would dare contradict you. What do you say?'

'Bah!' said the commissioner, not very convinced. 'We'll see.'

Montalbano left, feeling certain that Bonetti-Alderighi, though troubled by scruples, would do as he had suggested.

*

Before setting out from Montelusa, he called headquarters.

'Hallo? Hallo? Whozzat onna line?'

'Montalbano here, Cat. Pass me Inspector Augello.'

'I can't pass 'im t'ya 'cause 'e ain't here. But he was here before. He waited for you and seeing as how you din't show up, he left.'

'Do you know the reason he left?'

'Yes, sir, because of the reason that there was a fire.'

'A fire?'

'Yes, sir. And an arsenal fire, too, like the firemen said. And 'Spector Augello went there wit' officers Gallo and Galluzzo, seeing as how Fazio wasn't around.'

'What did the firemen want from us?'

'They said they was puttin' out this arsenal fire. Then 'Spector Augello grabbed the phone and talked to 'em hisself.'

'Do you know where this fire broke out?'

'It broke out inna Pisello districk.'

Montalbano had never heard of such a district. Since the fire station was nearby, he raced down there and introduced himself. They told him the fire, a definite case of arson, had broken out in the Fava district.

'Why did you call us?'

'Because they discovered two corpses in a crumbling old farmhouse. Old people, apparently, a man and a woman.'

'Did they die in the fire?'

'No, Inspector. The flames had already surrounded the ruined house, but our men got there in time.'

'So how did they die?'

'It looks like they were murdered, Inspector.'

NINE

Leaving behind the national route, Montalbano had to take a narrow, uphill dirt road that was all rocks and holes. The car groaned from the effort like a living being. At a certain point he could proceed no further, because the way was blocked by fire engines and other vehicles that had parked all around.

'Hey, you! Where do you think you're going?' a fireman asked him rudely, seeing him get out of the car and proceed on foot.

'I'm Inspector Montalbano. I was told that—'

'OK, OK,' the fireman said brusquely. 'You can go ahead, your men are already here.'

It was hot. The inspector took off the tie and jacket he'd put on to go see the commissioner. Still, despite this alleviation, after a few steps he was already sweating like a pig. But where was the fire?

He got his answer just round a bend. The landscape was suddenly transformed. There was no tree, shrub or plant of any kind to be seen, not a single blade of grass, only a form-less expanse, uniformly dark-brown in colour, completely charred. The air was heavy, as on days when the *sirocco* is particularly fierce, but it stank of burning, and here and there a wisp of smoke rose up from the ground. The rustic house stood another hundred yards away, blackened by fire. It was halfway up the side of a small hill, at the top of which flames were still visible, and silhouettes of men rushing about.

Somebody coming down the trail blocked his path, hand held out.

'Ciao, Montalbano.'

It was a colleague of his, chief inspector at Comisini.

'Ciao, Miccichè. What are you doing in these parts?'

'Actually, I should be the one asking you that question.'

'Why?'

'This is my territory. The firemen didn't know whether the Fava district was part of Vigàta or Comisini, so, just to be sure, they notified both police stations. The murder victims should have been my responsibility.'

'Should have?'

'Well, yes. Augello and I called up the commissioner, and I suggested we divvy them up, one corpse each.'

He laughed. He was expecting a chuckle from Montal-bano in turn, but the inspector seemed not even to have heard him.

'But the commissioner ordered us to leave both of them to you, since you're handling the case. Best of luck, see you around.'

He went away whistling, obviously pleased to be rid of the hassle. Montalbano continued walking under a sky that turned darker and darker with each step. He started to wheeze and was having some difficulty breathing. He began to feel troubled, nervous, but couldn't say why. A light breath of wind had risen, and the ash flew up in the air for a moment before falling back down impalpably. More than nervous, he realized he was irrationally scared. He picked up his pace, but then his quickened breath brought heavy, seemingly contaminated air into his lungs. Unable to go any farther alone, he stopped and called out, 'Augello! Mimì!'

Out of the blackened, tumbledown cottage came Augello, running towards the inspector and waving a white rag. When he was in front of him, he handed it to him: it was a little anti-smog mask.

'The firemen gave them to us. Better than nothing.'

Mimì's hair had turned all grey with ash, his eyebrows as well. He looked twenty years older.

Despite the mask, as he was about to enter the farmhouse, leaning on his assistant's arm, Montalbano smelt a strong odour of burnt flesh. He back-pedalled, and Mimì cast him a questioning glance.

'Is that them?' he asked.

'No,' Augello reassured him. 'There was a dog chained up behind the house. We can't work out who he belonged to. He was burnt alive. A horrible way to die.'

Why, was the way the Griffos died any better? Montalbano asked himself the moment he saw the two bodies.

The floor, once made of beaten earth, had now become a kind of bog from all the water the firemen had poured onto it. The two bodies were practically floating.

They lay face down, each killed by a single shot to the nape of the neck after being ordered to kneel down in a windowless little room, perhaps once a larder, that, as the house fell into ruin, had turned into a shithole that gave off an unbearable stench. The spot was fairly well shielded from the view of anyone who might look into the big single room that had once made up the whole house.

'Can a car make it up here?'

'No. It can get up to a certain point, then you have to go the last thirty yards on foot.'

The inspector imagined the old couple walking in the night, in the darkness, ahead of somebody holding them at gunpoint. They must have stumbled over the rocks, fallen and hurt themselves, but they had to get back up and keep moving, maybe even with the help of a few kicks from their executioner. And, of course, they hadn't rebelled, had not cried out, had not begged for mercy, but had remained silent, frozen in the awareness that they were about to die. An interminable agony, a real Via Crucis, those last thirty yards.

Was this ruthless execution the line that Balduccio Sinagra had said must not be crossed? The cruel, cold-blooded murder of two trembling, defenceless old people? No, come on. That couldn't have been the limit; this double murder wasn't what Balduccio Sinagra was bailing out of. He and his ilk had done far worse, goat-tying and torturing old and young alike. They'd even strangled, then dissolved in acid, a ten-year-old boy, guilty only of being born into the wrong family. Therefore what he was looking at was still within their limits. The horror, invisible for now, lay another shade beyond. He felt slightly dizzy for a moment, and leant on Mimi's arm.

'You all right, Salvo?'

'It's this mask, it's sort of oppressive.'

No, the weight on his chest, the shortness of breath, the aftertaste of infinite sadness, the feeling of oppression, in short, was not caused by the mask. He bent forward to have a better look at the corpses. And that was when he noticed something that finally bowled him over.

Under the mud one could see the shapes of the woman's right arm and the man's left arm. The two arms were extended and touching each other. He leaned even further forward to look more closely, all the while clinging to Mimi's arm. And he saw the victims' hands: the fingers of the woman's right hand were interlaced with those of the man's left hand. They had died holding hands. In the night, in their terror, with only the darker darkness of death before them, they had sought each other out, found each other, comforted each other as they had surely done so many other times over the course of their lives. The grief, the pity, assailed the inspector, two sudden blows to the chest. He staggered, and Mimì was quick to support him.

'Get out of here, you're not levelling with me,' said Augello.

Montalbano turned his back and left. He looked around. He couldn't remember who, but somebody from the Church had once said that hell does indeed exist, though we don't know where it is. Why didn't he try visiting these parts? Maybe he'd get an idea as to its possible location.

Mimì rejoined him, looking him over carefully.

'How do you feel, Salvo?'

'Fine, fine. Where are Gallo and Galluzzo?'

'I sent them off to lend the firemen a hand. They didn't have anything to do here anyway. And you too, why don't you go? I'll stay behind.'

'Did you inform the prosecutor? And the crime lab?'

'Everybody. They'll get here sooner or later. Go.'

Montalbano didn't budge. He just stood there, staring at the ground.

'I made a mistake,' he said.

'What?' said Augello, puzzled. 'A mistake?'

'Yes. I took this business of the old couple too lightly from the start.'

'Salvo,' Mimì reacted, 'didn't you just see them? The poor wretches were murdered on Sunday night, on their way home from the excursion. What could we possibly have done? We didn't even know they existed!'

'I'm talking about afterwards, after the son came and told us they'd disappeared.'

'But we did everything we could!'

'That's true. But I, for my part, did it without conviction. Mimì, I can't stand it here any more. I'm going home. I'll see you back at the office about five.'

'All right,' said Mimì.

He kept watching the inspector, with concern, until he saw him disappear behind a bend.

*

Back home in Marinella he didn't even open the refrigerator to see what was inside. He didn't feel like eating; his stomach was in knots. He went into the bathroom and looked at himself in the mirror. The ash, aside from turning his hair and moustache grey, had highlighted his wrinkles, turning them a pale, sickly white. He washed only his face, stripped down naked, letting his suit and underwear fall to the floor, put on his bathing suit and ran down to the beach.

Kneeling down in the sand, he dug a wide hole with his hands, stopping only when the water began to well up from the bottom. He grabbed a handful of seaweed still green and threw it into the hole. Then he lay face down and stuck his head inside. He inhaled deeply, once, twice, thrice, and with each new breath of air, the smell of the brine and algae cleansed his lungs of the ash that had entered them. Then he stood up and dived into the sea.

With a few vigorous strokes he propelled himself far from shore. Filling his mouth with sea water, he gargled for a long time, rinsing palate and throat. After this, he let himself float for half an hour, not thinking of anything.

He drifted like a branch, like a leaf.

*

Returning to headquarters, he phoned Dr Pasquano, who answered in his customary fashion.

'I was expecting your irritating call. Actually, I was wondering if something had happened to you, since I hadn't heard from you yet. I was worried, you know! What do you want? I plan to work on the two corpses tomorrow.'

'In the meantime, Doctor, you need only answer me with a simple yes or no. As far as you can tell, were they killed late on Sunday night?'

'Yes.'

'A single shot to the nape of the neck, execution-style?'

'Yes.'

'Were they tortured before they were killed?'

'No.'

'Thank you, Doctor. See how much breath I saved you? That way you'll still have plenty left, when you're on death's doorstep.'

'How I'd love to perform your autopsy!' said Pasquano.

*

For once Mimì Augello was punctual, showing up at five o'clock on the dot. But he was wearing a long face. It was clear he was stewing about something.

'Did you find time to rest a little, Mimì?'

'When would I have done that? We had to wait for Judge Tommaseo, who in the meantime had driven his car into a ditch.'

'Have you eaten?'

'Beba made me a sandwich.'

'And who's Beba?'

'You introduced her to me yourself. Beatrice.'

So he was already calling her Beba! Things must be proceeding very nicely. But then why was Mimì wearing that funereal face? He didn't have time to probe any further, however, because Mimì asked him a question he hardly expected.

'Are you still in touch with that Swedish woman, what's her name, Ingrid?'

'I haven't seen her in a while. But she did call me last week. Why do you ask?'

'Can we trust her?'

Montalbano hated it when somebody answered a question with another question. He did it himself at times, but always with a specific purpose in mind. He played along.

'What do you think?'

'Don't you know her better than I do?'

'What do you need her for?'

'If I tell you, do you promise not to think I'm crazy?'

'Do you think I'm capable of that?'

'Even if it's a really big deal?'

The inspector got bored with the game. Mimì hadn't even noticed how absurd the dialogue had become.

'Listen, Mimì, Ingrid's discretion I can vouch for. As for thinking you're crazy, I've done that so many times already that it won't make much difference if it happens one more time.'

'Well, I didn't sleep a wink last night.'

Beba was coming on strong!

'Why not?'

'There was this letter, one of the ones Nenè Sanfilippo wrote to his lover. You have no idea, Salvo, how hard I've been studying them! I practically know them by heart.'

You're such an arsehole, Salvo! Montalbano reproached himself. *All you ever do is think ill of Mimì, and here's the poor guy working through the night!*

Having duly rebuked himself, the inspector deftly overcame that brief moment of self-criticism.

'OK, OK. What was in the letter?'

Mimì waited a moment before deciding to answer.

'Well, he gets very angry, at first, because she shaves off her body hair.'

'What's there to get angry about? All women shave their armpits nowadays.'

'It wasn't her armpits.'

'Ah,' said Montalbano.

'All her hair, understand?'

'Yes.'

'Then, in the letters that follow, he starts to get into the novelty of it.'

'OK, but how's this of any importance to us?'

'It's important, believe me! Because I think, after losing sleep and my eyesight to boot, I've figured out who Nenè Sanfilippo's lover is. Some of the descriptions he gives, the little details, are better than a photograph. As you know, I really like to look at women.'

'Not just look at them.'

'OK. And I've become convinced that I recognize this woman. Because I'm sure I've met her. It would take very little to make a positive identification.'

'Very little! Mimì, what on earth are you thinking! You want me to go to this lady and say, "I'm Inspector Montalbano, ma'am. Er, would you please drop your panties for a moment?" Why, she'd have me put away, at the very least!'

'That's why I thought of Ingrid. If it's the woman I think it is, I actually saw her a few times with Ingrid in Montelusa. They must be friends.'

Montalbano twisted his mouth.

'You're not convinced?' asked Mimì.

'Oh, I'm convinced all right. But the whole idea has one major problem.'

'What?'

'I don't think Ingrid would be capable of betraying a friend.'

'Who ever said anything about betrayal? We just need to find a way, any way at all, to create a situation where she might blurt something out.'

'How, for example?'

'Bah, I don't know, you could invite Ingrid out for dinner, then take her to your place, give her something to drink, a little of that red wine of ours that the girls are so crazy about, and—'

'And then start talking about body hair? She's likely to have a fit if I mention certain things with her! She doesn't expect it from me.'

Mimì's jaw dropped in surprise.

'She doesn't expect it? Do you mean to tell me that, between you and Ingrid ... Never?'

'What are you thinking of?' said Montalbano, irritated. 'I'm not like you, Mimì!'

Augello looked at him for a moment, then joined his hands in prayer, eyes raised to the heavens.

'What are you doing?'

'Tomorrow I'm going to write a letter to His Holiness,' Mimì replied coyly.

'Saying what?'

'That you should be canonized while still alive.'

'Spare me the moronic humour,' the inspector said gruffly.

Mimì quickly turned serious again. With certain subjects, when dealing with Montalbano, one had to tread lightly.

'Anyway, as for Ingrid, give me a little time to think about it.'

'OK, but don't take too long, Salvo. You know, it's one thing to kill someone over a question of infidelity, and it's something else—'

'I am well aware of the difference, Mimì. And you're not exactly the person to be teaching me about it. Compared to me, you're still wrapping your arse in nappies.'

Augello took this in without reacting. He'd pushed the wrong button, talking about Ingrid. He had to try to dispel the inspector's bad mood.

'Salvo, there's another thing I wanted to talk to you about. Yesterday, after we ate, Beba invited me over to her place.'

Montalbano's gloom immediately lifted. He held his breath. Had what was supposed to happen between Mimì and Beatrice already happened, just like that? If Beatrice slept with Mimì too quickly, the affair might soon be over, and Mimì would inevitably go back to his Rebecca.

'No, Salvo, we didn't do what you're thinking,' said Augello, as if he could read Montalbano's mind. 'Beba's a nice girl. And very serious.'

How did Shakespeare put it? Oh, yes, 'These words content me much.' If Mimì spoke this way, there was hope.

'At a certain point she went to change her clothes. Left to myself, I picked up a magazine that was on the coffee table. When I opened it, a photo that had been inserted between the pages fell out. It showed the inside of a coach, with the passengers in their seats. In the background, you could see Beba from behind, with a frying pan in her hand.'

'When she came back out, did you ask her when . . .'

'No, it would have seemed, well, indiscreet. I put the photo back, and that was that.'

'So why are you telling me about it?'

'Something occurred to me. If people are taking souvenir photos on these tours, it's possible there are some in circulation from the excursion to Tindari, the one the Griffos went on. If we could find these photos, maybe they could tell us something, even if I don't know what.'

Well, there was no denying that Mimì had a very good idea. And he was obviously waiting for some words of praise. Which never came. Coldly, perfidiously, the inspector didn't want to give him the satisfaction. On the contrary.

'Did you read the novel, Mimì?'

'What novel?'

'If I'm not mistaken, along with the letters, I gave you some sort of novel that Sanfilippo—'

'No, I haven't read it yet.'

'Why not?'

'What do you mean, why not? I've been racking my brains with those letters! And before I get to the novel, I want to find out if my hunch about Sanfilippo's lover is correct.'

He got up.

'Where are you going?'

'I have an engagement.'

'Look, Mimì, this isn't some kind of hotel where you can—'

'But I promised Beba I'd take her to—'

'All right, all right, just this once. You can go,' Montalbano conceded, magnanimously.

✻

'Hello, Malaspina Tours? Inspector Montalbano here. Is your driver Tortorici there?'

'Just walked in. He's right here beside me. I'll put him on.'

'Good evening, Inspector,' said Tortorici.

'Sorry to disturb you, but I need some information.'

'At your service.'

'Tell me something, on your tours, do people usually take photos on the bus?'

'Well, yes ... but ...'

He seemed tongue-tied, hesitant.

'Well, do they take them or not?'

'I'm ... I'm sorry, Inspector. Could I call you back in five minutes, not a second longer?'

He called back before the five minutes were up.

'I apologize again, Inspector, but I couldn't talk in front of the accountant.'

'Why not?'

'You see, Inspector, the pay's not so good here.'

'What's that got to do with it?'

'Well, I ... supplement my wages, Inspector.'

'Explain yourself better, Tortorici.'

'Almost all the passengers bring cameras. When we're about to leave, I tell them they're not allowed to take pictures inside the coach. They can take as many as they like when we get to our destination. The only person allowed to take pictures when we're on the road is me. They always fall for it. Nobody complains.'

'Excuse me, but if you're driving, how can you take pictures?'

'I ask the ticket man or one of the passengers to do it for me. Then I have them developed and sell them to anyone who wants a souvenir.'

'Why didn't you want the accountant to hear you?'

'Because I never asked his permission to take pictures.'

'All you'd have to do is ask, and there'd be no problem.'

'Right. And with one hand he'd give me permission, and with the other he'd ask for a cut. My wages are peanuts, Inspector.'

'Do you save the negatives?'

'Of course.'

'Could I have the ones from the last excursion to Tindari?'

'I've already had all those developed! After the Griffos disappeared, I didn't have the heart to sell them. But now that they've been murdered, I'm sure I could sell 'em all, and at double the price!'

'I'll tell you what. I'll buy the developed photos and

you can keep the negatives. That way you can sell them however you like.'

'When do you want them?'

'As soon as you can get them to me.'

'Right now I have to go to Montelusa on an errand. Is it all right if I drop them off at the station tonight about nine o'clock?'

✳

One good turn deserved another. After her father-in-law's death, Ingrid and her husband had moved into a new house. He looked for the number and dialled it. It was dinner time, and the Swedish woman, when possible, liked to eat at home.

'You token I lissin,' said the female voice that answered the phone.

Ingrid may have changed houses, but she hadn't changed her habit of hiring housekeepers who she went looking for in Tierra del Fuego, on Mount Kilimanjaro, or inside the Arctic Circle.

'This is Montalbano.'

'Watt say you?'

She must have been an Australian Aborigine. A conversation between her and Catarella would have been memorable.

'Montalbano. Is Signora Ingrid there?'

'She mangia mangia.'

'Could I speak to her?'

Many minutes passed. If not for the voices in the background, the inspector would have thought he'd been cut off.

'Hey, who is this?' Ingrid finally asked, suspicious.

'Montalbano.'

'Oh, it's you, Salvo! The maid said there was some "Contrabando" on the phone. How nice to hear your voice!'

'I feel like a heel, Ingrid, but I need your help.'

'So you only remember me when you need me for something?'

'Come on, Ingrid. It's a serious matter.'

'OK. What do you want me to do?'

'Could we have dinner together tomorrow night?'

'Sure. I'll drop everything. Where shall we meet?'

'At the Marinella Bar, as usual. At eight, if that's not too early for you.'

He hung up, feeling unhappy and embarrassed. Mimì had put him in an awkward position. What kind of expression, what words, would he use to ask the Swedish woman if she had a girlfriend with no body hair? He could already see himself, red-faced and sweaty, muttering incomprehensible questions to an increasingly amused Ingrid . . . He suddenly froze. Maybe there was a way out. Since Nenè Sanfilippo had recorded his erotic correspondence on the computer, wasn't it possible that . . . ?

He grabbed the keys to the Via Cavour apartment and dashed out.

TEN

As fast as he was racing out of the office, Fazio was rushing in. And inevitably, as in the finest slapstick movies, they collided. Since they were the same height and were walking with heads down, they nearly locked horns like stags in love.

'Where are you going? I need to talk to you,' said Fazio.

'So let's talk,' said Montalbano.

Fazio locked the office door and sat down, smiling with satisfaction.

'It's done, Chief.'

'Done?' asked an astonished Montalbano. 'In one go?'

'Yes, sir, in one go. Father Crucillà's a clever man. He's the kind of priest that's likely to have a rear-view mirror to look in when he's saying Mass, so he can spy on his flock. Anyway, to cut a long story short, when I got to Montereale I went straight to the church and sat down in the first row of pews. There wasn't a soul around. After a little bit,

Father Crucillà comes out of the sacristy dressed up in his vestments, followed by an altar boy. I think he was taking the holy oil to somebody's deathbed. When he passed in front of me, seeing a new face, he looked at me. And I looked back at him. I stayed glued to that pew for practically two hours, and then he finally came back. We looked at each other again. He went into the sacristy for about ten minutes, then came back out with the altar boy still behind him. When he was right in front of me, he waved at me, spreading all five fingers, nice and clear. What do you think he meant?'

'He wanted you to come back to the church at five.'

'That's what I thought, too. See how clever he is? If I was any old churchgoer, I'd've thought he was just waving, but if I was the man sent by you, then he wasn't just waving, he was giving me a five o'clock appointment.'

'What did you do?'

'I went and had lunch.'

'In Montereale?'

'No, Chief, I'm not as dumb as you think. There's two trattorias in Montereale and I know a lot of people there. I didn't want to be seen about town. And since I had time, I went over Bibera way.'

'So far?'

'Yeah, but I thought it was worth it. I heard there was a place there where you eat like a god.'

'What's it called?' Montalbano asked at once with keen interest.

'Peppuccio's, it's called. But the cooking stinks. Maybe it wasn't a good day, maybe the owner, who's also the chef, was in a bad mood. If you're ever out that way, be sure to avoid Peppuccio's. Anyway, at ten to five I was back in the church. This time there were a few people there, two men and maybe seven, eight women. All old. At five o'clock sharp, Father Crucillà came out of the sacristy and looked over his parishioners. I had the impression he was looking for me. Then he went into the confessional and drew the curtain. A lady followed and stayed there for at least fifteen minutes. What could she have to confess?'

'Nothing, I'm sure,' said Montalbano. 'They go to confess just to talk to somebody. You know how it is for old people, don't you?'

'So I got up and sat down in a pew near the confessional. After the first old lady came out, another old lady went in. This one took a good twenty minutes. When she finished, it was my turn. I knelt down, made the sign of the cross, and said, "Don Crucillà, I'm the man sent by Inspector Montalbano." He didn't say anything at first, then he asked me my name. I told him, and he said, "We can't do it today. Tomorrow morning, before early Mass, come back here to confess." "I'm sorry, but what time is early Mass?" I asked. He says: "At six. But you must come at quarter to six. And tell the inspector to be ready, because we're definitely going to do it tomorrow, at nightfall." Then he said, "Now rise, make the sign of the cross, go back to where you were seated, and say five Hail Marys and three Our Fathers, make the sign of the cross again and leave."'

'So what'd you do?'

'What was I supposed to do? I said the five Hail Marys and three Our Fathers.'

'So why didn't you get back sooner, if you took care of all this so quickly?'

'My car broke down and I lost some time. So how do we leave it?'

'We're going to do as the priest says. Tomorrow morning, at quarter to six, you're going to hear what he has to tell you and then report back to me. If he said we can do it at nightfall, that probably means around six thirty or seven. Our actions will depend on what he tells us. Four of us will go, and we'll take one car, to keep a low profile. It'll be me, you, Mimì and Gallo. We'll talk again tomorrow. Now I've got some things to do.'

Fazio left, and Montalbano dialled Ingrid's home phone number.

'You token I lissin,' said the same voice as before.

'Who's tokens same man's token before. Contrabando.'

It worked like a charm. Ingrid came to the phone in thirty seconds.

'Salvo, what is it?'

'Change of plan, sorry. We can't meet tomorrow evening.'

'When can we, then?'

'Day after tomorrow.'

'A big hug.'

That was Ingrid. And that was why Montalbano so liked and admired her. She demanded no explanations, and wouldn't have given any herself, for that matter. She merely registered the situation. Never had he met a woman so womanly as Ingrid, who at the same time wasn't at all like a woman.

At least according to the notions we little men have formed about our little women, Montalbano concluded in his mind.

*

In front of the Trattoria San Calogero, walking briskly along, he came to a sudden halt, the way donkeys do when they decide, for mysterious reasons, to stop and not move another inch, whippings and kicks to the belly notwithstanding. He looked at his watch. Barely eight o'clock. Too early to eat. But the work that awaited him in Via Cavour promised to be long and would certainly take all night. Maybe he could start now and take a break around ten ... But what if he started feeling hungry before then?

'So, Inspector, you going to make up your mind or not?'

It was Calogero, the owner of the trattoria, watching him from the doorway. That was all he needed.

The room was totally empty. Eating at eight o'clock in the evening was for the Milanese; Sicilians don't start thinking about dinner until after nine.

'What's good tonight, Calò?'

'Lookee here,' Calogero replied proudly, pointing to the refrigerated display case.

Death strikes fish in the eyes, turning them milky. The eyes on these fish were bright and sparkly, as though they were still swimming in the water.

'Grill me four bass.'

'No first course?'

'No. What have you got for appetizers?'

'*Purpiteddri* that'll melt in your mouth. You won't need to use your teeth.'

It was true. The baby octopi, tender in the extreme, dissolved in his mouth. With the bass, after sprinkling it with a few drops of 'carter's dressing' – olive oil seasoned with garlic and hot pepper – he took his time.

The inspector had two ways to eat fish. The first, which he used reluctantly and only when he had little time, was to bone it, gather all the edible parts on his plate, and then set about eating them. The second, which gave him far more satisfaction, consisted of earning every single bite, removing the bones as he went along. It took longer, true, but that additional bit of time served to smooth the way, so to speak. As one was cleaning each already dressed bite, the brain would pre-activate the senses of taste and smell so that one seemed to eat the fish twice.

*

By the time he got up from the table, it was nine thirty. He decided to take a stroll to the port. The truth of the matter was that he had no desire to see what he was expecting to see in Via Cavour. Some large trucks were being loaded onto the mail boat for Sampedusa. Few passengers, no tourists. It wasn't the season yet. He dawdled for an hour or so, then made up his mind.

*

Entering Nenè Sanfilippo's flat, he made sure the windows were well shuttered and let no light filter out, then went into the kitchen. Sanfilippo had, among other things, the essentials for making coffee, and Montalbano used the largest pot he could find, a four-cupper. As the coffee was boiling, he had a look around the flat. Beside the computer, the one Catarella had worked on, was a shelf full of diskettes, CD-ROMs, CDs, and video cassettes. Catarella had put the computer disks in order and had stuck in a little piece of paper on which he'd written in block letters: DIRTY DISQUETTES. Porno stuff, therefore. Montalbano counted the video cassettes, thirty in all. Fifteen had been bought at a sex shop and had colourful labels and unambiguous titles; five had been recorded by Nenè himself and each given a different woman's name: *Laura*, *Renée*, *Paola*, *Giulia* and *Samantha*. The other ten were commercial movie cassettes, all strictly American, and all with titles promising sex and violence. He took out the cassettes with the women's names and went into the bedroom, where Nenè Sanfilippo had an enormous television screen. The coffee was stale. He drank one cup, went back to the bedroom, took off his jacket and shoes, inserted the first cassette he came across, *Samantha*, stretched out on the bed, putting two pillows behind his head, and turned on the tape as he lit himself a cigarette.

The set consisted of a double bed, the same one that Montalbano was lying on. The shot was a fixed-frame. The camera still sat in position on the chest of drawers in front of him, ready for another erotic take that would never happen. Higher up, directly above the bureau, were two small floodlights, properly aimed, that would be turned on at the appointed time. The speciality of this Samantha, a redhead barely five foot one, tended towards the acrobatic. She moved about so much and assumed positions so complex that she often ended up off-camera. Nenè Sanfilippo, in this sort of general review of the *Kama Sutra*, seemed perfectly at ease. The audio was terrible. The few words spoken could barely be heard. In compensation, the moans, grunts, sighs and groans boomed forth at full volume, like television commercials. The entire viewing took forty-five minutes. Falling victim to a lethal boredom, the inspector put in the second cassette, *Renée*. It barely gave him time to notice that the set was exactly the same and that Renée was a girl of about twenty, very tall and very thin but with enormous tits, and in full possession of all her body hair. He didn't feel like watching the whole tape, and the thought passed through his mind that he could use the fast-forward on the remote, stopping here and there to watch. It was only a fleeting thought, however, because no sooner did he see Nenè begin to penetrate Renée doggy-style than an irresistible wave of lethargy hit him in the head like a crowbar, forcing him to shut his eyes and plunging him irremediably into a leaden sleep. His last thought was that there is no better soporific than pornography.

*

He woke up with a start, unable to understand whether he'd been roused by a screaming Renée in the throes of an earth-shaking orgasm or by the violent kicking at the front door as the doorbell rang without interruption. What was happening? Groggy with sleep, he got up, turned off the tape, and, heading towards the door to open up just as he was – dishevelled, in shirtsleeves, trousers falling down (but when had he unfastened them to get more comfortable?), barefoot – he heard a voice he did not immediately recognize shout, 'Open up! Police!'

This completed his confusion. Wasn't he the police?

He opened the door. To his horror, the first thing he saw was Mimì Augello in proper firing position (knees bent, arse slightly protruding, arms extended, both hands wrapped around the butt of the pistol), behind him the widow Concetta Lo Mascolo (née Burgio) and behind her a throng of people crammed onto the landing and both staircases, above and below. At a single glance he recognized the entire Crucillà family (the father Stefano, retired, in a nightshirt, his wife in a terry-cloth bathrobe, the daughter

Samanta – this one without the *h* – in a provocative long sweater); Mr Mistretta in underpants and T-shirt with, inexplicably, his misshapen black tote bag in hand; and Pasqualino De Dominicis, the child arsonist, between his daddy in pyjamas and his mummy Gina in a baby-doll nightie that was as gauzy as it was outdated.

At the sight of the inspector, two phenomena occurred: time stopped and everyone turned to stone. The widow Concetta Lo Mascolo (née Burgio) took advantage of this to improvise a dramatic monologue that was part didactic, part explanatory.

'*Madonna mia, Madonna mia*, what a terrible fright! I'd just drifted off to sleep when all of sudden I thought I was hearing the same symphony I heard when the dear departed was alive! The slut going ah ah ah ah, with him making like a pig! Exactly like before! What! A ghost comes back to his house and brings his slut back with him? An' he starts – excuse my language – he starts fucking like he's still alive? It chilled my bones, I tell you! Scared to death, I was! So I called the police. The last thing I could've imagined was that it was Mr Inspector, come to do his personal business right here! The last thing!'

The conclusion reached by the widow Concetta Lo Mascolo (née Burgio), which was shared by all present, rested on iron-clad logic. Montalbano, already lost at sea, hadn't the strength to react. He stood in the doorway, in shock. It was Mimì Augello who finally reacted. Putting his gun back in its holster, he pushed the inspector violently back inside the flat with one hand and at the same time started yelling so loudly that the tenants began to flee at once.

'That's enough! Go back to bed! Move it! There's nothing to see here!'

Then, closing the door behind him, dark-faced, he came towards the inspector.

'What the fuck do you think you're doing, bringing a woman in here! Tell her to come out, so we can think of a way to get her out of the building without triggering another insurrection.'

Montalbano didn't answer, but went into the bedroom, followed by Mimì.

'Is she hiding in the bathroom?' asked Augello.

The inspector turned the tape back on, lowering the volume.

'There's the girl,' he said.

He sat down on the edge of the bed. Augello gawked at the television screen, then suddenly collapsed into a chair.

'Why didn't I think of that sooner?'

Montalbano pushed the freeze-frame button.

'Mimì, the fact of the matter is that we took on the Sanfilippo and Griffo murders, you and I both, without getting involved, neglecting certain things that needed to be done. Maybe we've got too many other things on our minds to think clearly. Perhaps we're more concerned with our personal lives than with the investigations. End of story. We're starting over. Did you ever ask yourself why Sanfilippo stored the correspondence with his lover on his computer?'

'No, but since he was in that line of work, computers, that is...'

'Have you ever received any love letters, Mimì?'

'Sure.'

'And what did you do with them?'

'I kept some and got rid of the rest.'

'Why?'

'Because some were important and—'

'Stop right there. They were "important", you say. Important because of their contents, of course, but also because of the way they were written: the handwriting, the mistakes, the words crossed out, the capital letters, the paragraph breaks, the colour of the paper, the address on the envelope ... In short, when you looked at that letter you could easily call to mind the person who had written it. True or not?'

'True.'

'But if you copy it onto a computer, that letter loses all value – well, maybe not *all* value, but most of it. It also loses its value as evidence.'

'How do you mean?'

'You can't very well have the handwriting analysed, can you? But anyway, having printed copies of letters in the computer is still better than nothing.'

'I don't follow, sorry.'

'Let's assume Sanfilippo's liaison is a dangerous one, not in the same sense as Laclos, of course, but—'

'Who's this Laclos?'

'Never mind. I mean dangerous in the sense where, if discovered, it could mean trouble, or death. Nenè Sanfilippo may have said to himself that, if we're caught, it might save our lives if I can produce the original correspondence. In short, he copies the letters onto the computer and then leaves the sheaf of originals in some obvious place, ready for an exchange.'

'Which never took place, since the originals have disappeared and he was killed just the same.'

'Right. But I'm convinced of one thing, and that is, that Sanfilippo, though he knew he was courting danger by getting involved with this woman, underestimated the danger itself. I have the impression – it's just an impression, mind you – that we're dealing with more than some jealous husband's revenge. But to continue, I said to myself: if Sanfilippo is depriving himself of the suggestive possibilities of a handwritten letter, is it possible he didn't keep at least a photograph or some kind of image of his mistress? And that's when I thought of the video cassettes.'

'And so you came here to look at them.'

'Yes, but I forgot that the minute I start watching a porno movie, I fall asleep. I was looking at the ones he recorded himself, in this room, with different women. But I don't think he would be so stupid.'

'What do you mean?'

'I mean that he must have taken some precautions to prevent other people from immediately discovering who she is.'

'Salvo, maybe it's because it's late, but—'

'Mimì, there are thirty cassettes here, and they all need to be looked at.'

'All of them?!'

'Yes, and I'll explain why. There are three different kinds of cassettes here. Five recorded by Sanfilippo, documenting his exploits with five different women. Fifteen are porno cassettes he bought somewhere. And ten are home videos of American movies. As I said, they must all be looked at.'

'I still haven't understood why we need to waste all this time. You can't record anything on commercially sold cassettes, whether they're normal films or porno.'

'That's where you're wrong. You can. You need only tinker with the cassette a certain way. Nicolò explained it to me once. Sanfilippo may have resorted to this method, you see. He takes the tape of some film, say, *Cleopatra*, he lets it run for fifteen minutes, then he stops it and begins recording whatever it is he wants to record over it. And what happens next? When an outsider puts the tape in the VCR, he thinks he's watching *Cleopatra*, so he stops it, takes it out and puts in another. Whereas that tape contained the very thing they were looking for. Is that clear now?'

'Clear enough,' said Mimì. 'Or enough to convince me to look at all the tapes. Even using the fast-forward, it's still going to be a long haul.'

'You'll have to grin and bear it,' was Montalbano's comment.

He slipped on his shoes, tied the laces and put on his jacket.

'Why are you getting dressed?' asked Augello.

'Because I'm going home. And you're staying here. Besides, you have an idea who the woman might be. You're the only person who would recognize her. If you find her on one of these tapes, and I'm sure you will, call me at once, no matter the hour. Have fun.'

He left the room, with Mimì unable to open his mouth.

As he was going down the stairs, he heard doors carefully opening on different floors: the tenants of Via Cavour 44 had stayed up waiting for the fiery woman who'd had sex with the inspector to come out. They would lose a night's sleep.

*

On the streets there wasn't a soul. A cat came out from a building and gave him a meow of greeting. Montalbano reciprocated with a 'Ciao, how are you?' The cat took a liking to him and followed him for a while. Then it turned back. The night air was beginning to dispel Montalbano's somnolence. His car was parked in front of headquarters.

A shaft of light filtered out from under the closed front door. He rang the bell, and Catarella came and opened up.

'What is it, Chief? You a need anyting?'

'Were you asleep?'

Just inside the entrance was the switchboard and a tiny room with a cot, where whoever was on duty could lie down.

'No, sir, Chief, I was figgerin' out a crossword puzzle.'

'The one you've been working on for two months?'

Catarella beamed proudly.

'No, Chief, that one I already figgered out. I started a bran new one.'

Montalbano went into his office. There was a packet on his desk, which he opened. Inside were the photos of the excursion to Tindari.

He began looking at them. They all showed smiling faces, de rigueur on these sorts of outings. Faces he now knew after seeing them at the station. The only people not smiling were the Griffos, of whom there were only two photos. In the first, the husband's head was half turned round, to look out of the rear window of the coach. The wife, on the other hand, was staring at the camera with a blank look on her face. In the second photo, she was leaning her head forward and one couldn't see her expression, while he was staring straight ahead, with no light in his eyes.

Montalbano looked at the first snapshot again. Then he started searching through his drawers, with increasing frenzy as he realized he couldn't find what he was looking for.

'Catarella!'

Catarella came running.

'Have you got a magnifying glass?'

'The kind that makes things look all biglike?'

'That's the one.'

'Fazio maybe's got one in 'is desk.'

He came back holding the glass triumphantly in the air.

'Got it, Chief.'

The car photographed through the rear window, practically glued to the back of the bus, was a Fiat Punto. Like one of Nenè Sanfilippo's cars. The licence plate was visible, but Montalbano was unable to make out the letters and numbers, not even with the help of the magnifying glass. There was probably no point getting one's hopes up. How many Fiat Puntos were there driving around Italy?

He slipped the photo in his jacket pocket, said goodbye to Catarella and got in his car. He felt as though he needed a good night's sleep.

ELEVEN

He slept hardly at all, three meagre hours of twisting and turning in bed, with the sheet wrapped round him as round a mummy. From time to time he would turn on the light and study the photo, which he'd put on the bedside table, as if some miracle might occur and suddenly make his eyesight so keen as to let him decipher the licence number of the Punto following the coach. He knew by sense of smell, like a hunting dog pointing at a shrub of sorghum, that therein lay the key that would open the right door. The ring of the phone at six was like a liberation. It had to be Mimì. He picked up the receiver.

'Did I wake you, Chief?'

It was Fazio, not Mimì.

'No, Fazio, don't worry about it. Did you go to confession?'

'Yes I did. And he gave me the usual penance, five Hail Marys and three Our Fathers.'

'Was anything decided?'

'Yes, sir. It's confirmed. It's gonna happen at nightfall. So, we're supposed to go—'

'Wait, don't talk about it over the phone. Go and get some sleep. I'll see you at the office about eleven.'

He thought of Mimì losing sleep watching Nenè Sanfilippo's home videos. It was better for him to stop and also go home to get a few hours' sleep. The business that awaited them at nightfall wasn't to be taken lightly. They all needed to be in the best shape possible. Fine, but he didn't have Nenè Sanfilippo's phone number. Christ, calling Catarella and trying to get it from him – since the number was surely lying about somewhere at the station – was out of the question. Fazio must know it. He was heading home and the inspector could reach him on his mobile. Fine, except that he didn't have Fazio's mobile number. As for Sanfilippo's number being in the phone book, hah! He opened the directory listlessly, and just as listlessly began searching for the number. It was there. But why, when looking for a number, does one always start from the premise that it's not in the phone book? Mimì answered on the third ring.

'Who's this?'

Mimì had answered in a low, cautious voice. Apparently he'd been thinking that the only person who might call would be a friend of Sanfilippo. Treacherously, Montalbano egged him on. He was brilliant at changing the sound of his voice, and assumed the tone of a belligerent thug.

'No, tell me who you are, arsehole.'

'First tell me who you are.'

Mimì hadn't recognized him.

'I'm looking for Nenè. Put him on.'

'He's not home. But you can give me a message and I'll—'

'Well, if there's no Nenè, then this must be Mimì.'

Montalbano heard a string of curses, then the irritated voice of Augello, who'd recognized him.

'Only a lunatic like you would think of fucking around on the phone at six in the morning. What's your problem, anyway? Why don't you see a doctor?'

'Find anything?'

'Nothing. If I'd found something, I'd have called you, wouldn't I?'

Augello was still upset over the prank.

'Listen, Mimì, since we've got something important to do this evening, I thought it'd be better if you leave off what you're doing and go and rest.'

'What do we have to do this evening?'

'I'll tell you later. We'll meet back at the office at three in the afternoon. Is that all right?'

'Yeah, that's all right. Because after looking at all these tapes, I'm starting to feel like becoming a Trappist monk. Tell you what: I'll look at two more, and then go home.'

The inspector hung up and dialled the office.

'Hallo! Hallo! Vigàta police talking! Whoozis onna line?'

'Montalbano.'

'Poissonally in poisson?'

'Yes. Tell me something, Cat. I think I remember you saying you had a friend in the Montelusa forensics lab.'

'Yes, sir, Chief. Cicco de Cicco. He's a rilly tall guy, a Neapolitan, in the sense that he's from Salerno, a real heart-warmer, sir. Just tink, one morning he calls me up and says . . .'

If he didn't stop him at once, Catarella was liable to tell him Cicco de Cicco's life story.

'Listen, Cat, you can tell me another time. What time does he usually get to the office?'

'He usually falls in roundabout nine o'clock. Say, like, in maybe two hours.'

'This De Cicco works in the photo lab, right?'

'Yes, sir, Chief.'

'I want you to do me a favour. Ring De Cicco and arrange to meet him. Some time this morning I want you to take him a—'

'I can't take to 'im, Chief.'

'Why not?'

'If you want, I'll take him whatever you want anyway, but De Cicco's not gonna be there no way this morning. De Cicco told me hisself in poisson last night when he phoned me.'

'So where's he going to be?'

'In Montelusa. At police headquarters. They're all meeting together.'

'What for?'

'Mr Commissioner brung a rilly rilly big crimologogist from Rome who's asposta give 'em a licture.'

'A lecture?'

'Yes, sir. An' De Cicco tol' me the licture's gonna show 'em how they're asposta do when they have to do peepee.'

Montalbano staggered.

'What the hell are you saying, Catarella!'

'I swear it, Chief.'

Then the inspector had a flash.

'Cat, it's not peepee, it's probably a PPA they're talking about. Which means Probable Profile of the Assailant. Understand?'

'No, sir, Chief. But what'm I asposta take to De Cicco?'

'A photograph. I need him to make me some enlargements.'

There was silence at the other end.

'Hey, Cat, you still there?'

'Yes, sir, Chief, I ain't budged. I'm still here. I's jes thinkin'.'

A good three minutes passed.

'Try to think a little faster, Cat.'

'Y'see, Chief, if you bring me the photo, I'll jes scannafayou.'

Montalbano balked.

'What do you want to do to me?'

'Not you, Chief, the photo. I wanna scan it.'

'Let me get this straight, Cat. Are you talking about the computer?'

'Yes, sir, Chief. An' if I don' scan it m'self, 'cause you rilly need a rilly good scanner, I'll bring it to a trusty friend a mine.'

'OK, thanks. See you in a bit.'

He hung up and straight away the telephone rang.

'Bingo!'

It was Mimì Augello, all excited.

'I was right on the mark, Salvo. Wait for me. I'll be at your place in fifteen minutes. Does your VCR work?'

'Yes. But there's no point in showing it to me, Mimì. You know that porno stuff only gets me down and knocks me out.'

'But this isn't porn, Salvo.'

He hung up and straight away the telephone rang.

'Finally!'

It was Livia. That 'finally', however, was said not with joy, but with utter coldness. The needle on Montalbano's personal barometer began to plummet towards 'Storm'.

'Livia! What a wonderful surprise!'

'Are you sure it's so wonderful?'

'Why wouldn't it be?'

'Because I haven't had any news from you for days. Because you can't be bothered to give me a ring! I've been calling and calling, but you're never at home.'

'You could have called me at work.'

'Salvo, you know I don't like to call you there. Do you know what I finally did, to get some news about you?'

'No. What?'

'I bought *Il Giornale di Sicilia*. Did you read it?'

'No. What did it say?'

'It says you've got your hands full with no less than three murders, an old couple and a twenty-year-old. The reporter even insinuated that you don't know whether you're coming or going. In short, he said you were over the hill.'

This might be an escape route. To say he was unhappy, left behind by the times, practically incapable of understanding or wanting anything. That way, Livia would calm down and maybe even feel sorry for him.

'Ah, that's so true, my Livia! Maybe I'm getting old, maybe my brain isn't what it used to be ...'

'No, Salvo, rest assured, your brain is the same as ever. And you're proving it by the lousy performance you're putting on. You want to be coddled? I won't fall for it, you know. I know you too well. Call me some time. When you've got a free moment, of course.'

She hung up. Why was it that every phone conversation with Livia had to end with a spat? They couldn't go on this way; a solution absolutely had to be found.

He went into the kitchen, filled the espresso pot, put it on the burner. While waiting, he opened the French windows and went out on the veranda. A day to lift the spirits.

Bright, warm colours, a lazy sea. He took a deep breath, and at that moment the phone rang again.

'Hello! Hello!'

There was nobody there, but the telephone started ringing again. How was that possible, if he had the receiver in his hand? Then he understood: it wasn't the phone, but the doorbell.

It was Mimì Augello, who'd arrived faster than a Formula 1 driver. He stood in the doorway, undecided as to whether to come inside, a smile cutting his face in two. He had a video cassette in one hand and was shaking it under the inspector's nose.

'Have you ever seen *The Getaway*, a film with—'

'Yeah, I've seen it.'

'Did you like it?'

'Rather.'

'This version's better.'

'Mimì, are you going to come inside or not? Follow me to the kitchen, coffee's ready.'

He poured a cup for himself and one for Mimì, who'd come in behind him.

'Let's go into the other room,' said Mimì.

He'd drunk down his cup in one gulp, surely scalding his pipes, but he was too pressed, too impatient to show Montalbano what he'd discovered and, above all, to glory in his own intuition. He slipped in the cassette, so excited that he tried to put it in upside down. He cursed, righted it and turned it on. After some twenty minutes of *The*

Getaway, which Mimì sped up, there was another five of blank screen, with only dancing white dots and fried audio. Mimì turned the sound off entirely.

'I don't think they say anything,' he said.

'What do you mean, "you don't think"?'

'Well, I didn't watch it straight through. I jumped around a bit.'

Then an image appeared. A double bed covered with a snow-white sheet, two pillows propped up as headrests, one leaning directly against the light-green wall. There were also two elegant bedside tables of light wood. It wasn't Sanfilippo's bedroom. Another minute passed without anything happening, but it was clear that somebody was fiddling with the camera, trying to get the focus right. All that white created too much glare. Darkness ensued. Then the same shot reappeared, but tighter, the bedside tables no longer visible. This time there was a woman of thirty or so on the bed, completely naked, with a magnificent tan, in a full-length shot. The hair removal stood out because, in that area, her skin was ivory white; apparently it had been shielded from the sun's rays by a G-string. At the first sight of her, the inspector felt a tremor. He knew her, surely! Where had they met? A second later, he corrected himself. No, he didn't know her, but he had, in a way, seen her before. In the pages of a book, in a reproduction. Because the woman, with her long, long legs and pelvis resting on the bed and the remainder of her body raised up by pillows, leaning slightly to the left, hands folded behind her head, was a dead ringer for Goya's *Naked Maja*. But it wasn't only her pose that gave Montalbano this mistaken impression: the unknown woman also wore her hair the same way as the Maja, and had the faintest hint of a smile on her face.

Like the Mona Lisa, the inspector thought, by this point thinking in terms of painterly comparisons.

The camera remained stationary, as though spellbound by the image it was recording. On the sheet and pillows, the unknown woman was perfectly at ease, relaxed and in her element. A creature of the bed.

'Is she the one you thought of when reading the letters?'

'Yes,' said Augello.

Can a monosyllable contain all the pride in the world? Mimì had managed to fit it all in there.

'But how did you do it? It seems like you've only seen her a few times in passing. And always with her clothes on.'

'You see, in the letters, he paints her. Actually, no. It's not a portrait. It's more like an engraving.'

Why, when people spoke of her, did this woman bring to mind the language of art?

'For example,' Mimì continued, 'he talks about the disproportion between the length of her legs and the length of her torso, which, if you look closely, should probably be a little longer. Then he describes her hair, the shape of her eyes—'

'I get the picture,' Montalbano cut him short, feeling envious. No doubt about it, Mimì had an eye for women.

Meanwhile the camera had zoomed in on her feet, then ever so slowly ascended the length of her body, lingering momentarily over the pubis, navel and nipples, before pausing at her eyes.

How was it that the woman's pupils shone with an inner light so intense as to surround her gaze in an aura of hypnotic phosphorescence? What was she, some sort of dangerous nocturnal animal? He looked more closely and reassured himself. Those were not the eyes of a witch. The pupils were merely reflecting the light of the floods used by Nenè Sanfilippo to better illuminate the set. The camera moved on to her mouth. The lips, two flames filling the screen, moved and parted; the cat-like tip of the tongue peeped out, traced the contour of the upper lip, then the lower lip. Nothing vulgar about it, but the two men watching were dumbstruck by the violent sensuality of the gesture.

'Rewind and turn the volume up all the way,' Montalbano said suddenly.

'Why?'

'She said something, I'm sure of it.'

Mimì obeyed. The moment the shot of the mouth reappeared, a man's voice murmured something incomprehensible.

'Yes,' the woman replied distinctly, then began running her tongue over her lips.

So there was sound. Not much, but it was there. Augello left it on high volume.

The camera then went down her neck, passing lightly over it like a loving hand, from left to right and right to left again, and again, an ecstatic caress. In fact, they heard a soft moan from the woman.

'That's the sea,' said Montalbano.

Mimì looked at him perplexed, struggling to take his eyes off the screen.

'What is?'

'That continuous, rhythmic sound that you hear. It's not some sort of rustling in the background. It's the sound the sea makes when it's a little rough. The house they're in must be right on the seashore, like mine.'

This time Mimì's look was one of admiration.

'What a sharp ear you've got, Salvo! If that's the sea we hear, then I know where they shot this video.'

The inspector leaned forward, grabbed the remote control and rewound the tape.

'What are you doing?' Augello protested. 'Aren't we going to keep watching? I told you I only saw parts of it!'

'You can watch the whole thing when you've been a good boy. In the meantime, could you give me a synopsis of what you did manage to see?'

'Well, it continues with the breasts, navel, tummy, mound of Venus, thighs, legs, feet. Then she rolls over and he redoes her whole body from behind. Finally she turns over on her back again, lies down more comfortably, puts a pillow under her buttocks and spreads her legs just enough so the camera can—'

'OK, OK,' Montalbano interrupted. 'So nothing else happens? Do we never see the man?'

'No. And nothing else happens. That's why I said it wasn't pornographic.'

'It's not?'

'No. That sequence is a love poem.'

Mimì was right, and Montalbano made no reply.

'Care to introduce me to this lady?' he asked.

'With great pleasure. Her name is Vanya Titulescu, thirty-one years old, Romanian.'

'A refugee?'

'Not at all. Her father was Minister of Health in Romania. She herself has a degree in medicine, but she doesn't practise here. Her future husband, already a celebrity in his field, was invited to Bucharest to give a series of lectures. They fell in love, or at least he fell in love with her, brought her back to Italy and married her. Even though he's twenty years her senior. But the girl jumped at the opportunity.'

'How long have they been married?'

'Five years.'

'Are you going to tell me who the husband is? Or do you plan to tell the story in instalments?'

'Doctor and Professor Eugenio Ignazio Ingrò, the transplant magician.'

A famous name. He was often in the papers, made television appearances. Montalbano tried to call him to mind, saw a hazy image of a tall, elegant man of few words. He really was considered a surgeon with magic hands, in demand all over Europe. He also had a clinic of his own in Montelusa, where he'd been born and still lived.

'Do they have any children?'

'No.'

'Excuse me, Mimì, but did you gather all this information this morning after watching the tape?'

Mimì smiled.

'No, I informed myself after I became convinced she was the woman in the letters. The tape was only a confirmation.'

'What else do you know?'

'That around here, in our area — more specifically, between Vigàta and Santolì — they have a villa by the sea, with a small private beach. And I'm sure that's where they shot the video. They must have taken advantage when the husband was travelling abroad.'

'Is he jealous?'

'Yes, but not excessively so. But that's probably also because her infidelity didn't spark any rumours, not that I know of, at least. She and Sanfilippo were very good at not letting anything about their affair leak out.'

'Let me ask you a more specific question, Mimì. Is Dr Ingrò the kind of person who would be capable of killing his wife's lover, or having him killed, if he discovered she was being unfaithful?'

'Why do you ask me? That's the kind of question you should ask Ingrid, who's her friend. Speaking of which, when are you going to see her?'

'We'd planned to meet tonight, but I had to postpone it.'

'Ah, that's right, you mentioned something important, something we're supposed to do at nightfall. What's this about?'

'I'll tell you in a minute. The cassette you should leave here, with me.'

'You want to show it to Ingrid?'

'Of course. So, to wrap things up temporarily, what's your take on the murder of Nenè Sanfilippo?'

'What do you think, Salvo? They don't come any clearer than this. Dr Ingrò, somehow or other, gets wise to their affair, and has the boy offed.'

'Why not her, too?'

'Because that would have triggered a huge scandal of international proportions. And he can't have any shadows hanging over his private life, since that might diminish his earnings.'

'But isn't he rich?'

'Extremely rich. At least, he would be if he didn't have an obsession that's siphoning off rivers of cash.'

'Gambling?'

'No, he doesn't gamble. Maybe at Christmas, playing gin rummy. No, his mania is for paintings. People say he's got paintings of enormous value stored in a variety of bank vaults. Apparently when he sees a painting he likes, he can't control himself. He'd be capable of having it stolen for him. One gossip told me that if the owner of a Degas proposed a trade for his wife, Vanya, he'd accept without hesitation. What is it, Salvo? Aren't you listening?'

Augello had realized that his boss's mind was far away. Indeed, the inspector was wondering why whenever anyone saw or mentioned Vanya Titulescu, the subject always turned to painting.

'So, you seem to think,' said Montalbano, 'that it was the doctor who ordered Sanfilippo's murder.'

'Who else, if not?'

The inspector's thoughts flew over to the photograph still lying on the bedside table. But he immediately let those thoughts go; he first had to wait for an answer from Catarella, the new oracle.

'So, now can you tell me what it is we're supposed to do tonight?' Augello asked.

'Tonight? Nothing. We're going to pick up Balduccio Sinagra's beloved grandson, Japichinu.'

'The fugitive?' asked Mimì, leaping to his feet.

'Yup, that's the one.'

'And you know where he's hiding?'

'Not yet. But a priest's gonna tell us.'

'A priest? What the fuck is going on? All right, you're

going to tell me the whole story from the beginning, leaving nothing out.'

Montalbano told him the whole story from the beginning, leaving nothing out.

'*Beddra Matre santissima!*' Augello commented when it was over, grabbing his head between his clenched fists. He looked like an illustration from a nineteenth-century acting manual, under the heading 'Dismay'.

TWELVE

Catarella first studied the photo the way the short-sighted do, sticking it right in front of his eyes, then the way the long-sighted do, holding it at arm's length. Finally, he frowned.

'Chief, definitely no way, the scanner I got can't do it. I gotta take it to my trusty friend.'

'How long will that take?'

'Two hours max, Chief.'

'Get back here as soon as you can. Who's going to man the switchboard?'

'Galluzzo. Uh, and Chief, I wanted to tell you, that orphan guy's been waitin' a talk t'you since early this morning.'

'Who's this orphan?'

'Griffo's his name, the guy whose mum and dad was killed, who says he can't unnastanna way I talk.'

Davide Griffo was dressed all in black, in deep mourning. Dishevelled, clothes full of wrinkles, looking spent.

Montalbano held out his hand to him, inviting him to sit down.

'Did they make you come for the official identification?'

'Yes, unfortunately. I arrived in Montelusa yesterday, late afternoon. They took me to see them. After ... afterwards, I went back to the hotel and threw myself down on the bed, clothes and all. I felt so bad.'

'I understand.'

'Is there any news, Inspector?'

'None so far.'

They looked each other in the eye, both dejected.

'You know something?' said Davide Griffo. 'It's not out of any desire for revenge that I'm so anxious for the killers to be caught. I just want to know why they did it.'

He was sincere. Not even he knew about what Montalbano called his parents' 'secret illness'.

'Why did they do it?' Davide Griffo asked. 'To steal Papa's wallet and Mama's bag?'

'Oh?' said the inspector.

'You didn't know?'

'That they took their wallet and bag? No. I was sure they would find the bag under your mother's body. And I didn't check your father's pockets. Anyway, neither the bag nor the wallet would have made any difference.'

'Is that what you think?'

'Absolutely. The people who killed your parents would eventually have let the wallet and bag turn up, duly cleaned of anything that might lead us to them.'

Davide Griffo looked lost in a memory.

'Mama never went anywhere without that little bag. I used to tease her about it sometimes. I would ask her what treasures she kept hidden in there.'

He was swept away in a surge of emotion, a kind of sob rising up from deep inside his chest.

'I'm sorry. Since I was given back their things, the clothes, the coins Papa had in his pocket, their wedding rings, the house keys … Well, I came here to ask your permission … in short, if I can go into the flat and start to take an inventory …'

'What do you intend to do with the flat? They owned it, didn't they?'

'Yes, they made a lot of sacrifices to buy it. When the time is right, I'll sell it. I don't have much reason to come back to Vigàta any more.'

Another stifled sob.

'Did your parents own any other property?'

'None whatsoever, as far as I know. They lived on their pensions. Papa had a little passbook with the Post Office, where he would deposit his and Mama's pension cheques … But there was very little left to set aside at the end of each month.'

'I don't think I've seen this passbook.'

'It wasn't there? Did you have a good look where Papa kept his papers?'

'It wasn't there. I went through all his papers very

carefully. Maybe the killers took it along with the wallet and handbag.'

'Why? What are they going to do with a postal passbook they can't use? It's a useless piece of paper!'

The inspector stood up. Davide Griffo did the same.

'I have no objection to you going into your parents' flat. On the contrary. If you should find anything among those papers that—'

He stopped short. Davide Griffo gave him a questioning glance.

'Please excuse me a minute,' the inspector said, and he left the room.

Cursing under his breath, he had realized that the Griffos' papers were still at the station, where he'd brought them from his house. In fact, the plastic rubbish bag was in the store room. It seemed like bad form to return those family mementos to the son in that package. He rifled through the closet, found nothing he could use, no cardboard boxes or even a more decent bag. He resigned himself.

Davide Griffo gave Montalbano a confused look as the inspector set the rubbish bag down at his feet.

'I took it from your parents' place, to put the papers inside. If you want, I could have them brought to you by one of my—'

'No, thanks. I've got my car here,' the other said stiffly.

✳

He hadn't wanted to tell the orphan, as Catarella called him (speaking of whom, how long had he been away now?), but there *was* a reason one might want to remove the postal passbook. A very plausible reason: to prevent others from knowing the amount on deposit. Indeed the amount in the passbook might even be the symptom of the secret illness that had caused the conscientious doctor to intervene. Just a hypothesis, of course, but one that needed to be verified. He called up Assistant Prosecutor Tommaseo and spent half an hour beating back the bureaucratic resistance the judge kept putting up. Finally Tommaseo promised he would see to the matter at once.

*

The post office was a stone's throw from police headquarters. A horrendous building. Begun in the 1940s, when Fascist architecture was rampant, it hadn't been finished until after the war, when tastes had changed. The office of the director was on the second floor, at the end of a corridor utterly devoid of human beings or objects, frightening in its desolation and loneliness. The inspector knocked on a door on which hung a plastic rectangle with the word 'Director' on it. Under the plastic rectangle was a sheet of paper with an image of a cigarette struck out by two intersecting red lines. Under this were the words, 'Smoking is strictly forbidden'.

'Come in!'

Montalbano went in and the first thing he saw was

an actual banner on the wall, repeating the admonition: 'Smoking is strictly forbidden.'

Or you'll have to answer to me, the President of the Republic seemed to be saying, staring sullenly from his portrait under the banner.

Under this was a high-backed armchair in which the director, Cavaliere Attilio Morasco, was sitting. In front of Cavaliere Morasco sprawled an enormous desk, entirely covered with papers. The director himself was a midget who looked like the late King Vittorio Emanuele III, with a crew-cut that gave him a head like Umberto I, and a handlebar moustache in the manner of the so-called 'Gentleman King'. The inspector felt absolutely certain he must be in the presence of a descendant of the House of Savoy, a bastard, one of the many sired by the Gentleman King.

'Are you Piedmontese?' Montalbano blurted out, staring at him.

The other looked flabbergasted.

'No, why? I'm from Comitini.'

He might be from Comitini, Paternò or Raffadali, it made no difference to Montalbano.

'You're Inspector Montalbano, aren't you?'

'Yes. Did Prosecutor Tommaseo phone you?'

'Yes,' the director admitted reluctantly. 'But a phone call is a phone call. You know what I mean?'

'Yes, of course I know what you mean. For me, for example, a rose is a rose is a rose is a rose.'

Cavaliere Morasco was unimpressed by the inspector's learned quotation of Gertrude Stein.

'I see that we agree,' he said.

'In what sense, may I ask?'

'In the sense that *verba volant* and *scripta manent*.'

'Could you explain?'

'Certainly. Prosecutor Tommaseo phoned me to tell me that you have authorization to conduct investigations concerning a postal passbook belonging to the late Alfonso Griffo. That's fine, though I consider this, how shall I say, an advance notice. Until I receive a request and written authorization, I cannot allow you to violate the postal code of secrecy.'

These words so steamed up the inspector that for a moment he was in danger of taking off through the ceiling.

'I'll come back later.'

He started to rise. The director stopped him with a gesture.

'Wait. There may be a solution. Could I see some identification?'

The danger of take-off increased. With one hand, Montalbano anchored himself to the chair he was sitting in, and with the other he held out his ID card.

The Savoy bastard examined it at great length.

'After the prosecutor's call, I imagined you'd come running here. So I drafted a declaration, which you will sign, and which says that you relieve me of all responsibility in the matter.'

'I'm happy to relieve you,' said the inspector.

He signed the declaration without reading it and put his ID card back in his pocket. Cavaliere Morasco stood up.

'Wait for me here. This will take about ten minutes.'

Before going out, he turned around and pointed to the photo of the President of the Republic.

'Did you see?'

'Yes,' said Montalbano, confused. 'It's Ciampi.'

'I wasn't referring to the president, but to what's written above him. Smo-king is strict-ly for-bid-den. I mean it. Don't take advantage of my absence.'

As soon as the man closed the door, Montalbano felt a violent need to smoke. But it was forbidden, and rightly so, since, as everyone knows, passive cigarette smoke kills millions, whereas smog, dioxin and lead in petrol do not. He got up, went downstairs to the ground floor, happened to see three employees smoking, went outside, plonked himself on the pavement, smoked three cigarettes in a row, went back inside – now there were four employees smoking – climbed the stairs, walked down the deserted corridor, opened the door to the director's office without knocking and entered. Cavaliere Morasco, sitting at his desk, looked at him disapprovingly, shaking his head. Montalbano regained his chair with the same guilty look he used to have when he arrived late for school.

'We have the printout,' the director solemnly declared.

'Could I see it?'

Before giving it to him, the cavaliere checked to make sure the inspector's liberating signature was still there on his desk.

But the inspector didn't understand a single thing on the printout, especially because the figure at the bottom seemed excessive.

'Could you explain this for me?' he asked, again with the tone he used to use at school.

The director leaned forward, practically stretching his entire body across the desk, and snatched the paper out of the inspector's hands in irritation.

'Everything is perfectly clear!' he said. 'From the printout one can see that the monthly pension of Mr and Mrs Griffo came to three million lire or, broken down individually, one million eight hundred thousand for him, and one million two hundred thousand for her. At the time of collection, Mr Griffo would withdraw his own pension, in cash, for their monthly needs, and leave his wife's pension on deposit. This was their standard procedure. With a few rare exceptions, naturally.'

'But even assuming they were extremely tight and thrifty,' the inspector said, thinking aloud, 'it still doesn't add up. I believe I saw that there were almost a hundred million in that passbook!'

'You saw correctly. To be precise, ninety-eight million three hundred thousand lire. But there's nothing so unusual about that.'

'There isn't?'

'No, because, without fail, on the first of each month for the last two years, Alfonso Griffo would deposit two million lire. Which makes a total of forty-eight million, added to their usual savings.'

'And where was he getting these two million per month?'

'Don't ask me,' the director said, offended.

'Thank you,' said Montalbano, standing up. And he held out his hand.

The director stood up, walked around his desk, looked the inspector up and down and shook his hand.

'Could I have the printout?' Montalbano asked.

'No,' the Savoy bastard replied drily.

The inspector left the office and, once out on the pavement, lit a cigarette. He'd guessed right. They'd made off with the passbook because those forty-eight million lire were the symptom of the Griffos' fatal illness.

*

After he'd been back at headquarters ten minutes, Catarella returned wearing the desolate expression of an earthquake victim. He had the photo in his hand and set it down on the desk.

'Even my trusty friend's scanner couldn't do it. If you want, I'll take it to Cicco de Cicco, 'cause that crimolological thing's not happenin' till tomorrow.'

'Thanks, Cat, but I'll take it there myself.'

'Salvo, why on earth don't you learn how to use a

computer?' Livia had asked him one day, adding, 'You have no idea how many problems you could solve with it!'

Well, here was one little problem the computer hadn't been able to solve. It had only made him waste his time. He reminded himself to tell this to Livia, just to keep the polemic going.

He put the photo in his jacket pocket, left the station, and got in his car. He decided, however, to pass by Via Cavour before going to Montelusa.

'Mr Griffo's upstairs,' the concierge informed him.

When he opened the door, Davide Griffo was in shirt-sleeves, scrubbing brush in hand. He was cleaning the flat.

'It was getting too dusty.'

He showed the inspector into the dining room. On the table, in little piles, were the papers Montalbano had given him shortly before. Griffo intercepted his gaze.

'You were right, Inspector. The passbook's not here. Did you want to tell me something?'

'Yes. I went to the post office and found out how much your parents had in that passbook account.'

Griffo made a gesture as if to say that there wasn't any point in discussing this.

'Not much, I'm sure.'

'Ninety-eight million three hundred thousand lire, to be exact.'

Davide Griffo turned pale.

'There must be a mistake!' he stammered.

'No mistake, I assure you.'

Davide Griffo, his knees turning to jelly, collapsed in a chair.

'But how can that be?'

'Over the last two years, your father deposited two million lire in the account every month. Do you have any idea who might have been giving him that money?'

'I haven't the vaguest idea! They never mentioned any extra earnings to me. I can't understand it. Two million a month is a respectable stipend. What could my father have done, at his age, to earn it?'

'It wasn't necessarily a stipend.'

Davide Griffo turned even paler, and went from being confused to looking downright scared.

'Do you think there could be a connection?'

'Between the two million a month and the murder of your parents? It's a possibility that must be taken into serious consideration. That's exactly why the killers took the passbook: so we wouldn't think there was any cause-and-effect relationship.'

'But if it wasn't a stipend, what was it?'

'Bah,' said the inspector. 'I'll make a conjecture. But first I have to ask you something, and I want you to be truthful. Would your father have ever done anything dishonest for money?'

Davide Griffo didn't answer right away.

'It's hard to judge, right offhand ... I don't think so, I don't think he would. But he was, well, vulnerable.'

'How?'

'He and Mama were very attached to money. So, what's your conjecture?'

'Your father might, for example, have served as a front man for someone involved in some illegal business.'

'Papa wouldn't have agreed to anything like that.'

'Even if the business had been presented to him as legal?'

This time Griffo didn't answer. The inspector stood up.

'Well, if you can think of any explanation...'

'Yes, of course,' said Griffo, looking distracted. He walked Montalbano to the door.

'I was just remembering something Mama said to me last year. I had come to see them, and at one point, when Papa wasn't around, Mama said to me in a low voice, "When we're no longer here, you're going to have a pleasant surprise." Of course, sometimes Mama wasn't really all there, poor thing. She never brought it up again. And I forgot all about it.'

＊

At Montelusa Central Police, Montalbano had the receptionist phone Cicco de Cicco. He had no desire to run into Vanni Arquà, the chief of forensics who had replaced Jacomuzzi. They shared a mutual antipathy. De Cicco arrived in a hurry and took the photo from him.

'I was expecting worse,' he said, looking at it. 'Catarella said they tried scanning it onto the computer, but...'

'Think you can tell me the number on that licence plate?'

'I think so, Inspector. I'll give you a ring this evening, in any case.'

'If I'm not in, leave a message with Catarella. But make sure he writes the numbers and letters down correctly, otherwise we're liable to come up with a licence plate from Minnesota.'

*

On the drive back, a stop at the Saracen olive tree seemed almost obligatory. He needed a pause for reflection, a real one, not like what politicians call a pause for reflection, which is in fact a lapse into a deep coma. He climbed astride the usual branch, leaning back against the trunk, and lit a cigarette. He immediately felt uncomfortable, however, as the knots and nubs in the wood dug into the inside of his thighs. He had an odd sensation, as if the olive tree didn't want him sitting there and was trying to make him change position.

Some of the shit that goes through your head . . . !

He held out a bit longer, then couldn't stand it any more and climbed off the branch. He went to his car, grabbed a newspaper, returned to the olive tree, spread the pages out on the ground and lay down on top of them, after removing his jacket.

Viewed from below, from this new perspective, the tree looked bigger and more intricate. He saw complex ramifications he couldn't see before, from inside. Some words came to mind, 'There's a Saracen olive tree, a big one ... which solved everything for me.' Who had said them? And what had the tree solved? Then his memory came more clearly into focus. It was Pirandello who'd said those words, to his son, a few hours before dying. And they referred to *The Giants of the Mountain*, his unfinished novel.

He lay there for a good half-hour, on his back, never once taking his eyes off the tree. And the longer he looked, the more the tree opened up to him, the more it told him how the play of time had slashed and twisted it, how the water and wind, year after year, had forced it to take its present form, not by whim or chance, but by necessity.

His eyes remained fixed on three thick branches that for a brief stretch ran almost parallel before each took off on a personal fantasy of sudden zigzags, backward turns, sidesteps, detours, arabesques. One of the three, the middle one, looked slightly lower than the other two, but with its twisted little offshoots it grabbed at the two branches above, as if wanting to cling to them for the duration of the stretch they had in common.

Tilting his head to get a better look, Montalbano realized that the three branches were not born independently of one another in their common proximity, but all originated from the same point, a sort of great, wrinkly boil protruding from the trunk.

It was probably a light gust of wind that shifted some leaves, but a sudden ray of sunlight shone right in the inspector's eyes, blinding him. Squinting hard, he smiled.

Whatever De Cicco ended up telling him that evening, Montalbano was now certain that the person at the wheel of the car behind the bus was Nenè Sanfilippo.

*

They lay in wait behind a shrub of boxthorn, pistols cocked. Father Crucillà had led them to a secluded farmhouse he said was Japichinu's secret hideout. Before leaving them, however, the priest had made a point of advising them that they should approach very carefully; he wasn't sure whether Japichinu was ready to give himself up without reacting. Most important, the fugitive was armed with an assault rifle and had shown on many occasions that he knew how to use it.

The inspector had therefore decided to go by the rule book, and had sent Fazio and Galluzzo behind the house.

'By now they must be in position,' said Mimì.

Montalbano said nothing. He wanted to give his two men enough time to find the right spot for positioning themselves.

'I'm going in,' Augello said, impatient. 'Cover me.'

'OK,' the inspector consented.

Mimì began to crawl along the ground. The moon was shining, otherwise his movements would have been invisible. The farmhouse door, strangely, was wide open. Not so strangely, come to think of it: Japichinu obviously wanted to give the impression that the house was abandoned, when in fact he was lurking inside, assault rifle in hand.

In front of the door, Mimì half stood up, stopped on the threshold, leaned his head in for a look. Then, stepping lightly, he went inside. He reappeared moments later, waving an arm in the inspector's direction.

'There's nobody here,' he said.

'What could be going through his head?' Montalbano asked himself nervously. 'Doesn't he realize he could come under fire?'

At that moment, feeling himself shudder with fear, he saw the barrel of a machine gun emerge from the little window vertically above the door. Montalbano leapt to his feet.

'Mimì! Mimì!' he shouted.

Then he stopped, thinking he was singing *La Bohème*.

The machine gun fired and Mimì fell.

The same burst that killed Mimì woke the inspector up.

He was still lying on the pages of the newspaper, under the olive tree, drenched in sweat. At least a million ants had taken possession of his body.

THIRTEEN

Few, and at first glance insubstantial, were the ultimate differences between the dream and the reality. The secluded little farmhouse pointed out by Father Crucillà as Japichinu's secret hideout was the same as the one Montalbano had dreamt, except that this one, instead of a little window, had an open balcony directly over the door, which was also wide open.

Unlike in the dream, the priest did not run off in haste.

'You might,' he said, 'be needing me.'

And Montalbano, in his mind, had duly knocked on wood. Father Crucillà, crouching behind a huge sorghum bush with the inspector and Augello, eyed the house and shook his head in concern.

'What's wrong?' asked Montalbano.

'I don't like the look of the door and balcony. The other times I've been to see him, it was all closed up, and you had to knock. Be careful, I mean it. I can't swear that

Japichinu is ready to turn himself in. He keeps a machine gun always within reach, and he knows how to use it.'

When he was sure that Fazio and Gallo had reached their positions behind the house, Montalbano looked at Augello.

'I'm going in now. You cover me.'

'What kind of novelty is this?' Mimì reacted. 'We've always done it the other way around.'

Montalbano couldn't tell him he'd seen him die in a dream.

'This time we're doing it differently.'

Mimì didn't answer. He merely crouched down with his ·38. He could tell, by the inspector's tone of voice, when there was room for discussion and when there was not.

Night hadn't fallen yet. There was that grey light that precedes darkness, making it possible to distinguish silhouettes.

'How come he hasn't turned on the lights?' asked Augello, gesturing with his chin towards the darkened house.

'Maybe he's waiting for us,' said Montalbano.

And he rose to his feet, out in the open.

'What are you doing? What are you doing?' Mimì said in a whisper, trying to grab him by the jacket and pull him down. Then all of a sudden a terrifying thought occurred to him.

'Have you got your gun?'

'No.'

'Take mine.'

'No,' the inspector repeated, taking two steps forward. He stopped and cupped his hands around his mouth.

'Japichinu! This is Montalbano. I'm unarmed.'

There was no answer. The inspector advanced a short distance, calmly, as though out for a stroll. About ten feet from the door, he stopped again and said in a voice only slightly louder than normal, 'Japichinu! I'm coming inside now. So we can talk in peace.'

Nobody answered, nobody moved. Montalbano raised his hands and entered the house. It was pitch dark inside. He stepped slightly to one side, so as not to be visible in the doorway. And that was when he smelled it, that odour he had smelled so many times, which always gave him a vague feeling of nausea. Before turning on the light, he already knew what he would see. Japichinu lay in the middle of the room, on top of what looked like a red blanket but was in fact his blood. Throat slashed. He must have been taken by surprise, treacherously, when he turned his back to his assassin.

'Salvo! Salvo! What's happening?'

It was Mimì Augello. Montalbano appeared in the doorway.

'Fazio! Gallo! Mimì! Come!'

They all came running, the priest following behind, out of breath. Then, at the sight of Japichinu, they froze. The first one to move was Father Crucillà, who knelt beside the dead man, unconcerned by the blood soiling his frock, blessed him, and began to murmur some prayers. Mimì, for his part, touched the corpse's forehead.

'They must have killed him not two hours ago.'

'What do we do now?' asked Fazio.

'The three of you are going to get in one car and go,' said Montalbano. 'You'll leave me the other car. I want to stay and have a little talk with the priest. Just remember: we never came to this house, and we never saw Japichinu's corpse. Anyway, we're not authorized to be here; it's outside our territory. There could be some hassles.'

'All the same—' Mimì Augello started to say.

'All the same, my arse. We'll meet back at the office.'

They filed out like beaten dogs, obeying against their will. The inspector heard them muttering intensely as they walked away. The priest was lost in prayer. He had more than his share of Hail Marys, Our Fathers and requiems to recite, with the load of murders on Japichinu's shoulders, wherever he might be sailing at that moment. Montalbano climbed the stone staircase that led to the room above and turned on the light. There were two cots with only their mattresses, a bedside table between them, a shabby armoire and two wooden chairs. In one corner, a small altar consisting of a low table covered with an embroidered white tablecloth. On the altar stood three statuettes: the Virgin Mary, the Sacred Heart of Jesus and Saint Calogero. Each statue had a little light burning in front of it. Japichinu was a religious boy, as his grandfather Balduccio had said. So religious he even had a spiritual father. The only problem was that the boy and the priest both mistook superstition for religion. Like most Sicilians, for that matter. The inspector remembered once having seen a crude votive painting from the early twentieth century, depicting a *viddrano*, a peasant, fleeing from two plumed carabinieri in hot pursuit. On the upper right, the Madonna was leaning down from the clouds, showing the fugitive the best path of escape. The scroll bore the words: *For excaping the cluches of the law*. On one of the cots, lying crosswise, was a Kalashnikov. He turned off the light, went downstairs, pulled up one of the two wicker chairs and sat down.

'Father Crucillà.'

The priest, who was still praying, roused himself and looked up.

'Eh?'

'Pull up a chair and sit down. We need to talk.'

The priest obeyed. He was congested and sweating.

'How am I ever going to tell Don Balduccio?'

'There's no need.'

'Why?'

'Because by now he's already been told.'

'By whom?'

'By the killer, naturally.'

Father Crucillà struggled to grasp this. He kept staring at the inspector and moving his lips without forming any words. Then he understood and, eyes bulging, bolted out of his chair, reeled backwards, slipped on the blood but managed to remain standing.

Now he's going to have a stroke and die, thought Montalbano, alarmed.

'In God's name, what are you saying?!' the priest wheezed.

'I'm just saying how things stand.'

'But Japichinu was sought by the police, the carabinieri, the Secret Service!'

'Who don't usually slit the throats of people they're trying to arrest.'

'What about the new Mafia? Or the Cuffaros?'

'Father, you just don't want to accept that you and I have both been taken for a ride by that sly fox Balduccio Sinagra.'

'What proof do you have—'

'Sit back down, if you don't mind. Would you like a little water?'

Father Crucillà nodded yes. Montalbano grabbed a jug full of water, still nice and cool, and handed it to the priest, who put his lips to it at once.

'I have no proof and don't believe we ever will.'

'And so?'

'Answer me first. Japichinu wasn't staying here alone. He had a bodyguard who even slept beside him at night, didn't he?'

'Yes.'

'What's his name, do you know?'

'Lollò Spadaro.'

'Was he a friend of Japichinu's or one of Don Balduccio's men?'

'One of Don Balduccio's. It was the don who wanted it this way. Japichinu didn't even like him, but he said with Lollò around, he felt safe.'

'So safe that Lollò was able to kill him without any problem.'

'How can you think such a thing! Maybe they cut Lollò's throat before doing the same to Japichinu!'

'Well, Lollò's body's not upstairs. And it's not down here, either.'

'Maybe it's out there, outside the house!'

'Sure, we could look for it, but there's no point. You forget that my men and I surrounded the house and carefully searched the whole area. And we didn't stumble over Lollò's body anywhere.'

Father Crucillà wrung his hands. The sweat was pouring down his face.

'But why would Don Balduccio set up a scene like this?'

'He wanted us as witnesses. What should I have done, in your opinion, as soon as I discovered the murder?'

'I don't know ... Whatever you usually do. Call the forensics lab, the judge ...'

'And that would have allowed him to play the despairing grandfather, to scream that it was the new Mafia that killed his beloved grandson, who he loved so much he would rather have seen in jail and who he actually succeeded in persuading to turn himself in to me. And you, a priest, were even there ... As I said, he took us for a ride. But only so far. Because in five minutes I'm going to leave and it'll be exactly as if I'd never been here before. Balduccio's going to have to come up with a new plan. But if you see him, give him some advice: tell him he'd better bury his grandson on the sly, without any fanfare.'

'But you ... How did you arrive at these conclusions?'

'Japichinu was a hunted animal. He was suspicious of everything and everyone. You think he would have turned his back on someone he didn't know extremely well?'

'No.'

'Japichinu's Kalashnikov is on his bed. Do you think he would have let himself piddle around here downstairs, unarmed, in the presence of someone he didn't absolutely trust?'

'No.'

'And tell me another thing: were you told what course of action Lollò was supposed to take if Japichinu was arrested?'

'Yes. He was supposed to let himself be captured, too, without reacting.'

'And who gave him this order?'

'Don Balduccio himself.'

'That's what Balduccio told you. Whereas he told Lollò something completely different.'

Father Crucillà's throat was dry, and he set to the jug of water again.

'Why did Don Balduccio want his grandson to die?'

'To be honest, I don't know. Maybe the boy screwed up, maybe he didn't recognize his grandfather's authority. You know, wars of succession don't only happen among kings and captains of industry...'

He stood up.

'I'm going to go. You want a lift in my car?'

'No, thanks,' the priest replied. 'I'd like to stay a little longer and pray. I was very fond of him.'

'Suit yourself.'

At the door, the inspector turned around. 'I wanted to thank you.'

'For what?' asked the priest, alarmed.

'In all the different conjectures you made as to who might have killed Japichinu, you didn't once mention the bodyguard. You could have said it was Lollò Spadaro, who'd sold himself to the new Mafia. But you knew that never in a million years would Lollò betray Balduccio Sinagra. And your silence confirmed my hunch beyond a shadow of a doubt. Oh, one last thing. When you leave, don't forget to turn off the light and lock the door. I wouldn't want any stray dogs ... Understand?'

He went out. The night was completely dark. Before reaching his car, he stumbled over some rocks and holes in the ground. It reminded him of the Griffos' calvary, with their killer kicking them from behind, cursing, rushing them to the place and the hour of their death.

'Amen,' he said, heart aching.

On his way back to Vigàta, he became convinced that
Balduccio would follow the advice he was sending him
through the priest. Japichinu's corpse would end up at the
bottom of some rocky cliff. No, the grandfather knew how
religious his grandson was. He would have him buried
anonymously in consecrated ground. In somebody else's
coffin.

✻

Passing through the front door to headquarters, he found
things unusually quiet. Could everyone have left, even
though he had told them to wait for him to return?
No, they were there, Mimì, Fazio and Gallo, each seated
at his desk, face gloomy as after a defeat. He called them
into his office.

'I want to tell you something. Fazio must have told you
what happened between me and Balduccio Sinagra. Well,
do you believe me? You must believe me, because I've never
lied to you before, not about anything big, at least. From
the very first, I realized that Don Balduccio's request that I
arrest Japichinu, because he'd be safer in jail, didn't make
sense.'

'So why did you give it any consideration?' Augello
asked polemically.

'To see what he was up to. And to thwart his plan, if I
could work out what it was. Which I did, and then I made
the proper counter-move.'

'Which was what?' asked Fazio this time.

'Not letting our discovery of Japichinu's body become official. That's what Balduccio wanted: for us to be the ones to discover it, which would have provided him with an alibi. You see, he was expecting me to inform the judge that he'd intended for us to capture his grandson safe and sound.'

'After Fazio explained things to us,' Mimì resumed, 'we reached the same conclusion as you, that is, that it was Balduccio who had his grandson killed. But why?'

'At the moment it's not clear. But something'll come out sooner or later. As far as we're concerned, the whole business ends here.'

The door flew open, crashing against the wall with such force that the windows rattled. Everybody jumped. Naturally, it was Catarella.

'Oh, Chief! Chief! Cicco de Cicco called just now! He made the development! An' it worked! I wrote the number down on this piece a paper here. He made me repeat it to him five times!'

He set a half sheet of squared notebook paper on the inspector's desk and said, 'Beg your pardon 'bout the door.'

He went out. And reclosed the door so hard that a crack in the paint near the handle widened slightly.

Montalbano read the licence-plate number and looked at Fazio.

'Have you got Nenè Sanfilippo's licence-plate number within reach?'

'Which car? The Punto or the Duetto?'

Augello pricked up his ears.

'The Punto.'

'That one I know by heart: BA 927 GG.'

'They correspond,' said Mimì. 'But what does it mean? Would you explain?'

*

Montalbano explained, telling them how he'd found out about the postal passbook and the money on deposit; how, following up on what Mimì himself had suggested to him, he'd studied the photos from the excursion to Tindari and discovered that a Fiat Punto had been riding on the coach's rear bumper; and how he'd brought the photo to the Montelusa forensics lab to have them enlarge it. The whole time the inspector was speaking, Augello maintained a suspicious expression.

'You already knew,' he said.

'I already knew what?'

'That the car following behind the coach was Sanfilippo's. You knew it before Catarella gave you that slip of paper.'

'Yes,' the inspector admitted.

'And how did you know?'

A tree, a Saracen olive tree told me. That would have been the correct answer, but Montalbano didn't have the courage to say it.

'I had an intuition,' he said instead.

Augello let it drop.

'This means,' he said, 'that the Griffo and Sanfilippo murders are closely connected.'

'We can't say that yet,' the inspector disagreed. 'The only thing we know for sure is that Sanfilippo's car was following the coach the Griffos were in.'

'Beba even said Alfonso Griffo kept turning around to look at the road. Apparently he wanted to make sure Sanfilippo's car was still behind them.'

'Right. Which tells us that there was a connection between Sanfilippo and the Griffos. But we have to stop there. Maybe Sanfilippo did pick them up in his car on the drive back, at the last stop before Vigàta.'

'Don't forget that Beba said it was Alfonso Griffo himself who asked the driver to make that extra stop, which means they must have planned it together before-hand.'

'Right again. But this does not allow us to conclude that Sanfilippo killed the Griffos himself, or that he in turn was shot as a consequence of the Griffos' murders. The infidelity hypothesis still holds.'

'When are you going to see Ingrid?'

'Tomorrow evening. But you, tomorrow morning, try to gather some information on Eugenio Ignazio Ingrò, the transplant doctor. I'm not interested in what the papers have to say, but in the other stuff, the whispers.'

'I've got somebody, a friend in Montelusa, who knows him pretty well. I'll find some excuse to pay him a visit.'

'But, Mimì, I'm warning you: kid gloves. It should be

the furthest thing from everyone's mind that we might be interested in the doctor and his cherished consort, Vanya Titulescu.'

Mimì, offended, pulled a frown.

'Do you take me for some kind of idiot?'

*

The moment he opened the refrigerator, he saw it.

Caponata! Fragrant, colourful, abundant, it filled an entire soup dish, enough for at least four people. It had been months since Adelina, his housekeeper, last made it for him. The bread, in its plastic bag, was fresh, bought that morning. The notes of the triumphal march of *Aïda* came spontaneously, naturally, to his lips. Humming, he opened the French windows after turning on the light on the veranda. Yes, it was a cool night, but still warm enough to eat outside. He set the little table, brought the dish, the wine, and the bread outside, and sat down. The telephone rang. He covered the dish with a paper napkin and went to answer it.

'Hello? Inspector Montalbano? This is Orazio Guttadauro.'

He'd been expecting this phone call. He'd have bet his arse on it.

'What can I do for you, sir?'

'First of all, please accept my apologies for being forced to call you at this hour.'

'Forced? By whom?'

'By circumstances, Inspector.'

Clever, this lawyer.

'What circumstances are you referring to?'

'My client and friend is worried.'

Was he afraid to mention Balduccio Sinagra's name over the phone, now that a fresh corpse had been added to the mix?

'Oh, is he? And why's that?'

'Well ... he hasn't heard from his grandson since yesterday.'

Since yesterday? Balduccio Sinagra was starting to cover himself.

'What grandson? The exile?'

'Exile?' the lawyer repeated, genuinely puzzled.

'No need to be so formal, Counsel. Nowadays "exile" and "fugitive" mean pretty much the same thing. Or so they would have us believe.'

'Yes, of course,' said the lawyer, still dazed.

'But how could he hear from his grandson if he was on the run?'

One roguish turn deserved another.

'Er ... well, you know how it is, mutual friends, people passing through . . .'

'I see. And what has this got to do with me?'

'Nothing,' Guttadauro was quick to affirm. And he repeated, clearly pronouncing the words, 'None of this has anything to do with you.'

Message received. Balduccio Sinagra was letting him know that he had taken the advice relayed to him by Father

Crucillà. Of Japichinu's murder there would be no mention. Japichinu could just as easily have not been born, if not for the people he'd killed.

'Why, Mr Guttadauro, do you feel the need to communicate your friend and client's worry to me?'

'Oh, it was just to let you know that, despite this agonizing worry, my friend and client has been thinking of you.'

'Of me?' said Montalbano, on his guard.

'Yes. He asked me to send you an envelope. He says there's something inside that may interest you.'

'Listen, Mr Guttadauro. I'm going to bed. I've had a rough day.'

'I entirely understand.'

The damn lawyer was being ironic.

'You can bring me the envelope tomorrow, at the station. Good night.'

He hung up, went back out on the veranda, then reconsidered. Returning inside, he picked up the phone and dialled.

'Livia, darling, how are you?'

There was silence at the other end.

'Livia?'

'My God, Salvo, what's happening? Why are you phoning me?'

'Why shouldn't I phone you?'

'Because you only phone when something's bothering you.'

'Oh, come on!'

'No, really, it's true. When you're not feeling bothered, I'm always the first to ring.'

'OK, you're right, I'm sorry.'

'What did you want to tell me?'

'That I've been thinking a lot about our relationship.'

Livia – Montalbano distinctly heard it – held her breath. She didn't speak. Montalbano continued.

'I realized that we're often bickering, too often. Like a couple who've been married for years and are feeling the strain of living together. But the good part is, we don't live together.'

'Go on,' said Livia in a faint voice.

'So, I said to myself: why don't we start all over again, from the beginning?'

'I don't understand. What do you mean?'

'Livia, what would you say if we got engaged?'

'Aren't we already?'

'No. We're married.'

'OK. So how do we begin?'

'Like this: Livia, I love you. And you?'

'Me too. Good night, my love.'

'Good night.'

He hung up. Now he could stuff himself with the caponata without fearing any more phone calls.

FOURTEEN

He woke up at seven, after a night of dreamless sleep so leaden he had the impression, upon opening his eyes, that he was still in the same position as when he first lay down. It was certainly not the most glorious of mornings — scattered clouds giving the impression of sheep about to gather into flocks — but one could clearly see that it did not promise any major bouts of ill humour. He slipped on a pair of shabby old trousers, stepped down from the veranda and, barefoot, went for a walk along the beach. The cool air cleansed his skin, lungs and thoughts. Back inside, he shaved and went into the shower.

In the course of every investigation that came his way, there was always one day — actually, a specific moment on a certain day — when an inexplicable sense of physical well-being, a happy lightness in the interaction of his thoughts, a harmonious conjunction of his muscles, made him feel as if he could walk endlessly along a road, eyes closed, without once stumbling or running into anything or anyone. As happens, sometimes, in the land of dreams. It didn't last very long, but it was enough. By now he knew from experience that from this point on – it was like the buoy at the bend in the sea-lane, the sign of the approaching turn – every piece of the puzzle, the investigation in other words, would fall into place, all by itself, without any effort. It was almost enough just to will it so. And this was what was going through his head in the shower, even though many things, indeed almost everything, still remained obscure.

*

It was quarter past eight when he slowed down to park the car in front of the station, then he reconsidered and drove on to Via Cavour. The concierge gave him a dirty look and didn't even say hello: she'd just finished washing the floor at the entrance, and now the inspector's shoes were going to muck it all up again. Davide Griffo looked less pale. He'd recovered a little. He didn't seem surprised to see Montalbano and immediately offered him a cup of coffee, which he'd just made.

'Did you find anything?'

'Nothing,' said Griffo. 'And I looked everywhere. There's no passbook, and there's nothing in writing that might explain Papa's two million lire a month.'

'Mr Griffo, I need you to help me remember something.'

'I'm at your disposal.'

'I believe you told me your father didn't have any close relatives.'

'That's right. He had a brother, whose name I forget, but he was killed in the American bombing raids in 1943.'

'Your mother, however, did have some close relations.'

'Exactly. A brother and a sister. The brother, Zio Mario, lives in Comiso and has a son who works in Sydney. We talked about him, remember? You asked me—'

'I remember.' The inspector cut him short.

'The sister, Zia Giuliana, used to live in Trapani, where she became a schoolteacher. She remained single, never wanted to get married. But neither Mama nor Zio Mario saw much of her, though she and Mama got a little closer in recent years, to the point that Mama and Papa went to visit her two days before she died. They stayed in Trapani for almost a week.'

'Any idea why your mother and her brother had fallen out with this Giuliana?'

'My grandfather and grandmother, when they died, left almost all of the little they had to Giuliana, practically disinheriting the other two.'

'Did your mother ever tell you why . . .'

'She hinted at it. Apparently my grandparents felt abandoned by Mama and Zio Mario. My mother got married very young, you see, and my uncle had left home to go to work before he was even sixteen. Only Zia Giuliana stayed with her parents. As soon as my grandparents died — Grandma died first — Zia Giuliana sold what she owned here and moved to Trapani.'

'When did she die?'

'I can't really say exactly. At least two years ago.'

'Do you know where she lived in Trapani?'

'No. I didn't find anything relating to Zia Giuliana in this apartment. I do know, however, that she owned her place in Trapani. She'd bought it.'

'One last thing: your mother's maiden name.'

'Di Stefano. Margherita Di Stefano.'

One good thing about Davide Griffo: he was generous with his answers and frugal with his questions.

*

Two million lire a month. More or less what a low-level clerk makes by the end of his career. But Alfonso Griffo had been retired for some time and was getting by on his pension — his combined with his wife's. Or, more accurately, he'd been able to get by because for two years he'd been receiving a considerable supplement: two million lire a month. From another perspective, a derisory sum. If this were a case of systematic blackmail, for example. And yet, no matter how attached he might be to money, Alfonso Griffo, lacking the courage or imagination, could never have resorted to blackmail, assuming he had no scruples about it. Two million lire a month. For serving as a front man, as the inspector had first hypothesized? Usually, however, a front man gets a cut of the profits or is paid off all at once, certainly not by the month. Two million lire a month. In a sense, it was the modesty of the sum that made things more difficult. Still, the regularity of the deposits must indicate something. An idea began to form in the inspector's mind. There was a coincidence that intrigued him.

✳

He stopped in front of city hall and went upstairs to the records office. He knew the clerk there, a certain Crisafulli.

'I need some information.'

'At your service, Inspector.'

'If someone who was born in Vigàta dies in another town, is the death reported here too?'

'There's a provision for such cases,' Mr Crisafulli replied evasively.

'Is it ever respected?'

'Generally, yes. But it takes time, you see. You know how these things go. And I should add that if the death occurs in a foreign country, forget about it. Unless a family member takes the trouble himself to—'

'No, the person I'm interested in died in Trapani.'

'When?'

'A little over two years ago.'

'What was his name?'

'Her name was Giuliana Di Stefano.'

'We can look that up right away.'

Mr Crisafulli touched a few keys on the computer towering in one corner of the room, then looked up at Montalbano.

'She died in Trapani on the sixth of May, 1997.'

'Does it say where she resided?'

'No. But if you wish, I could tell you in about five minutes.'

Here Mr Crisafulli did something strange. He went to his desk, opened a drawer, took out a small metal flask, unscrewed the cap, took a sip, then rescrewed the cap, leaving the flask out. Then he went back and fiddled with the computer. Seeing that the ashtray on the table was full of cigar butts whose odour had permeated the room, the inspector lit up a cigarette himself. He had just put it out when the clerk announced, in a faint voice, 'Found it. She lived in Via Libertà 12.'

Was the man not feeling well? Montalbano wanted to ask him, but didn't do so in time. Mr Crisafulli raced back to his desk, grabbed the flask and took another gulp.

'Cognac,' he explained. 'I'm retiring in two months.'

The inspector gave him a questioning look. He didn't get the connection.

'I'm a clerk of the old school,' the man said. 'It used to take me months to find a record like that. Now, whenever I do it this fast, my head starts to spin.'

✳

To get to Trapani, Via Libertà, took him two and a half hours. Number 12 was a small three-storey building surrounded by a well-tended garden. Davide Griffo had told him that Zia Giuliana used to own the flat she lived in. After her death, it might have been resold to people she didn't even know, in which case the proceeds would almost certainly have gone to some charitable institution. Next to the closed entrance gate was an intercom with only three names. The flats must be pretty big. He pushed the button on top, next to the name 'Cavallaro'. A woman's voice answered.

'Yes?'

'Excuse me, ma'am. I need some information concerning the late Miss Giuliana Di Stefano.'

'Ring flat two, the middle one.'

The name tag next to the middle button read 'Baeri'.

'Jesus, what's the hurry! Who is it?' asked the voice of another woman, this one elderly, after the inspector had rung three times without answer and given up hope.

'Montalbano's the name.'

'What do you want?'

'I'd like to ask you a few questions about Miss Giuliana Di Stefano.'

'Go ahead.'

'Right here, over the intercom?'

'Why, will it take long?'

'Well, it'd be better if—'

'OK, I'll buzz you in,' said the elderly voice. 'Now, do

as I say. As soon as the gate opens, come in and stop in the middle of the path. If you don't, I won't open the front door.'

'All right,' said the inspector, resigned.

Standing in the middle of the path, he didn't know what to do. Then he saw some shutters open on a balcony, and out came an old lady in a wig, dressed all in black, a pair of binoculars in hand. She raised these to her eyes and looked carefully, as Montalbano began inexplicably to blush, feeling naked. The lady went back inside, reclosed the shades, and a short while later the inspector heard the metal click of the front door being opened. Naturally, there was no lift. On the second floor, the door with the name 'Baeri' on it was closed. What further test awaited him?

'What did you say your name was?' asked the voice on the other side of the door.

'Montalbano.'

'And what is your profession?'

If he said he was a police inspector, the lady might have a stroke.

'I work at the ministry.'

'Have you got an ID?'

'Yes.'

'Slide it under the door.'

With the patience of a saint, the inspector obeyed.

Five minutes of absolute silence passed.

'I'm going to open now,' said the old lady.

Only then, to his horror, did the inspector notice that

the door had four locks. And certainly inside there must be a padlock and chain. After some ten minutes of various noises, the door opened and Montalbano was able to make his entrance into the Baeri household. He was led into a large sitting room with dark, heavy furniture.

'My name is Assunta Baeri,' the old lady began, 'and your ID says that you're with the police.'

'That's correct.'

'Well, isn't that nice,' Mrs (Miss?) Baeri said sarcastically.

Montalbano didn't breathe.

'The thieves and killers do whatever they please, and the police go off to football matches with the excuse that they need to maintain order! Or they serve as escorts to Senator Ardolì, who doesn't need any escort, because all he's gotta do is look at somebody and they die of fright.'

'Mrs Baeri, I—'

'*Miss* Baeri.'

'Miss Baeri, I'm sorry to disturb you, but I came to talk to you about Giuliana Di Stefano. This used to be her flat, didn't it?'

'Yes.'

'Did you buy it from the deceased?' What a question! 'Before she died, of course.'

'I didn't buy anything! The "deceased", as you call her, left it to me, loud and clear, in her will! Thirty-two years, I lived with her. I even paid rent. Not much, but I paid it.'

'Did she leave you anything else?'

'Ah, so you're not with the police after all, but with the tax bureau! Yes, sir, she left me another flat, too, but a teeny-weeny one. I rent it out.'

'Anyone else? Did she leave anything to anybody else?'

'Who else?'

'I don't know, some relative . . .'

'There was her sister, who she made up with after they hadn't spoken for years; she left her some little thing.'

'Do you know what this little thing might be?'

'Of course I know! She drew up her will right in front of me, and I've even got a copy of it. To her sister she left her stable and hide. Not much, just something to remember her by.'

Montalbano was flummoxed. Could one bequeath one's hide to somebody? Miss Baeri's next words cleared up the misunderstanding.

'No, not much at all. Do you know how much land is in a hide?'

'I couldn't honestly say,' the inspector replied, recovering himself.

'Giuliana, when she left Vigàta to come and live here, wasn't able to sell the stable and the land around it, which apparently was out in the middle of nowhere. So, when she made her will, she decided to leave them to her sister. They're not worth much.'

'Do you know exactly where this stable is?'

'No.'

'But it must be specified in the will. You said you have a copy of it.'

'Oh, *Madunnuzza santa!* What, you want me to start looking for it?'

'If you'd be so kind...'

The old lady stood up, mumbling to herself, went out of the room, and returned less than a minute later. She'd known perfectly well where the copy of the will was. She handed it rudely to Montalbano, who skimmed through it and finally found what he was looking for.

The stable was termed a 'one-room rural construction'; as for the measurements, a twelve-by-twelve-foot box. Around it was a quarter of an acre of land. Not much, as Miss Baeri had said. The building was in a district called the Moor.

'Thank you very much, and please excuse the disturbance,' the inspector said politely, getting up.

'Why are you interested in that stable?' asked the woman, also standing up.

Montalbano hesitated. He had to think up a good excuse. But Miss Baeri continued, 'I ask you because you're the second person who's enquired about it.'

The inspector sat back down, and Miss Baeri did likewise.

'When was that?'

'The day after poor Giuliana's funeral, when her sister

and her husband were still here. They were sleeping in the room in the back.'

'Explain to me what happened.'

'I'd completely forgotten about it; I only remembered it just now because we were talking about it. Anyway, the day after the funeral, it was almost time to eat. The phone rang and I went and answered it. It was a man who said he was interested in the stable and the land. I asked him if he knew that Giuliana had died and he said no. He asked me who he could talk to about it. So I put Margherita's husband on, since it was his wife who'd inherited it.'

'Did you hear what was said?'

'No, I left the room.'

'Did the man who phoned say what his name was?'

'He might have, but I can't remember any more.'

'Afterward, did Mr Griffo talk about the phone call in your presence?'

'When he went into the kitchen, Margherita asked him who was on the phone, and he said it was somebody from Vigàta who lived in the same building as them. But that was all he said.'

Bull's eye! Montalbano leapt up.

'I have to go now, thank you very much, please excuse me,' he said, making for the door.

'Just tell me one thing. I'm curious,' said Miss Baeri, following hard on his heels. 'Why don't you simply ask Alfonso these things?'

'Alfonso who?' asked Montalbano, having already opened the door.

'What do you mean, Alfonso who? Margherita's husband.'

Jesus! The lady knew nothing about the murders! She obviously had no television and didn't read the newspapers.

'I'll ask him,' the inspector assured her, already on his way down the stairs.

✳

At the first phone booth he saw, he stopped and got out of the car, went in, and immediately noticed a small red light flashing. The telephone was out of order. He spotted another. Also broken.

He cursed the saints, realizing that the smooth run he'd been on until that moment was beginning to be broken up by small obstacles, harbingers of bigger ones ahead. At the third booth, he was finally able to call headquarters.

'Oh, Chief! Chief! Where you been hidin' out? All mornin' I been—'

'Tell me about it another time, Cat. Can you tell me where the Moor is?'

First there was silence, then a little giggle of what was supposed to be derision.

'How'm I sposta know, Chief? You know what it's like in Vigàta these days. There's Smallies everywhere.'

'Put Fazio on at once.'

Smallies? Were there so many Pygmies among the immigrant population?

'What can I do for you, Chief?'

'Fazio, can you tell me where the district called the Moor is located?'

'Just a sec, Chief.'

Fazio had activated his computer brain. Inside his head he had, among other things, a detailed map of the municipal area of Vigàta.

'It's over by Monteserrato, Chief.'

'Explain to me how you get there.'

Fazio explained. Then he said, 'Sorry, but Catarella insists on talking to you. Where are you calling from?'

'From Trapani.'

'What are you doing in Trapani?'

'I'll tell you later. Pass me Catarella.'

'Hallo, Chief? I just wanted to say that this morning—'

'Cat, what is a Smallie?'

'Somebody from Smallia, Chief, in Africa. Inn't that what they're called? Or is it Smallians?'

He hung up, sped off in his car, then stopped in front of a large hardware shop. Self-service. He bought himself a crowbar, a big pair of pliers, a hammer and a small hacksaw. When he went to pay, the cashier, a dark, pretty girl, smiled at him.

'Have a good robbery,' she said.

He didn't feel like answering. He went out and got back in his car. Shortly afterwards, he happened to look at his watch. It was almost two, and a wolf-like hunger came over him. He saw a trattoria called, according to its sign, DAL BORBONE, with two articulated lorries parked in front. Therefore the food must be good. A brief but ferocious battle ensued between the angel and the devil inside him. The angel won, and he continued on to Vigàta.

'Not even a sandwich?' the devil whined.

'No.'

*

Monteserrato was the name of a line of hills, of considerable height, separating Montelusa from Vigàta. They practically began at the sea and continued on for three or four miles inland. Atop the last ridge stood a large, old farming estate. It was an isolated spot. And so it had remained, despite the fact that at the time of the public-works construction craze, in their desperate search for a place that might justify the building of a highway, bridge, overpass or tunnel, the authorities had linked it to the Vigàta–Montelusa provincial road with a ribbon of asphalt. Old Headmaster Burgio had once spoken to Montalbano of Monteserrato a few years back. He had told him of how, in 1944, he'd made an excursion to Monteserrato with an American friend, a journalist to whom he'd taken an immediate liking. They'd walked for hours across the countryside, then began climbing, stopping occasionally to rest. When they came within view of the estate, and its high enclosure of walls, they were stopped by two dogs of a sort that neither the headmaster nor the American had ever seen before. With a greyhound's body but a very short, curled, piglike tail, long ears as on a hunting dog, and a ferocious look in the eye. The dogs literally immobilized them, snarling whenever they made the slightest move. Finally somebody from the estate came past on horseback and accompanied them. The head of the family took them to see the remains of an ancient monastery, where Burgis and the American saw an extraordinary fresco, a nativity, on a damp, deteriorating wall. One could still read the date: 1410. Also portrayed in the painting were three dogs, in every way identical to the ones that had cornered them on their arrival. Many years later, after the asphalt road was built, Burgio had decided to go back there. The vestiges of the monastery no longer existed; in their place now stood a vast garage. Even the wall with the fresco had been knocked down. Around the garage one could still find little pieces of coloured plaster on the ground.

*

The inspector found the little chapel that Fazio had told him to look for; ten yards beyond began a dirt road that descended down the hillside.

'Be careful, it's very steep,' Fazio had said.

Talk about steep! It was practically vertical. When he was halfway down, he stopped the car, got out, and looked out from the edge of the road. The panorama that unfolded before him could be seen as either hideous or beautiful, depending on the observer's tastes. There were no trees, no other houses than the one whose roof was visible about a hundred metres down. The land was not cultivated. Left to itself, it had produced an extraordinary variety of wild plants. Indeed, the tiny house was utterly buried under the tall grass, except, of course, for the roof, which clearly had been redone a short while before, its tiles intact. With a sense of dismay, Montalbano saw electrical and telephone wires, originating at some distant, invisible point, leading into the former stable. They were incongruous in that landscape, which appeared to have looked this way since the beginning of time.

FIFTEEN

At a certain point along the dirt road, on the left-hand side, the repeated comings and goings of a car had opened a kind of trail through the tall grass. It led straight up to the door of the former stable, a door recently remade in solid wood and fitted with two locks. In addition, a chain of the sort used to protect motorbikes from theft was looped through two screw eyes and secured by a big padlock. Beside the door was a tiny window, too small for even a five-year-old child to pass through, blocked by iron bars. Beyond the bars, one could see that the pane was painted black, either to prevent one from seeing in or to keep the light from filtering out at night.

Montalbano had two possible courses of action: either return to Vigàta and ask for reinforcements or set about breaking and entering, even though he was convinced this would be a long and arduous task. Naturally, he opted for the latter. Removing his jacket, he picked up the little hacksaw he'd been lucky enough to buy in Trapani and got down to work on the chain. After fifteen minutes, his arm began to ache. After half an hour, the pain had spread halfway across his chest. After an hour, the chain broke, with the help of the crowbar, which he used for leverage, and the pliers. Drenched in sweat, he removed his shirt and spread it out on the grass, hoping it would dry a little. He sat down in the car and rested. He didn't even feel like smoking a cigarette. When he felt sufficiently rested, he attacked the first of the two locks with the set of picklocks he now carried with him at all times. He tinkered for about half an hour before deciding it was useless. He got nowhere with the second lock either. Then he had an idea that at first seemed ingenious to him. He opened the glove compartment of the car, got his pistol, loaded it, aimed and fired at the higher of the two locks. The bullet hit its target, ricocheted off the metal and lightly grazed his side, the same one he'd injured a few years before. The only result he achieved was to have deformed the keyhole. Cursing, he put the pistol back in its place. Why was it that the policemen in American movies always succeed in opening doors with this method? The fright brought on another round of sweating. He took off his vest and spread it out next to his shirt. Armed with hammer and chisel, he started working on the wood of the door, all around the lock he had shot at. After an hour or so, he thought he'd done enough digging. A good shoulder-thrust should definitely open the door now. He took three steps back, got a running start and crashed his shoulder into the door. But it didn't budge. The pain shooting through his entire shoulder and chest was so great that tears came to his eyes. Why hadn't the damn thing opened? Easy: he'd forgotten that, before putting his shoulder to the door, he had to reduce the second lock to the same state as the first. Now his trousers, damp with sweat, were bothering him. He took them off, too, laying them next to the shirt and vest. After yet another hour, the second lock also began to feel shaky. His shoulder had swollen and started throbbing. He worked with the hammer and crowbar. The door resisted, inexplicably. Suddenly he was overwhelmed by an uncontrollable rage: like Donald Duck in a cartoon, he began kicking and punching the door, screaming like a madman. Limping, he returned to the car. His left foot ached, he took off his shoes, and at that moment, he heard a noise: by itself, and exactly like in a cartoon, the door decided to give in, collapsing into the room. Montalbano ran back to the house. The former stable, plastered and whitewashed, was completely empty. Not a single piece of furniture, not even a piece of paper. Nothing whatsoever, as if it had never been used, except, at the base of the walls, a number of electrical outlets and telephone jacks. The inspector stood there staring at the emptiness, unable to believe his eyes. When it got dark, he made up his mind. He picked up the door, leant it against its frame, gathered up his vest, shirt and trousers, tossed them into the back seat of the car, put on only his jacket and, after turning the headlights on, headed home to Marinella, hoping nobody would stop him along the way. *Nuttata persa e figlia fimmina.*

*

He took a much longer route home, but it spared him the trouble of passing through Vigàta. He had to drive slowly because of the shooting pains in his right shoulder, which was as puffy as a loaf of bread fresh out of the oven. He pulled up in the parking area in front of his house, groaning as he gathered up his shirt, vest, trousers and shoes, then turned off the headlights and got out of the car. The lamp outside the front door wasn't on. He took two steps forward and froze. Right next to the door there was a shadow. Somebody was waiting for him.

'Who are you?' he asked angrily.

The shadow didn't answer. The inspector took another two steps and recognized Ingrid. She was gawking at him, unable to speak.

'I'll explain later,' Montalbano felt compelled to say as he searched for his keys in the trousers he was carrying on his arm. Ingrid, having slightly recovered, took the shoes from his hand. The door opened at last. In the light, Ingrid examined him with curiosity and asked, 'Have you been performing with the Chippendales?'

'Who are they?'

'Male strippers.'

The inspector said nothing and took off his jacket.

Upon seeing his swollen shoulder, Ingrid didn't scream or ask for any explanation. She merely said, 'Have you got any liniment in the house?'

'No.'

'Give me the keys to your car and get in bed.'

'Where are you going?'

'There must be a chemist open somewhere, don't you think?' said Ingrid, picking up the house keys as well.

Montalbano undressed – he needed only to remove his socks and pants – and got into the shower. The big toe on his left foot was now as large as a medium-sized pear. Once out of the shower, he went and looked at his watch, which he'd put on his bedside table. It was already nine thirty; he'd had no idea. He dialled the number of headquarters, and as soon as he heard Catarella, he transformed his voice.

'Allo? Zis is Monsieur Hulot. Je cherche Monsieur Augelleau.'

'Are you Frinch, sir? From Frince?'

'Oui. Je cherche Monsieur Augelleau, or, as you say, Augello.'

'He ain't here, Mr Frinch.'

'Merci.'

He dialled Mimì's home phone. He let it ring a long time, but got no answer. As a last resort, he looked up Beatrice's number in the phone book. She picked up at once.

'Montalbano here, Beatrice. Forgive me for intruding, but—'

'You want to talk to Mimì?' the divine creature cut in. 'I'll put him on.'

She wasn't the least bit embarrassed. Mimì, on the other hand, was, and immediately began making excuses.

'Salvo, I happened to be in the area, you see, when I realized I was just outside Beba's door—'

'For heaven's sake, Mimì, there's no problem,' Montalbano conceded magnanimously. 'Let me apologize, first of all, for disturbing you.'

'But not at all! I wouldn't dream of it! What can I do for you?'

Could the Chinese have done any better in the way of ceremoniousness?

'I wanted to ask you if we could meet at the office tomorrow morning, say around eight. I've made an important discovery.'

'What?'

'The connection between the Griffos and Sanfilippo.'

He heard Mimì exhale the way one does when kicked in the stomach. Then Mimì stammered, 'Wh-where are you? I'll come and meet you right away.'

'I'm at my place. But Ingrid's here.'

'Oh. Let me tell you, Salvo, squeeze her anyway, even if, after what you just said, the infidelity theory doesn't really hold up any more.'

'Listen, don't tell anyone where I am. I'm going to disconnect the phone now.'

'Of course, of course,' Mimì said insinuatingly.

Montalbano went to lie down, limping all the way. It took him half an hour to find the right position. He closed his eyes and reopened them at once. Hadn't he invited Ingrid to dinner? How was he going to get dressed, stand up on his feet, and go out to a restaurant? The word 'restaurant' immediately gave him a feeling of emptiness in the pit of his stomach. How long had it been since he'd eaten? He got up and went into the kitchen. Enthroned in the refrigerator was a serving dish full of red mullet *all'agrodolce*. Reassured, he went back to bed. He was nodding off when he heard the front door open.

'I'll be right there,' Ingrid called from the dining room.

She came in a few minutes later carrying a small bottle, an elastic bandage and a roll of gauze.

'I want to pay off my debt,' she said.

'What debt?' asked Montalbano.

'Don't you remember? When we first met. I sprained an ankle and you brought me here and gave me a massage...'

Now he remembered, of course. She had been lying half naked on the bed when Anna, a policewoman from Montelusa who'd fallen in love with him, had barged in. The girl had got the wrong idea and made his life hell. Had Livia and Ingrid ever met? Maybe at the hospital, the time he was wounded...

Under Ingrid's slow, continuous caresses he felt his eyelids begin to droop. He surrendered to a delicious somnolence.

'Pull yourself up. I have to wrap you now . . . Keep your arm raised . . . Turn a little more towards me.'

He obeyed, a satisfied smile on his lips.

'I'm done,' said Ingrid. 'In half an hour you'll start feeling better.'

'What about the big toe?' he asked, his mouth gluey.

'What did you say?'

Without speaking, the inspector pulled his foot out from under the sheet. Ingrid got back to work.

✲

He opened his eyes. From the dining room came the sound of a man's voice, speaking softly. He looked at his watch: past eleven. He felt quite a bit better. Had Ingrid called a doctor? He got up and, just as he was – in his underwear, with his shoulder, chest and big toe all wrapped up – he went to investigate. It wasn't a doctor – actually, it was a doctor, but he was on television, talking about some miraculous weight-loss programme. Ingrid was sitting in an armchair. Seeing him enter, she sprang to her feet.

'Feeling better?'

'Yes. Thanks.'

'I got dinner ready, if you're hungry.'

The table had been set. The mullet, taken out of the refrigerator, wanted nothing more than to be eaten. They sat down. As they were serving the fish, Montalbano asked, 'Why didn't you wait for me at the Marinella Bar?'

'For more than an hour, Salvo?'

'You're right, I'm sorry. Why didn't you come in your car?'

'I haven't got it at the moment. It's at the garage. A friend gave me a ride to the bar. Then, when you didn't show up, I decided to go for a walk and came here. I knew you'd come home sooner or later.'

While they were eating, the inspector looked at Ingrid. She was becoming more and more beautiful. At the corners of her mouth she now had a little line that made her look more mature, more aware. What an extraordinary woman! It had never even occurred to her to ask him how he'd managed to injure his shoulder. She ate for the pleasure of eating; the mullet had been carefully apportioned, three each. And she drank with gusto: she was already on her third glass when Montalbano was still on his first.

'What did you want from me?'

The question baffled the inspector.

'I don't understand.'

'Salvo, you called me up to tell me—'

The video cassette! It had completely slipped his mind.

'I wanted to show you something. But let's finish eating first. Want some fruit?'

Then, sitting Ingrid down in the armchair, he picked up the cassette.

'But I've already seen that film!' she protested.

'We're not here to watch the film, but something that was taped over it.'

He put the cassette in, turned it on and sat down in the other armchair. Then, with the remote control, he fast-forwarded it until the shot of the empty bed appeared, with the cameraman trying to bring the picture into focus.

'Looks like a promising start,' Ingrid said, smiling.

Then came the darkened screen. The image reappeared, and now Nenè Sanfilippo's mistress, in the pose of the *Naked Maja*, lay on the bed. A second later Ingrid was on her feet, surprised and troubled.

'But that's Vanya!' she nearly yelled.

Montalbano had never seen Ingrid so upset, never, not even the time she was framed to look like, or almost like, the chief suspect in a crime.

'Do you know her?'

'Of course.'

'Are you friends?'

'Pretty good friends.'

Montalbano turned off the video.

'How did you get that tape?'

'Could we go and talk in the other room? Some of the pain has come back.'

He got into bed. Ingrid sat down on the edge.

'I'm uncomfortable like this,' the inspector complained.

Ingrid got up, pulled him up and put the pillow behind his back so he could remain half sitting. Montalbano was starting to enjoy having a nurse.

'How did you get that cassette?' Ingrid asked again.

'My second-in-command found it at Nenè Sanfilippo's place.'

'And who's he?'

'You don't know? He's that twenty-year-old who was murdered a few days ago.'

'Right, I heard some mention of that. But why did he have that tape?'

Ingrid was being utterly sincere. She seemed truly amazed by the whole business.

'Because he was her lover.'

'What? A boy like that?'

'Yes. She never talked about it with you?'

'Never. At least, she never mentioned his name. Vanya is very reserved.'

'How did the two of you meet?'

'Well, in Montelusa the only comfortably married foreign women are me, two English ladies, an American, two Germans and Vanya, who is Romanian. We've formed a kind of club, just for fun. Do you know who Vanya's husband is?'

'Yes, Dr Ingrò, the transplant surgeon.'

'Well, from what I can gather, he's not a very nice man. For a while, though she's at least twenty years younger, Vanya was happy living with him. Then love faded, for him too. They began to see less and less of each other, and he was often travelling the world.'

'Did she have lovers?'

'Not that I know of. She remained very faithful, in spite of everything.'

'What do you mean, in spite of everything?'

'Well, they stopped sleeping with each other. And Vanya's a woman who—'

'I get the picture.'

'Then, suddenly, about three months ago, she changed. She became sort of more cheerful and sadder at the same time. I realized she was in love. So I asked her, and she said yes. As far as I could tell, it was a great physical passion, mostly.'

'I'd like to meet her.'

'Who?'

'What do you mean, who? Your friend, Vanya.'

'But she left about two weeks ago!'

'Do you know where she is?'

'Of course. She's in a village near Bucharest. I have her address and phone number. She wrote me a couple of lines. She says she had to go back to Romania because her father became ill after falling into disfavour and losing his ministerial post.'

'Do you know when she'll be back?'

'No.'

'Do you know Dr Ingrò very well?'

'I've probably met him three times at the most. Once was when he came to my house. He's very elegant, but unpleasant. Apparently he owns an extraordinary collection of paintings. Vanya says it's a kind of illness, his collection mania. He's spent an incredible amount of money on it.'

'Listen, I want you to think before answering: would he be capable of killing or having somebody kill Vanya's lover, if he ever discovered her infidelity?'

Ingrid laughed.

'You must be kidding! He doesn't give a shit about Vanya any more!'

'But don't you think her husband might have made her leave Vigàta to separate her from her lover?'

'Yes, that's possible. But if he did it, it was only to avoid nasty rumours and gossip. He's not the type of man to take things any further.'

They looked at each other in silence. There was nothing else to say. Something then occurred to Montalbano.

'If you don't have your car, how are you going to get home?'

'Call a cab?'

'At this hour?'

'Then I'll sleep here.'

Montalbano felt the sweat begin to bead on his forehead.

'What about your husband?'

'Don't worry about him.'

'Look, tell you what. Just take my car and go.'

'What about you?'

'I'll have somebody come and pick me up tomorrow morning.'

Ingrid stared at him in silence.

'Do you think of me as a bitch on heat?' she asked, dead serious with a kind of sadness in her eyes.

The inspector felt embarrassed.

'I'm happy for you to stay,' he said sincerely.

As if she'd always lived in that house, Ingrid opened a drawer in his dresser and took out a shirt.

'OK if I wear this?'

*

In the middle of the night, Montalbano, drowsy with sleep, realized there was a woman's body lying next to his. It could only be Livia. He reached out and put his hand on a smooth, solid buttock. All at once an electric shock ran through him. Christ, it wasn't Livia. He pulled his hand abruptly away.

'Put it back,' Ingrid said in a thick voice.

*

'It's six thirty. Coffee's ready,' said Ingrid, touching him delicately on his damaged shoulder.

The inspector opened his eyes. Ingrid had only his shirt on.

'Sorry to wake you up so early. But you yourself said, before falling asleep, that you had to be at your office by eight.'

He got up. He felt less pain, but the tight bandaging made it hard to move. Ingrid removed it for him.

'I'll wrap you up again after you wash.'

They drank their coffee. Montalbano had to use his left hand, as the right was still numb. How would he manage to wash himself? Ingrid seemed to read his mind.

'Leave it to me,' she said.

In the bathroom, she helped the inspector out of his briefs. She took off the shirt she was wearing. Montalbano carefully avoided looking at her. Ingrid, on the other hand, acted as if they'd been married for ten years.

In the shower, she lathered him up. Montalbano had no reaction. He felt, to his delight, like he was a little boy again, when loving hands used to perform the same task on his body.

'I see apparent signs of awakening,' said Ingrid, laughing.

Montalbano looked down and blushed violently. The signs were more than apparent.

'Forgive me. I'm mortified.'

'About what?' Ingrid asked. 'For being a man?'

'Turn on the cold water, it's for the best,' said the inspector.

Then came the torment of being dried off. When he put on his briefs, he sighed in satisfaction, as if to signal that the danger was past. Before wrapping him back up, Ingrid got dressed. That way everything, for the inspector, could proceed more calmly. Before going out, they drank another cup of coffee. Ingrid got into the driver's seat.

'Now, I want you to drop me off at the station, and you can continue on to Montelusa in my car,' said Montalbano.

'No,' said Ingrid. 'I'll drive you to the station and take a taxi from there. It's easier than having to bring the car back to you later.'

*

For half of the drive they sat in silence. One thought kept stewing in the inspector's brain, however, and at a certain point he mustered up the courage and asked, 'What happened between us last night?'

Ingrid laughed.

'Don't you remember?'

'No.'

'Is it important for you to remember?'

'I'd say so.'

'All right. You know what happened? Nothing, if that's what your scruples want.'

'And what if I didn't have any scruples?'

'Then everything happened. Whatever works best for you.'

There was silence.

'Do you think our relationship has changed since last night?' Ingrid asked.

'Absolutely not,' the inspector replied frankly.

'Then why all the questions?'

Her reasoning made sense. And Montalbano asked no

more questions. As she pulled up in front of the station, she asked, 'Do you want Vanya's telephone number?'

'Of course.'

'I'll call you later this morning.'

As Ingrid, after opening the door, was helping Montalbano out of the car, Mimì Augello appeared in the police station's doorway and came to a sudden stop, keenly interested in the scene. Ingrid dashed off after kissing the inspector lightly on the mouth. Mimì kept looking at her from behind until she was out of his sight. With great effort, the inspector hoisted himself up onto the pavement.

'I'm one big ache,' he said, walking past Augello.

'See what happens when you get out of shape?' said Mimì, smirking.

The inspector would have bashed his teeth in but was afraid he might seriously injure his arm.

SIXTEEN

'All right, Mimì, listen carefully to what I say, but don't let it distract you from your driving. I've got a bad shoulder and can't afford any more damage. And, most important, don't interrupt me with questions or I'll lose my train of thought. Save them all for the end, after I've finished. OK?'

'OK.'

'And don't ask me how I found these things out.'

'OK.'

'And no useless details, OK?'

'OK. Before you begin, can I ask you one question?'

'Just one.'

'In addition to your arm, did you also hurt your head?'

'What's that supposed to mean?'

'You're driving me mad with all this asking if things are OK! Are you obsessed or something? I'll just say OK to everything you ask, even about things I don't know. OK? You can begin.'

'Margherita Griffo had a brother and a sister, Giuliana, a schoolteacher, who lived in Trapani.'

'Is she dead?'

'You see? You see?' the inspector burst out. 'You even promised! And still you come out with some stupid question! Of course she's dead, if I say *she had* and *she lived*!'

Augello didn't breathe.

'Margherita hasn't spoken to her sister since they were young. An inheritance squabble. One day, however, the two sisters get back in touch. When Margherita learns that Giuliana is dying, she goes with her husband to see her. They're put up at Giuliana's flat. Also living with the dying woman, from time immemorial, is a friend of hers, Miss Baeri. The Griffos learn that Giuliana, in her will, has left her sister a former stable with a bit of land around it, in a district of Vigàta called the Moor. Which is where we're now going. It was only a token of affection, worth nothing. The day after the funeral, when the Griffos are still in Trapani, some bloke rings up, saying he's interested in the former stable. He doesn't know that Giuliana is dead. Miss Baeri passes the phone to Alfonso Griffo, which makes sense, since his wife now owns the property. The two men talk over the phone. As to the contents of their conversation, Alfonso seems evasive. All he tells his wife is that the man lives in the same building as them.'

'Christ! Nenè Sanfilippo!' Mimì cried out, letting the car swerve.

'Either you drive safely or I'm not going to tell you

anything else. The fact that the stable's owners live on the floor above him seems to Sanfilippo a fantastic coincidence.'

'Wait. Are you sure it's a coincidence?'

'Yes, it's a coincidence. And, incidentally, if I have to put up with your questions, they have to be intelligent. It's a coincidence. Sanfilippo didn't know that Giuliana was dead, and he had no reason to pretend otherwise. He didn't know that the former stable had been bequeathed to Mrs Griffo, because the will hadn't been made public yet.'

'OK.'

'A few hours later, the two men meet.'

'In Vigàta?'

'No, in Trapani. As far as Sanfilippo's concerned, the less he's seen with the Griffos, the better. But I would bet my balls that Sanfilippo fed the old man some line about a stormy, dangerous love affair . . . where, if they're found out, there could be a massacre . . . Anyway, he needs the stable, to turn it into a pied-à-terre. But there are rules that must be respected: the inheritance tax is not to be declared; if it's discovered, Sanfilippo must pay; the Griffos are not to set foot on the property; from that day forward, if the Griffos and Sanfilippo should cross paths, they're not even to say hello to each other; and they must not speak to their son about any of this. As fond as they are of money, the old couple accept the conditions and pocket the first two million lire.'

'But why did Sanfilippo need a place that was so isolated?'

'Certainly not to turn it into a slaughterhouse. Among other things, there's no water, there's not even a toilet. If nature calls, you have to do it outside.'

'And what then?'

'You'll work it out for yourself. See that little chapel there? Just past it, there's a track, on the left. Turn there, and go very slowly, because it's full of holes.'

The door was still leaning against the frame, exactly as he had left it the previous evening. Nobody had been inside. Mimì moved it aside, they entered and the room immediately looked smaller than it was.

Augello looked all around in silence.

'They've cleaned it out,' he said.

'See all those outlets?' said Montalbano. 'He had electricity and a phone put in, but not a toilet. This was his office, where he came to work each day for his employer.'

'Employer?'

'Of course. He worked for some third party.'

'And who would that be?'

'The same people who told him to find a secluded place, far from everyone and everything. Shall I venture a few guesses? First, drug-traffickers. Second, paedophiles. Then you have the whole gamut of weirdos who use the Internet. From here, Sanfilippo could connect with the whole world. He would surf the Web, make contact, communicate and then report back to his bosses. The arrangement went without a hitch for two years. Then something serious happened, and he had to clear out, cut all ties and cover his tracks. On the instructions of his superiors, Sanfilippo convinces the Griffos to go on a nice excursion to Tindari.'

'But for what purpose?'

'He probably fed the poor old people some bullshit, like maybe the dangerous husband had found out about his affair and was going to kill them too, for being accomplices ... So he had this great idea: why don't they go on Malaspina's excursion to Tindari? It would never dawn on the enraged cuckold to look for them on the bus ... They need only stay away from home for a day, and in the meantime some friends would intervene and try to pacify the jealous husband ... And he, too, would make the same excursion, but in his car. Scared out of their wits, the old couple agree to do it. Sanfilippo says he'll keep track of the situation's developments by mobile phone. But before getting back to Vigàta, the old man must ask the bus driver to make an extra stop. That way Sanfilippo can bring them up to date on things. Everything unfolds as planned. Except that at the last stop before Vigàta, Sanfilippo tells the two that nothing's been resolved yet; they'd be better off spending the night away from home. So he takes them in his car and then turns them over to their executioner. At that moment he doesn't know yet that he, too, has been marked for death.'

'But you still haven't told me why it was necessary to

send the Griffos away. They probably didn't even know where their property was!'

'Somebody had to get into their flat and remove all documents pertaining to that same property. Their copy of the will, for instance, or some letter from Giuliana where she says she intends to remember her sister with this bequest. That sort of thing. And the bloke who goes looking for this stuff also finds the postal passbook showing a sum that looks too high for two impoverished retirees, so he snatches that, too. But it's a mistake, because that's what will arouse my suspicion.'

'To be honest, Salvo, I don't find this business of the excursion to Tindari very convincing, at least not the way you tell it. What need was there to do it? Those guys, with the slightest excuse, could've marched into the Griffos' flat and done whatever they wanted!'

'Yes, but then they would have had to kill them right then and there in their flat, which would have alarmed Sanfilippo, to whom the killers would certainly have said they had no intention of killing the old people, but only terrorizing them the right amount ... And bear in mind that it was in everybody's interest to make us believe there was no connection between the Griffos' disappearance and Sanfilippo's murder. In fact, how long did it take us to realize the two cases were interrelated?'

'Maybe you're right.'

'No maybe about it, Mimì. Then, after they clear this

place out with Sanfilippo's help, they take the boy off with them. Maybe with the excuse that they need to talk about setting up his office somewhere else. In the meantime they go into his flat and do the same thing they did at the Griffos'. They take the electricity and phone bills for this place, for example, which we were unable to find, in fact. And Sanfilippo they send home late at night and—'

'What need was there to send him home? They could have killed him wherever they took him.'

'Three mysterious disappearances in the same building?'

'True.'

'Sanfilippo goes home, it's almost morning, he gets out of his car, sticks his key in the door and whoever was waiting for him calls to him.'

'So how do we proceed from here?' Augello asked, after a brief pause.

'I don't know,' Montalbano replied. 'We can leave this place, for starters. There's no point in calling forensics for fingerprints. They probably scrubbed the place with lye, including the ceilings.'

They got in the car and left.

'You've certainly got a lively imagination,' Mimì commented after thinking over the inspector's reconstruction of events. 'When you retire you could start writing novels.'

'I would definitely write mysteries. But it's not worth the trouble.'

'Why do you say that?'

'Because certain critics and professors, or would-be critics and professors, consider mystery novels a minor genre. And, in fact, in histories of literature they're never even mentioned.'

'What the hell do you care? Do you want to enter literary history alongside Dante and Manzoni?'

'I'd die of shame.'

'So just write them and be content with that.'

After a short spell, Augello resumed talking.

'All of which means that my whole day yesterday was a waste.'

'Why?'

'What do you mean, why? Have you forgotten? All I did all day was gather information on Dr Ingrò, as we'd decided when we thought Sanfilippo was killed over an illicit love affair.'

'Ah, yes. Tell me about him anyway.'

'He's truly a worldwide celebrity. He has a very exclusive clinic, all his own, between Vigàta and Caltanissetta, where only a few choice VIPs go. I went and had a look at it from the outside. It's a big house surrounded by a very high wall, with enormous grounds. They even land helicopters in there. Two armed guards are posted outside. I asked some questions, and they told me the place was temporarily closed. The doctor, in any case, can operate pretty much wherever he likes.'

'Where is he at the moment?'

'You know what? That friend of mine who knows him

said he's holed up at his seaside villa between Vigàta and Santolì. Says it's a bad time for him.'

'Maybe he found out about his wife's affair.'

'Maybe. My friend also said that a little over two years ago the doctor went through another bad period but later recovered.'

'Obviously that time, too, his fair consort—'

'No, Salvo, that time there was a better reason, I'm told. Nothing certain, just rumours. But apparently he over-extended himself for a vast sum, to buy a painting. He didn't have the cash. He bounced a few cheques and was threatened with legal action. Then he came up with the money and everything went back to normal.'

'Where does he keep the paintings?'

'In a vault. At home he only hangs reproductions.'

After another silence, Augello asked guardedly, 'So, what did you get out of Ingrid?'

Montalbano bristled.

'I don't like that kind of talk, Mimì.'

'I just meant, did you find anything out about Vanya, Ingrò's wife!'

'Ingrid knew that Vanya had a lover, but didn't know his name. In fact, she hadn't made any connection between her friend and the murdered Sanfilippo. At any rate, Vanya's gone back to Romania to visit her sick father. She left before her lover was killed.'

They were pulling in to headquarters.

'Just out of curiosity, did you read Sanfilippo's novel?'

'Believe me, I didn't have time. I thumbed through it. It's odd: some pages are well written, others are terrible.'

'Would you bring it to me this afternoon?'

*

On their way in, Montalbano noticed that Galluzzo was at the switchboard.

'Where's Catarella? I haven't seen him since this morning.'

'He was summoned to Montelusa, Inspector, for a follow-up computer course. He'll be back this evening around five thirty.'

'So, how should we proceed?' Mimì asked again, having followed his boss inside.

'Listen, Mimì, I was ordered by the commissioner to work only on small stuff. In your opinion, the Griffo and Sanfilippo murders, are they small stuff or big stuff?'

'Big. Really big.'

'So it's not our job. I want you to write me a report, in which you're to present only the facts, not what I think. That way, he'll assign it to the captain of the Flying Squad. Provided that, in the meantime, the captain's recovered from the runs or whatever his problem was.'

'We're going to serve up a hot case like this to those guys?' Augello asked, outraged. 'They won't even thank us for it!'

'Do you care so much about being thanked? Try instead to write that report well. Then bring it to me in the morning so I can sign it.'

'What's that supposed to mean, write it well?'

'It means you should season it with things like "having arrived at said premises", "in lieu of", "from which it may be surmised", "the above notwithstanding". That way they'll feel as though they're on their own turf, in their own language, and they'll take the case seriously.'

✳

He relaxed for an hour. Then he called Fazio.

'Any news about Japichinu?'

'Nothing. Officially, he's still at large.'

'How's that jobless guy who set himself on fire doing?'

'Better, but he's still not out of danger.'

Then Gallo came in and told him about a group of Albanians who had escaped from a concentration camp, called by some a reception camp.

'Did you track them down?'

'Not a single one of 'em, Chief. And nobody'll ever find 'em, either.'

'Why not?'

'Because these escapes are arranged on the sly with other Albanians who've put down roots here. A colleague of mine in Montelusa doesn't agree. He says some Albanians escape and go back to Albania and that, all things considered, they discovered they were better off at home.

A million lire a head to come here, and two to go back. The boatmen always make a killing.'

'Is that some kind of joke?'

'I don't think so,' said Gallo.

The telephone rang. It was Ingrid.

'I've got Vanya's number for you.'

Montalbano wrote it down. Instead of saying goodbye, Ingrid said, 'I talked to her.'

'When?'

'Just before ringing you. We had a long conversation.'

'Should we meet?'

'Yes, I think it's best. I even have my car back.'

'Good, that way you can change my bandages. See you at one o'clock, at the Trattoria San Calogero.'

Something in Ingrid's voice didn't sound right. She seemed troubled.

*

Among the many gifts the good Lord had given her, Ingrid also had a knack for punctuality. They went into the restaurant, and the first thing the inspector saw was a couple sitting at a table for four: Mimì and Beba. Augello sprang to his feet. Though the proud owner of a poker face, he was blushing slightly. He gestured for the inspector and Ingrid to join them at his table. The scene from a few days earlier was repeated in reverse.

'We don't want to disturb you ...' said Montalbano hypocritically.

'But it's no disturbance at all!' countered Mimì, even more hypocritically.

The women introduced themselves, smiling. The smiles they exchanged were open and sincere, and the inspector thanked heaven. Eating with two women who didn't hit it off would have been an ordeal. But Montalbano's sharp detective's eye noticed something that troubled him: there was some sort of tension between Mimì and Beatrice. Or was it merely that his presence made them feel awkward? They all ordered the same thing: seafood antipasto and a giant platter of grilled fish. Halfway through a grilled sole, Montalbano became convinced that his second-in-command and Beba must have been having a little spat when he and Ingrid interrupted them. Christ! He had to make sure the two made up by the time they got up from the table. He was racking his brain trying to think of a solution when he saw Beatrice place her hand lightly over Mimì's. Augello looked at the girl, the girl looked at him. For a few seconds, they drowned in each other's eyes. Peace! They'd made peace! The meal went down better for the inspector.

*

'Let's take separate cars to Marinella,' Ingrid said as they were leaving the trattoria. 'I have to be back in Montelusa soon. I've got an appointment.'

Montalbano's shoulder was feeling much better. As she was changing the bandages, she said, 'I'm a little confused.'

'By the phone call?'

'Yes. You see—'

'Later,' said the inspector. 'Let's talk about it later.'

He was basking in the cool sensation of the salve that Ingrid was massaging into his skin. And he liked — why not admit it? — feeling the woman's hands practically caressing his shoulders, arms and chest. All of a sudden he realized he was sitting there with eyes closed, about to start purring like a cat.

'I've finished,' said Ingrid.

'Let's go out on the veranda. Want some whisky?'

Ingrid consented. For a spell they sat in silence, staring at the sea. Then the inspector began, 'How did you happen to ring her?'

'Well, it was a sudden impulse, really, when I was looking for the postcard to give you her number.'

'OK. Go on.'

'As soon as I said it was me, she seemed terrified. She asked me if anything had happened. I felt in an awkward position. I wondered if she knew her lover had been murdered, but in any case she'd never told me his name. So I replied, no, nothing had happened, I just wanted to know how she was doing. Then she said she would be away for a long time. And she started crying.'

'Did she explain why she had to stay away?'

'Yes. I'll try to give you the facts in order, though what she told me was confused and fragmented. One evening Vanya, knowing that her husband was out of town and would be away for a few days, brought her lover to her villa near Santolì, as she'd done many times before. As they were sleeping, they were woken up by someone entering the bedroom. It was Dr Ingrò. "So it's true," he muttered. Vanya says her husband and the boy looked at each other a long time. Then the doctor said, "Come with me," and he went into the living room. Without a word, the boy got dressed and joined the doctor. What struck my friend most was that . . . well, she had the impression that the two already knew each other. And rather well.'

'Wait a minute. Do you know how Vanya and Nenè Sanfilippo first met?'

'Yes, she told me the time I asked her if she was in love, right before she left. They met by chance, at a bar in Montelusa.'

'Did Sanfilippo know who your friend was married to?'

'Yes, Vanya told him.'

'Go on.'

'Then the husband and Nenè – Vanya, at this point in her story, said to me, "His name is Nenè" – the husband and Nenè went back into the bedroom and—'

'She said "his name *is*"? She used the present tense?'

'Yes. I noticed it myself. She still doesn't know that her lover was murdered. So, as I was saying, the two came back and Nenè, with eyes lowered, mumbled that their relationship had been a terrible mistake, that it was his fault, and that they must never see each other again. And then he left. Ingrò did the same a short while later, without saying a word. Vanya didn't know what to do; she felt disappointed by Nenè's aloofness. She decided to stay at the villa. Late the following morning, the doctor returned. He told Vanya that she had to go back to Montelusa at once and pack her bags. Her flight to Bucharest had already been booked. Somebody would drive her to the Catania airport at dawn. Left alone in the house that evening, Vanya tried to ring Nenè, but he was nowhere to be found. The next morning she left. To her friends, including me, she explained her departure with the excuse that her father was sick. She even told me that the time her husband came to tell her that she had to leave, he wasn't resentful or offended or embittered, but only worried. Then, yesterday, the doctor phoned her and advised her to stay away from here as long as possible. And there you have it.'

'But why do you feel confused?'

'Because ... in your opinion, is that normal behaviour for a husband who's just caught his wife in bed, in his house, with another man?'

'You yourself said they no longer loved each other!'

'And does the young man's behaviour seem normal to you? Since when have you Sicilians become more Swedish than the Swedish?'

'See, Ingrid, Vanya's probably right when she says Ingrò and Sanfilippo knew each other ... The boy was an excellent computer technician, and there must be plenty of computers at the Montelusa clinic. When Nenè first hooked up with Vanya, he didn't know she was the doctor's wife. When he finds out – maybe because she told him – they're already taken with each other. It's all so clear.'

'Bah!' said Ingrid, sceptical.

'Look: the boy says he's made a mistake. And he's right, because he's definitely lost his job. And the doctor sends his wife away because he's afraid of the consequences, the gossip ... Say the two got some bright idea, like running away together ... Better not to let them have the opportunity.'

From the look Ingrid gave him, Montalbano realized that she was not convinced by his explanations. But since that was the way she was, she didn't ask any more questions.

*

After Ingrid left, he remained seated on the veranda. The trawlers were heading out of the port to fish through the night. He didn't want to think about anything. Then he heard a harmonious sound, very close by. Somebody was whistling softly. Who? He looked around. There was nobody. It was him! He was the one whistling! As soon as he realized this, he couldn't whistle any more. Therefore there *were* moments when, like a double, he could actually whistle. He started laughing.

'Dr Jekyll and Mr Hyde,' he mumbled.

'Dr Jekyll and Mr Hyde.'

'Dr Jekyll and Mr Hyde.'

The third time he was no longer laughing. In fact, he had turned dead serious. His forehead was sweating a little.

He filled his glass with straight whisky.

*

'Chief! Chief!' said Catarella, running after him. 'I gots this letter here I's a sposta give to you poissonally since yesterday. 'Sfrom that lawyer Guttadadaro, who said I'm only sposta give it to you poissonally in poisson!'

He dug it out of his jacket pocket, and handed it to Montalbano. The inspector opened it.

Esteemed Inspector, the person you know, my client and friend, had intended to write you a letter expressing his increased admiration in your regard. He changed his mind, however, and asked instead that I inform you he will be calling you by phone. Most respectfully yours, Guttadauro.

He tore it up into little pieces and went into Augello's office. Mimì was at his desk.

'I'm writing the report,' he said.

'Fuck it,' said Montalbano.

'What's going on?' Augello asked, alarmed. 'I don't like the look on your face.'

'Did you bring me the novel?'

'Sanfilippo's? Yes.'

He pointed at a large envelope on the desk. The inspector picked it up and put it under his arm.

'What's wrong?' Augello insisted.

The inspector didn't answer.

'I'm going home to Marinella. Don't let anyone ring me there. I'll be back at the station around midnight. I want you all here.'

SEVENTEEN

Once outside the police station, his great desire to hole up at Marinella and start reading suddenly disappeared the way the wind sometimes does, uprooting trees one moment and vanishing the next, as if it had never existed. He got into his car and drove towards the port. When he arrived in the neighbourhood, he stopped the car and got out, taking along the envelope. The truth of the matter was that he couldn't muster up the courage to read it: he was afraid of finding in Nenè Sanfilippo's words a stinging confirmation of an idea that had occurred to him after Ingrid had left. He walked slowly, deliberately, to the lighthouse and sat down on the flat rock. He smelled the strong, acrid odour of the *lippo*, the greeny down that grows on the lower half of the rocks, the part in contact with the sea. He glanced at his watch: there was still an hour of light remaining. He could, if he wanted, start reading right there. But he still didn't feel like it; he wasn't up to it. What if Sanfilippo's writing turned out in the end to be a pile of shit, the constipated fantasy of a dilettante who thinks he can write a novel just because he learned how to parse sentences in school? Which isn't even taught any more. Another sign — as if he needed any more — of just how far he was getting on in years. But to keep holding those pages in his hand, unable to decide one way or another, made his skin crawl. Maybe it was better to go back to Marinella and start reading on the veranda. He would be breathing the same sea air.

*

At a glance he realized that Nenè Sanfilippo, to hide what he really had to say, had resorted to the same method he used in filming the naked Vanya. In that instance the tape had begun with some twenty minutes of *The Getaway*; here the first pages were copied from a famous novel: Asimov's *I, Robot*.

It took Montalbano two hours to read the whole thing. The closer he got to the end, the clearer what Nenè Sanfilippo was saying became to him, and the more often his hand reached out for the whisky bottle.

The novel had no ending. It broke off in the middle of a sentence. But what he'd read was more than enough for him. From the pit of his stomach a violent spasm of nausea rose up and seized his throat. He ran to the bathroom, barely able to stand, knelt down in front of the toilet and started to vomit. He vomited the whisky he'd just drunk, vomited what he'd eaten that day as well as what he'd eaten the day before, and the day before that, and he felt, with his sweaty head now entirely inside the toilet bowl and a sharp pain in his side, as if he were endlessly vomiting up the entire time of his life on earth, going all the way back to the pap he was given as a baby, and when, at last, he'd expelled even his own mother's milk, he kept on vomiting poison bitterness, bile, pure hatred.

He managed to stand up, holding onto the sink, but his legs could barely support him. He was sure he was getting a fever. He stuck his head under the running tap.

'Too old for this profession,' he muttered.

He lay down on the bed and closed his eyes.

*

He didn't stay there long. When he got up his head was spinning, but the blind rage that had overwhelmed him was now turning into lucid determination. He called the office.

'Hallo? Hallo? This the Vigàta pol—'

'Montalbano here, Cat. Put Inspector Augello on, if he's there.'

He was there.

'What is it, Salvo?'

'Listen to me carefully, Mimì. I want you and Fazio, right now, to take a car, not a squad car, mind you, and drive towards Santolì. I want to know if Dr Ingrò's villa is being watched.'

'By whom?'

'No questions, Mimì. If it's being watched, it's certainly not by us. And you must try to determine if the doctor is alone or with others. Take as long as you need to be sure of what you're seeing. I summoned all the men for a midnight meeting. Cancel the order; it's no longer necessary. When you've finished in Santolì, let Fazio go home and come to Marinella to tell me how things stand.'

✻

He hung up and the telephone rang. It was Livia.

'How come you're already home at this hour?' she asked.

She was pleased, but more than pleased, she was happily surprised.

'And if you know I'm never home at this hour, why did you call?'

He'd answered a question with a question. But he needed to stall. Otherwise Livia, knowing him as she did, would realize that something wasn't right with him.

'You know, Salvo, for the last hour or so something strange has been happening to me. It's never happened to me before, or at least, it's never been so strong as now. It's hard to explain.'

Now it was Livia who was stalling.

'Give it a try.'

'Well, it's as though you were here.'

'I'm sorry, but—'

'OK. See, when I came home, I didn't see my dining

room, I saw yours. Not exactly, though; it was my room, of course, but at the same time, it was yours.'

'As in dreams.'

'Yes, something like that. And since that moment, it's as though I've been split in two. I'm in Boccadasse, but at the same time I'm with you, in Marinella. It's ... really beautiful. I called because I knew you'd be at home.'

To hide his emotions, Montalbano tried to make a joke of it.

'The fact is, you're curious.'

'About what?'

'About the layout of my house.'

'But I already—' Livia reacted. She broke off, suddenly remembering the little game he'd suggested they play: getting engaged, starting all over again. 'I'd like to get to know it.'

'Why don't you come?'

He'd been unable to control his tone, and a sincere question had come out. Livia took notice.

'What's wrong, Salvo?'

'Nothing. A bad mood, it'll pass. An ugly case.'

'Do you really want me to come?'

'Yes.'

'I'll catch the afternoon flight tomorrow. I love you.'

*

He had to find a way to pass the time while waiting for Mimì. He didn't feel like eating, even though he had emptied his guts of everything possible. His hand, as if of its own will, took a book off the shelf. He glanced at the title, *The Secret Agent*, by Joseph Conrad. He recalled having liked it, even a lot, but couldn't remember anything else. It often happened that if he read the opening lines of a novel, or the conclusion, a little compartment in his memory would open up, and characters, situations, phrases would come tumbling out. 'Mr Verloc, going out in the morning, left his shop nominally in charge of his brother-in-law.' That's how the book began, but these words didn't tell him anything. 'He passed on unsuspected and deadly, like a pest in the street full of men.' These were the final words, and they said too much. Then a sentence from the book came back to him, 'No pity for anything on earth, including themselves, and death enlisted for good and all in the service of humanity...' He hastily put the book back in its place. No, his hand had not acted by itself, independently of his mind; it had been guided, unconsciously of course, by him, by what was inside him. He sat down in the armchair and turned on the television. The first image he saw was of prisoners in a concentration camp, not one of Hitler's, but a contemporary one. It wasn't clear where, because the faces of people subject to horror are the same everywhere. He turned it off. He went out on the veranda, sat there staring at the sea, trying to breathe with the same rhythm as the surf.

✻

Was it the door or the phone? He looked at his watch: past eleven, too early for Mimì.

'Hello? Sinagra here.'

Balduccio Sinagra's faint voice, which always sounded ready to break like a spider's web in a gust of wind, was unmistakable.

'If you have anything to say to me, Sinagra, ring me at the station.'

'Wait. What's wrong, you scared? This phone's not bugged. Unless yours is.'

'What do you want?'

'I wanted to tell you that I feel bad, really bad.'

'Because you haven't heard from your beloved grandson Japichinu?'

It was a shot fired straight at the balls. And for a moment, Balduccio Sinagra remained silent, long enough to absorb the blow and catch his breath.

'I'm convinced that my grandson, wherever he is, is better off than I am, because my kidneys don't work no more. I need a transplant, or I'll die.'

Montalbano said nothing. He let the falcon fly in ever smaller, concentric circles.

'But do you know,' resumed the old man, 'how many patients like me need this operation? Over ten thousand, Inspector. While waiting for your turn, you have all the time in the world to die.'

The falcon had stopped circling and was now ready to swoop down on the target.

'And then you have to be sure that the surgeon operating on you is good, dependable ...'

'Someone like Dr Ingrò?'

The inspector had reached the target first; the falcon had dawdled too long. He'd managed to defuse the bomb Sinagra had in his hand. And he would not be able to say, yet again, that he had manipulated Inspector Montalbano like a marionette at the puppet theatre. The old man's reaction was authentic.

'My compliments, Inspector,' he said, 'my sincerest compliments.'

And he continued: 'Dr Ingrò is the right man. But I'm told he had to close down his hospital here in Montelusa. Seems he's not in the best of health himself, poor man.'

'What do the doctors say? Is it serious?'

'They don't know yet. They want to be sure before they decide on a treatment. Bah, we're all in the hands of the Lord, dear Inspector!'

He hung up.

At last the doorbell rang. He was making a pot of coffee.

*

'There's nobody watching the villa,' Mimì said as he came in. 'And until a little over half an hour ago, when I left to come here, he was alone.'

'Somebody may have gone there in the meantime.'

'If so, Fazio will call me from his mobile phone. But you're going to tell me right now why you're suddenly so fixated on Dr Ingrò.'

'Because they're still keeping him in limbo. They haven't decided whether to let him continue working or kill him like they did the Griffos and Nenè Sanfilippo.'

'So the doctor's mixed up in this too?' asked Mimì in astonishment.

'He's mixed up in it, all right,' said Montalbano.

'Says who?'

A tree, a Saracen olive tree. This would have been the correct answer. But Mimì would have thought him insane.

'Ingrid phoned Vanya, who's scared out of her wits because there are certain things she doesn't understand. For instance, the fact that Nenè knew the doctor really well but never said anything to her. Or the fact that her husband, when he caught her in bed with her lover, didn't get angry or upset. He only got worried. And just this evening, Balduccio Sinagra confirmed it all for me.'

'Jesus Christ!' said Mimì. 'What's Sinagra got to do with this? And why would he turn informer?'

'He didn't turn informer. He told me he needed a kidney transplant, and said he agreed when I mentioned Dr Ingrò's name. But he also said the good doctor wasn't in the best of health. You told me the same thing, remember? Except that the word "health" has different meanings for you and Balduccio.'

The coffee was ready. They drank it.

'You see,' the inspector resumed, 'Nenè Sanfilippo wrote the whole story, and quite clearly at that.'

'Where?'

'In the novel. He starts out by copying the pages of a famous book, then tells his own story, then adds another passage from the famous novel, and so on. It's a story about robots.'

'It's science fiction, which is why I thought—'

'You fell into the trap set up by Sanfilippo. His robots, which he calls, say, Alpha 715 or Omega 37, are made of metal and circuits, but they think and feel just like us. Sanfilippo's robot world is a carbon copy of our own.'

'What does the novel say?'

'It's the story of a young robot, Delta 32, who falls in love with a female robot, Gamma 1024, who is married to a world-famous robot, Beta 5, who knows how to replace broken robot parts with new ones. The surgeon robot — that's what we'll call him — is a man, sorry, a robot, who's in constant need of money, because he has a mania for expensive paintings. One day he incurs a debt he's unable to pay. And so a criminal robot, a gang leader, makes him an offer. That is, they'll give him all the money he wants, on the condition that he perform clandestine transplants on clients of their choosing, first-rate clients from all over the world, rich and powerful people who don't have the time or the desire to wait their turn. The doctor robot then asks how it will be possible to get the right spare parts in good time. They tell him this isn't a problem: they know how to find the spare parts. How? By scrapping a robot that meets the requirements and removing the part they need. The scrapped robot is then dumped into the sea or buried underground. We can serve any client, says the leader, whose name is Omicron I. All over the world, he explains, there are people imprisoned, in jails and special camps. And we have a robot in every one of these camps. And near every one of these camps, there is a landing strip. Those of us you see here, Omicron I continues, are just a tiny part of the whole. Our organization is at work all over the world; it's become globalized. And so Beta 5 accepts. Beta 5's requests will be relayed to Omicron I, who will in turn convey them to Delta 32, who, using a highly advanced Internet system, will communicate them to the ... let's call them operative services. And that's where the novel ends. Nenè didn't have a chance to write the conclusion. Omicron I wrote it for him.'

Augello sat there a long time, thinking. Apparently the full significance of what Montalbano had just told him hadn't dawned on him yet. Then he understood, turned pale, and said in a low voice, 'Baby robots, too, naturally.'

'Naturally,' the inspector confirmed.

'And how does the story continue, in your opinion?'

'You must start from the premise that the people who organized the whole affair bear a terrible responsibility.'

'I'll say. The death of—'

'Not just death, Mimì. Life, too.'

'Life?'

'Of course. The lives of those who've been operated on. They've paid a horrific price, and I'm not talking about money. I mean the death of another person. If this ever came out, they'd be finished, whatever their position, whether at the top of a government, economic empire or banking conglomerate. They'd lose face for ever. Therefore, the way I see it, things went as follows: one day, somebody finds out about the love affair between Sanfilippo and the doctor's wife. As of that moment, Vanya becomes a danger to the entire organization. She represents the potential link between the surgeon and the criminal organization. The two things must remain absolutely separate. What to do? Kill Vanya? No, that would put the doctor right in the middle of a murder investigation, which would be plastered all over the newspapers … The best thing is to close down the Vigàta headquarters. But first they inform the doctor of his wife's infidelity. He should be able to tell, from Vanya's reaction, whether she's wise to anything. Vanya, however, knows nothing. She's sent back to her native country. The organization then cuts off all the roads that might lead to her: the Griffos, the Sanfilippos …'

'Why didn't they kill the doctor too?'

'Because he can still be useful to them. His name is a guarantee for the customers. Like in advertising. So they decide to wait and see how things work out. If they work

out well, they'll let him start practising again. If not, they'll
kill him.'

'What are you going to do?'

'What can I do? Nothing, for now. Go on home, Mimì.
And thanks. Is Fazio still in Santolì?'

'Yes. He's waiting for my phone call.'

'Ring him, then. Tell him he can go home to bed.
Tomorrow morning we'll decide how to continue our
surveillance.'

Augello spoke with Fazio. Then he said, 'He's going
home. There are no new developments. The doctor is
alone. He's watching television.'

*

At three in the morning, after putting on a heavy jacket
because it was cool outside, the inspector got in his car and
drove off. Pretending it was simply for curiosity's sake,
he'd had Augello describe the exact location of Ingrò's villa
to him. On the way there, he thought again of Mimì's
expression after hearing his account of the transplant story.
He himself had reacted the way he did, nearly suffering
a stroke. Whereas Mimì had turned pale, yes, but didn't
really seem too upset. Self-control? Lack of sensitivity?
No, the reason was clearly much simpler: the difference in
age. He was fifty and Mimì was thirty. Augello was already
prepared for the year 2000, whereas he would never be.
Nothing more. Augello naturally knew that he was entering

an era of pitiless crimes committed by anonymous people, who had Internet addresses or sites or whatever they're called, but never a face, a pair of eyes, an expression. No, he was too old by now.

He stopped about twenty yards from the villa and, turning off the headlights, stayed there without moving. He carefully studied the place through binoculars. Not a single ray of light could be seen in the windows. Dr Ingrò must have gone to bed. He got out of the car and, treading lightly, approached the gate. He stayed there some ten minutes without moving. Nobody came forward, nobody called from the darkness to ask what he wanted. With a tiny pocket torch, he examined the lock on the gate. There was no alarm. Was it possible? Then he realized that Dr Ingrò didn't need any security systems. With the friends he had, only a fool would be crazy enough to rob his villa. It took him a moment to pick the lock. There was a broad lane, lined with trees. The garden must have been kept in perfect order. There were no dogs, since at this hour they would have already attacked him. With the picklock he opened the front door as well. A large foyer led into an entirely glass-walled salon and to other rooms. The bed-rooms were upstairs. He climbed a luxurious staircase covered with thick, soft carpeting. In the first room there wasn't anybody. In the second room, however, there was. Someone was breathing heavily. With his left hand, the inspector felt around for the light switch; in his right, he held a pistol. He wasn't fast enough. The lamp on one of the bedside tables came on.

Dr Ingrò was lying on the bed, fully dressed, shoes included. He showed not the least bit of surprise at seeing an unknown man, with a gun, no less, in his room. He'd clearly been expecting as much. The room smelled stuffy, sweaty, rancid. Dr Ingrò was no longer the man the inspector remembered seeing two or three times on television. He was unshaven, his eyes red, his hair sticking straight up.

'Have you decided to kill me?' he asked in a soft voice.

Montalbano didn't answer. He was still standing in the doorway, motionless, the hand clutching the pistol at his side, but with the weapon in full view.

'You're making a mistake,' said Ingrò.

He reached out towards the bedside table – Montalbano recognized it from the tape of the naked Vanya – picked up the glass that was there and took a long drink of water, spilling some of it on himself. His hands were trembling. He set the glass down and spoke again.

'I could still be of use to you.'

He put his feet on the ground.

'Where are you going to find someone as skilled as me?'

As skilled, maybe not, but more honest, yes, thought the inspector. But he said nothing. He let the man stew in his juices. But maybe it was better to give him a little push.

The doctor was now standing up, and Montalbano ever so slowly raised the gun and pointed it at his head.

Then it happened. As if someone had cut the invisible rope holding him up, the man fell to his knees. He folded his hands in prayer.

'Have pity! Have pity!'

Pity? The kind of pity he'd shown for those who were slaughtered, literally slaughtered, for his sake?

The doctor was crying. Tears and spittle made the beard on his chin sparkle. Was this the Conradian character he'd imagined?

'I can pay you, if you let me go,' he whispered.

He thrust a hand in his pocket, extracted a set of keys, and held them out to Montalbano, who didn't move.

'These keys ... you can help yourself to all my paintings ... a vast fortune ... you'll be rich ...'

Montalbano could no longer restrain himself. He took two steps forward, raised his foot and shot it straight at the doctor's face. The man fell backwards, managing to scream this time.

'No! No! Not that!'

He held his face in his hands, the blood from his broken nose running between his fingers. Montalbano raised his foot again.

'That's enough!' said a voice behind him.

He turned around abruptly. In the doorway stood Augello and Fazio, both with guns drawn. They all looked one another in the eye and understood. And the performance began.

'Police,' said Mimì.

'We saw you break in, punk!' said Fazio.

'You were going to kill him, weren't you?' Mimì recited.

'Drop the gun,' ordered Fazio.

'No!' the inspector shouted and, grabbing Ingrò by the hair, he yanked him to his feet and pointed the gun at his head.

'If you don't get out of here, I'll kill him!'

OK, they'd all seen that scene a thousand times in any number of American movies, but, all things considered, they had to be pleased with the way they were improvising it. Now, as if on cue, it was Ingrò's turn to speak.

'Don't go!' he begged. 'I'll tell you everything! I'll confess! Save me!'

Fazio leapt forward and seized Montalbano while Augello held down Ingrò. Fazio and the inspector pretended to struggle, then the former gained the upper hand. Augello took control of the situation.

'Handcuff him!' he ordered.

But the inspector still needed to give some instructions. It was absolutely imperative that they all act in concert and follow the same script. He grabbed Fazio's wrist and, as if caught by surprise, Fazio let him take the gun away. Montalbano fired a shot that deafened them all and ran out. Augello freed himself from the doctor, who had been clutching his shoulders, weeping, and raced off in pursuit. At the bottom of the stairs, Montalbano tripped on the last step and fell face down, firing another shot. Mimì, still shouting 'Stop or I'll shoot,' helped him up. They went out of the house.

'He shit his pants,' Mimì said. 'He's cooked.'

'Good,' said Montalbano. 'Take him to Montelusa Central. On your way there, pull over at some point and look around, as if you're fearing an ambush. When he's in front of the commissioner, he has to tell us everything.'

'And what about you?'

'I escaped,' said the inspector, firing a shot in the air for good measure.

*

On the drive back to Marinella, he changed his mind. Turning the car round, he headed towards Montelusa. He took the outer ring road and finally pulled up at Via De Gasperi 38, home of his journalist friend, Nicolò Zito. Before buzzing the intercom, he checked his watch. Almost five in the morning. He had to buzz three long times before he heard Nicolò's voice, sounding half asleep and half enraged.

'Montalbano here. I need to talk to you.'

'Wait for me downstairs, otherwise you'll wake up the whole house.'

A few minutes later, sitting on a stair, Montalbano told

him the whole story, with Zito interrupting him from time to time with comments like, 'Wait!' and 'Oh, Christ!'

He needed an occasional pause. The story took his breath away.

'What do you want me to do?' Zito asked when the inspector had finally finished.

'This very morning, do a special report. Keep it vague. Say that Dr Ingrò apparently turned himself in because of an alleged involvement in illegal organ-trafficking ... You have to trumpet the news, make sure it reaches the national papers and networks.'

'What are you afraid of?'

'That they'll hush the whole thing up. Ingrò has some very important friends. Too important. And one more favour. On the one o'clock edition, pull out another story. Keeping it still vague, say that the fugitive Jacopo Sinagra, known as "Japichinu", has reportedly been murdered, and that he apparently belonged to the same organization that Dr Ingrò was working for.'

'But is it true?'

'I think so. I'm almost certain this is why his grandfather Balduccio Sinagra had him killed. Not because of any moral qualms, mind you. But because his grandson, fortified by his alliance with the new Mafia, could have had him liquidated whenever he wanted.'

*

It was seven in the morning when he finally managed to get to bed. He decided to sleep the whole morning. In the afternoon he would drive to Palermo to pick up Livia, on her way down from Genoa. He was able to sleep for two hours before the telephone woke him up. It was Mimì. But the inspector spoke first.

'Why did you guys follow me last night when I explicitly—'

'When you explicitly tried to pull the wool over our eyes?' Augello finished his sentence. 'But, Salvo, how can you possibly imagine that Fazio and I don't know what you're thinking? I ordered Fazio not to leave the area of the villa, even if I countermanded the order. We knew you'd be there sooner or later. And when you left your house, I followed you. I'd say we did the right thing.'

Montalbano accepted this and changed the subject.

'So, how'd it go?'

'What a fucking circus, Salvo. They all came running: the commissioner, the chief prosecutor ... And the doctor kept talking and talking ... They couldn't get him to stop ... I'll see you later at the office and tell you the whole story.'

'My name never came up, right?'

'No, don't worry. We explained that we happened to be passing by the villa when we noticed the gate and front door were wide open, which aroused our suspicion. But unfortunately the hitman escaped. See you later.'

'I won't be in today.'

'The fact is,' said Mimì, embarrassed, 'I won't be in tomorrow.'

'Where are you going?'

'To Tindari. Since Beba has to go there, as usual, for work...'

And maybe, on the way, he'd buy himself a set of kitchenware.

What Montalbano remembered of Tindari was the small, mysterious Greek theatre and the beach shaped like a pink-fingered hand ... If Livia stayed a few days, an excursion to Tindari might not be a bad idea.

Author's Note

This entire book — names, surnames (especially surnames), situations — is invented out of whole cloth. Any coincidence whatsoever is due to the fact that my imagination is limited.

This book is dedicated to Orazio Costa, my teacher and friend.

Notes

page 4 – **Charles Martel** – Mayor of the Palace of the Kingdom of the Franks and unifier, with his son Pépin the Short and grandson Charlemagne, of the Frankish realm. A fierce warrior and field general (Martel means 'hammer'), Charles stemmed the Arab advance into France at the Battle of Tours (more accurately the Battle of Poitiers) in 732.

page 5 – **the state monopoly** – In Italy, all tobacco products, domestic and foreign, are controlled by government monopoly.

page 5 – **defending the police against the students at Valle Giulia** – On 1 March 1968, at the University of Rome at Valle Giulia, protesting students reacted to heavy-handed tactics by riot police by hurling stones and setting fire to cars, resulting in injuries to both sides. In a now-famous poem written in response to this event, the radical poet, author, and filmmaker Pier Paolo Pasolini (1922–1975), while acknowledging the reasons behind the demonstration, declared his sympathies for the policemen, whom he called 'children of the poor', against the students, who for him were 'spoiled rich kids'.

page 5 – **with the exception of one who ... had been putting**

up with trials and incarceration ... and another who'd died in obscure circumstances – The author is alluding to the celebrated cases of Adriano Sofri (born 1942) and Mauro Rostagno (1942–1988). Sofri – founder and ex-leader of the now-defunct extreme left-wing group Lotta Continua – is currently serving a twenty-two-year sentence for having allegedly ordered the murder, in 1972, of police inspector Luigi Calabresi, himself widely believed responsible for the 'suicide' of an anarchist, Giuseppe Pinelli, who supposedly threw himself out the window of a police interrogation room when being questioned by the same Calabresi. (This latter event was immortalized by Nobel laureate Dario Fo in the play *The Accidental Death of an Anarchist.*) Sofri's ultimate conviction in 1996, after no less than eight trials – one of which came on a prior prosecutor's appeal of an acquittal, a judicial option that still exists in contemporary Italy – rested only on the much-belated confession (in 1988) and inconsistent testimony of one of Calabresi's killers, Leonardo Marino. There was no material evidence. The procedures and results of the case have been widely decried by both Italian and international legal experts. Sofri, a distinguished author and journalist, has always steadfastly maintained his innocence and even refuses to ask for a pardon – which would probably be granted if requested – since this would imply guilt.

Mauro Rostagno, another former member of Lotta Continua, was murdered in 1988, in a case that has never been officially solved despite the fact that several Mafia turncoats have testified that the Mob was behind the killing. Originally from the north of Italy, Rostagno had moved to Sicily in the 1980s, working as a journalist and commentator for an independent left-wing television station he had helped to found. His nearly nightly critiques of the local power alliances between the Mafia, business interests and government quickly won him the enmity of local chieftains. Curiously, there was a blackout on the night of his murder. Eight years later, it was discovered that Vincenzo Mastrantonio, technician and manager of the local chapter of the national power-grid company Enel at the time of the murder, had been the most trusted driver of Mafia boss Vincenzo Virga. Mastrantonio himself was murdered eight months after Rostagno.

page 6 – **burglars of Boccadasse ... Genoa's thieves** – Boccadasse, where Livia resides, is a district of Genoa.

page 7 – **a tray full of ten-thousand-lire notes** – In 1968, ten thousand lire was worth about £7.

page 8 – **'lupara'** – A sawn-off shotgun, traditionally the weapon of choice among mafiosi and bandits in Sicily. Modern times have witnessed the advent of more sophisticated weaponry.

page 14 – **Paolo Villaggio's immortal Fantozzi** – Ugo Fantozzi is an obsequious, tough-luck character created for television and films by comic actor Paolo Villagio (born 1932).

page 18 – **'Eight hundred thousand lire a month'** – About £250.

page 19 – **'Duetto'** – A classic model of the Alfa Romeo Spider of the early 1970s, popularized by Dustin Hoffman in the film *The Graduate.*

page 22 – **'Madunnuzza santa!'** – Blessed little Madonna (Sicilian dialect).

page 37 – **Via Crucis** – The path travelled by Christ on his way up to Mount Calvary, while carrying the cross.

page 50 – **'three million ... two million'** – About £930 and £620, respectively, at the time of the novel's writing.

page 51 – **Quasimodo** – Poet Salvatore Quasimodo (1901–1968), winner of the Nobel Prize in Literature in 1959, was a native Sicilian.

page 64 – **everyone ... was repenting about something** – Montalbano has his own ongoing polemic against the phenomenon of Mafia turncoats and other criminals who turn state's witness (called *pentiti*, or 'repenters') and are thereafter coddled and protected by the government. See, in particular, A. Camilleri, *The Snack Thief.*

page 81 – *sfincione* – Also called *sfinciuni* in dialect, this is a thick-crust sort of pizza or focaccia originally from the Palermo area. It was traditionally served during the Christmas season among the poor people as a way of presenting bread in a festive manner, with a variety of toppings. Versions differ all over Sicily, but typical toppings include chopped onions, tomatoes, black olives, anchovies, aubergine and *caciocavallo* cheese.

page 91 – *vù cumprà* – Term used for African street pedlars in Italy, in whose accent the question *Vuoi comprare* ('Do you want to buy?') comes out as *Vù cumprà*.

page 96 – **four to five billion lire** – £1,240,000 to £1,550,000.

page 119 – **'Having faith is always best' ... 'If you don't sleep, you still can rest'** – Montalbano is simultaneously mocking religion and the comforting adage for insomniacs: *Il letto è una gran cosa / Se non si dorme s'arriposa* (Of all things the bed is best / If you can't sleep you still can rest), quoted in A. Camilleri, *Voice of the Violin.*

page 126 – **couldn't bring himself to call them 'repenters', much less state's witnesses** – See note to page 64.

page 130 – **medical-service cards** – In order to use the public health-care system in Italy, one must present a government-issued medical card.

page 130 – **'certificate of living existence'** – *Certificato di esistenza in vita*, in Italian. This bureaucratic oddity was created, among other reasons, to prevent pensions from being paid out to people who are dead.

page 133 – **'the ROS'** – The Reperto Operativo Speciale, an elite unit of the carabinieri, the national police force.

page 138 – **'I've got a heart like a lion and another like a donkey'** – This is the literal translation of a Sicilian expression that means, more or less, 'I'm of two minds' or 'I'm torn'. Montalbano here purposely uses a Sicilian idiom to confuse the commissioner, who he knows will not understand it.

page 143 – **It was as if they were at Pontida** – On 7 April 1167, the Lombard League, a federation of north Italian communes in the province of Lombardy (Brescia, Bergamo, Cremona, Mantua and later Milan), was founded at the Convent of Pontida to fight the hegemonic designs of Holy Roman Emperor Frederick Barbarossa across the region. The solemn Oath of Pontida, taken on this occasion, has been grotesquely re-created in our time by the right-wing separatist, anti-immigrant party of Umberto Bossi, originally also called the Lombard League, now re-named the Northern League, which re-enacts the oath annually.

page 145 – **'Pisello districk' ... Fava district** – *Pisello* means pea and *fava* is broad bean, hence Catarella's confusion.

page 150 – **goat-tying** – My rendering of the Sicilian verb *incaprettare* (containing the word for goat, *capra*), which refers to a particularly cruel method of execution used by the Mafia.

Lying face down, the victim has a rope looped around his neck and then tied to his feet, which are raised behind his back, as in hog-tieing. Fatigue eventually forces the victim to lower his feet, strangling himself in the process.

page 158 – 'These words content me much' – *Henry VI, Part II,* Act 3, Scene 2.

page 197 – *'Beddra Matre santissima!'* – Most holy beautiful Mother (Sicilian dialect).

page 200 – 'passbook with the Post Office' – In Italy one can conduct a variety of transactions with the postal service, including banking.

page 203 – Vittorio Emanuele III ... Umberto I ... 'Gentleman King' – Three kings of Italy. The Gentleman King (*il re galantuomo*) was Vittorio Emanuele II. All the Italian kings since the foundation of the modern monarchy have been of the House of Savoy.

page 204 – *verba volant* and *scripta manent* – 'The spoken word flies' and 'the written word remains' (Latin).

page 205 – 'It's Ciampi' – Carlo Azeglio Ciampi, still the Italian President of the Republic, a largely ceremonial position. Executive power is invested in the office of the *presidente del Consiglio*, or prime minister.

page 206 – 'a hundred million' – About £31,000.

page 228 – Caponata – A zesty traditional southern-Italian dish, often served as an appetizer or side dish, made up of sautéed aubergine, tomato, green pepper, garlic, onion, celery, black olives, vinegar, olive oil and anchovies. In this instance, Montalbano eats a large helping of caponata as his main course.

page 241 – **'she left her stable and hide'** – In Italian, an insignificant inheritance is sometimes described idiomatically as *una stalla e una salma*, or 'a stable and a corpse'. In Sicilian, however, the term *salma* is also an ancient and sometimes modern unit of surface measurement, equivalent to 1.76 hectares, or about four and a half acres. As a Sicilian, Montalbano seems to be unaware of the Italian expression, since in this conversation he momentarily takes the term *salma* (rendered as 'hide') literally; he is also unaware of the rather obscure Sicilian unit of measure. A hide was a unit of measurement in medieval England of varying size, starting at about sixty acres. Translating *salma* as hide, while increasing the area some fifteen times, does, however, make it possible to reproduce the protagonist's incomprehension in this situation, as it rather fortuitously and symmetrically preserves the original term's double meaning of 'corpse' and 'land area'. What is inevitably lost is Camilleri's rather sly literalization of an idiomatic metaphor.

page 297 – **prepared for the year 2000** – This book was written in 1999 and first published in 2000.

Notes compiled by Stephen Sartarelli